**W9-CDY-657**

HOUSE for HAPPY MOTHERS

Center Point
Large Print

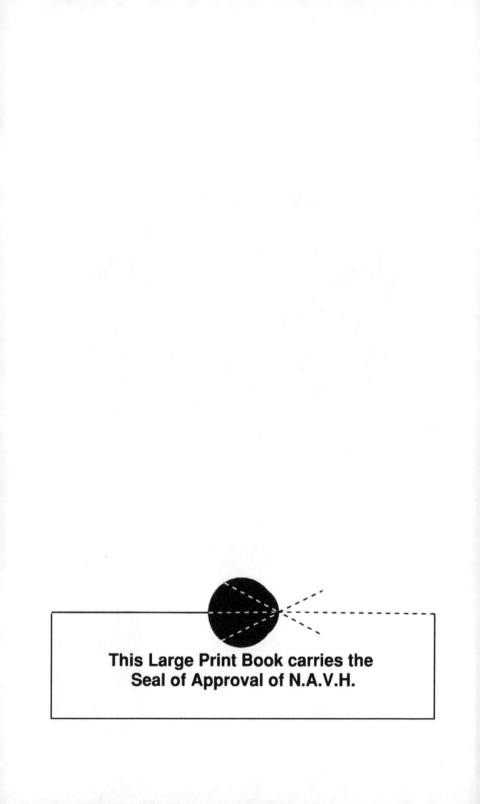

**This Large Print Book carries the
Seal of Approval of N.A.V.H.**

A HOUSE for HAPPY MOTHERS

AMULYA MALLADI

CENTER POINT LARGE PRINT
THORNDIKE, MAINE

This Center Point Large Print edition
is published in the year 2017 by arrangement with
Amazon Publishing, www.apub.com.

Originally published in the United States
by Amazon Publishing, 2016.

This is a work of fiction.
Names, characters, organizations, places,
events, and incidents are either products of the
author's imagination or are used fictitiously.

The text of this Large Print edition is unabridged.
In other aspects, this book may vary
from the original edition.
Printed in the United States of America
on permanent paper.
Set in 16-point Times New Roman type.

ISBN: 978-1-68324-298-7

Library of Congress Cataloging-in-Publication Data

Names: Malladi, Amulya, author.
Title: A house for happy mothers / Amulya Malladi.
Description: Center Point Large Print edition. | Thorndike, Maine :
Center Point Large Print, 2017.
Identifiers: LCCN 2016056200 | ISBN 9781683242987
    (hardcover : alk. paper)
Subjects: LCSH: Surrogate mothers—Fiction. | Large type books. |
Domestic fiction.
Classification: LCC PS3613.A45 H68 2017 | DDC 813/.54—dc23
LC record available at https://lccn.loc.gov/2016056200

For Søren, in good times and in bad.

PART 1:
Conception

Chapter One

Rock-a-bye baby in the tree top, when the wind blows, the cradle will rock . . .

The nursery rhyme played itself in her head over and over again as she tried to fall asleep.

When the bough breaks, the cradle will fall.

And down will come baby, cradle and all.

This one chance, she thought desperately. *God, give me this one last chance.*

"Please, please, please," she whispered under her breath.

And even though she was lying down in bed, she knew she was really on her knees.

By two in the morning, Priya finally gave up trying to sleep. She looked in disbelief at her husband, who was lying next to her. How could he sleep? Why wasn't he worried like she was? Why wasn't his head throbbing like hers, his mind tired of running through each and every dreadful possibility?

She nudged him.

"What?" Madhu mumbled, his eyes still closed.

"I can't sleep," Priya said.

"Just count them sheep," he mumbled again, then turned his back to her.

Even half-asleep, he had to crack a joke.

"Madhu, damn it, I'm freaking out here," she said in frustration.

"I'll give you a hundred dollars to go to sleep and five hundred to just be quiet," he said. He made some kissing sounds before continuing to snore.

Priya sighed.

He had a right to sleep. Hell, she should be sleeping.

But she hadn't in a week, not since they had flown to Hyderabad from California. It had been a stressful seven days. They had chosen a surrogate to carry their baby. Priya had had her eggs extracted. Dreadful process. And then Madhu had ejaculated into a cup. Their baby was made in a test tube and inserted into the surrogate. And now, in just a few hours, they would know if their surrogate was pregnant. They didn't always get pregnant. There were times when they didn't.

Oh God, please, please, Priya chanted silently, *please let her be pregnant.*

"You know what, you're insensitive for sleeping while I'm stewing over here," she said to Madhu's sleeping form. She doubted he heard her. "It's not like this is the neighbor's baby, you know."

Madhu didn't make a sound.

Obviously this was not the ideal way to have a baby. The easiest way would be to get knocked up—but that hadn't quite worked out for them. And now after three miscarriages and three failed

IVF treatments, each costing about $10,000, surrogacy had become the only way out. The only way to have a child, a family.

"Priyasha, don't be stupid; if you can't have a baby, maybe you're not meant to have a baby," her mother had said. "Have you thought about that instead of running around impregnating some strange woman with your child?"

Her mother, who went by Sush, short for Sushila, never shortened Priya's name as everyone else did.

"Your name means 'a dear wish,' and you are a dear wish, and that's what you'll always be," Sush liked to say. But what Sush said was in sharp contrast to what Sush did, which was consistently make Priya feel like a massive failure in every aspect of her life. Far from a dear wish. Far from the daughter Sush had wanted.

"My own child is exploiting my people," Sush said when Priya announced her decision over the phone. "I can't support this, Priyasha. I will never support this. It's an exploitation of the poor, and you should be ashamed of yourself."

When she first introduced the idea to Madhu, his eyes had all but bugged out.

"Are you fucking nuts?"

"Hear me out, Madhu," Priya had said.

"Are you fucking nuts?" he repeated.

Priya had sighed. "Yes," she said, giving in. "I'm nuts. I want a baby and goddamn it . . . come on, Madhu, this is our last chance. Hell, this is our only chance. Our only, only, last chance. I want this."

"No," Madhu had said. "Priya, this isn't some handcrafted Indian sari you buy at the fair-trade store. This is a baby. You can't just rent a body."

But Priya had sent him e-mail after e-mail with information about how safe it was, how effective it had been for others like them, and most important, how the money they would give the surrogate would help her family and improve the quality of her life.

"No," Madhu had said. "You want to help the poor, donate money."

"We already donate money," Priya said. "But now I want the donation to work for *me*."

"By definition, a charitable donation is selfless," Madhu said.

They went back and forth and back and forth until he finally caved. And though Madhu had agreed, he still stood on the sidelines. Once she had a child, it wouldn't matter how the baby got here, Priya thought, and until then she'd manage Madhu, she'd manage her guilt, their guilt . . . and then the baby would be here and it would be all right. Because once Priya had thought of them being a family—once that thought had ensconced itself inside her psyche—she couldn't devolve and just accept their being a couple. It was not enough.

• • •

Madhu rolled over now, deep in sleep, and faced Priya. She smiled at him. He would make a great dad, she thought, and gently touched his face. Would they have a daughter or a son? A daughter would get spoiled. If she wanted a pony, Madhu would get her the prettiest one. She would wrap him around her little finger. And if they had a boy? Oh, Madhu would run out and buy a cricket uniform and teach his son how to bowl and bat. He would adore his son. They would have one of those great relationships that went from being father and son to being friends as they grew older.

Yes, she could see Madhu would be a fabulous parent. But Priya wasn't so sure about herself. What kind of mother would she be? Her own had not been a stellar example of motherhood.

"Graphic designer? Why? You got a master's in urban development; why on earth would you not do something to help the weak in our world?" Sush had demanded when Priya changed career paths.

Priya's intentions had been noble. She had gotten her bachelor's degree in political science from Berkeley and went on to complete her master's at Ohio State University. She had planned on finding a job at an NGO and living her life fulfilling her mother's expectations of her, she really had, but she had always had a creative streak.

Sush never appreciated her daughter's painting

skills ("Painters make no money and help no one"), but her father, Andrew, had supported his daughter's "hobby."

Priya, however, was proud to have put her artistic skills to good use, the best use she could while earning a living. She ran a studio for an advertising agency. She managed the creatives, the writers and graphic designers—people more creative than she was—in a corporate setting, and she did her job well. The brainstorming, the creative part, was fantastic, but the administrative nonsense was just that. The endless staff meetings, the cover-your-ass e-mails, the hand-holding of unhappy clients, the divas and their egos that needed to be soothed time and again. But no job was perfect, and Priya was content with her professional career. She didn't want more. This was good.

Born and bred in the corporate world and a sales executive himself, Madhu didn't understand her lack of ambition, and when she complained about the politics and the corporate backstabbing, he would say, "You sound just like Sush."

Before the first miscarriage, she had painted regularly; some small pieces had ended up in galleries, and a few of those had actually sold. But even with those small successes, painting had always been a private meditation, a one-on-one communion with her deeper self, a visceral need to express. Once she started to lose the babies, something inside her shriveled. She couldn't paint like she used to.

"If our daughter wants to become a musician, we'll let her," she whispered now to Madhu's sleeping form. "We won't push her to be this or that, just herself."

He didn't stir, and Priya curbed the urge to wake him again so he could sit vigil with her as they waited for news that their child had been conceived.

Priya got exactly two hours of sleep before Madhu gently rocked her awake.

He was ready. She could smell the Dove soap on him, and his hair was still wet. She could hear the clashing of utensils downstairs. The maid washing dishes, getting ready to wash clothes. She could smell the filtered coffee that Sairam, her father-in-law, drank every morning, the same coffee that Madhu drank every morning back home in the Bay Area, rain or shine, whether he had time for it or not.

"Is it late?" Priya asked groggily.

"Not really," he said a little hesitantly, and Priya sat up.

"How late?" she demanded, her heart rate accelerating. If they couldn't even make it on time for this, how on earth would they get anything done once they had the baby?

"Relax, we still have an hour to get ready," he said.

Srirampuram was a two-hour drive from Hyderabad, but considering the traffic, they allotted three hours to get there on time.

Since she'd taken a bath before going to bed, Priya decided to forgo a shower and get ready as quickly as possible, as she knew they were going to lose time downstairs trying to avoid her mother-in-law's enormous South Indian–style breakfast.

"Eat, *Amma*, eat," Prasanna said. "Eat an *idli*. Or just a bowl of *sambhar*. You're too thin, Priya, I can see your collarbones."

"*Atha*, I'm really not feeling up to it," Priya said. Her stomach was churning with tension. "Just coffee today. Tomorrow, I promise I'll eat."

When Priya had first met Madhu's parents, she had called them by their first names, but she was soon advised by Madhu to call them *Atha* and *Mava*, mother-in-law and father-in-law, because that's what good Telugu Indians did. Priya, for her part, had told him not to call her parents anything but Andrew and Sush.

Priya watched Madhu plow into his breakfast. He missed eating food like this in California. Even though South Indian food was available, this was vacation eating; this was Amma-made food eating.

"Amma, leave her alone," Madhu said as he put another fresh *idli* on his plate.

"She's too thin, Madhu," Prasanna complained. "She must eat."

"It's OK if she doesn't eat one morning," Sairam said, though he did agree with his wife that Priya was too thin.

"Stick figures might be the norm in America, but here we like our women well rounded," Prasanna said authoritatively, and Priya all but choked on her coffee.

Madhu looked up from his *idli* and shook his head. "She looks fabulous," he said, and winked at Priya.

"I don't understand—" Prasanna began.

"You don't have to, Amma; she's my wife," Madhu said, standing up. "We have to go. Now wish us luck and stop nagging Priya about how she looks."

There were other husbands, Indian husbands, who always sided with their parents. Priya would hear Indian women, mostly the wives of Madhu's friends, bitch about how when they visited his parents it was all about them.

"*Arrey*, she tells him, in front of me, what she thinks I'm doing wrong in raising our children, and he just nods his head. It's so insulting," one would complain.

"Mine just hates me. Whines about everything I do, and he just sits there and takes it. If my parents said anything about my husband, I'd defend him. Is it too much to expect the same of him?" another would chime in.

Priya didn't have much to say when their eyes

turned to her. They expected her to narrate her own harrowing mother-in-law experiences, but what could she say? Madhu was always on her side.

"Good luck," Prasanna said, not angrily but in resigned acceptance that Priya would indeed not eat anything. "Whatever happens, Priya, keep your chin up, OK?"

Unlike Andrew and Sush, Prasanna and Sairam were all for having a baby the surrogate way. They didn't see it as an exploitation of the poor, as Sush did; they saw it as a way for them to have a grandchild while helping another family have a better life.

"You know, you could've eaten one measly *idli* and killed that whole breakfast chitchat," Madhu said as they merged into traffic. At 7:00 a.m., it was already chaos and would only get worse as the day progressed. There was no rush hour here—all hours were rush hour.

"So you prefer a 'well-rounded wife' instead of a healthy one?" Priya teased. She didn't want to fight today.

"Well, what exactly do you mean by 'well rounded'?" Madhu asked as he honked at a driver not going fast enough.

"Do you really think the guy in front of you can hear your honk over the others?" Priya asked.

The auto rickshaw moved out of Madhu's way.

"In India if you don't honk, you'll get nowhere."

"Now there's a guy honking at you," Priya said, turning around.

"God knows who he's honking at, but it ain't me," Madhu said.

Priya couldn't imagine driving on the roads of Hyderabad. The idea of being in a vehicle here was stressful enough without having to be the driver. The first time she came with Madhu to India, she had insisted that he not drive after hearing all the nightmarish stories about car accidents. But these were his streets, no matter how much they had changed. Madhu said he'd be damned if he let someone else drive him. To his credit, they were still alive and intact—not even a scratch on the car. Well, at least not any new ones.

"So," Priya said as Madhu managed to avoid hitting a scooter that decided to cut him off with little room to spare. Madhu called them the suicide squad—people he was saving from killing themselves. They were all over the streets—the woman with her baby, the scooter, the moped, the motorcycle, the auto rickshaw—they all merrily cut in and hoped for the best.

"So, what?" Madhu asked. If the driving was stressing him out, she couldn't tell. He was relaxed as he honked, braked, and changed gears.

"You still haven't told me," Priya said.

They had been discussing it for the past few

days, and Madhu got squeamish each time she brought up the topic.

"I don't want to talk about this," Madhu said, and Priya could see he was embarrassed.

"Come on, did you or did you not need any of the porno movies they gave you?" Priya asked with a smile.

"I don't want to talk about this," he repeated.

"You know I would've told you if it were me," Priya said. "And it isn't the first time you've had to . . . you know"—she paused for effect—"masturbate into a cup."

"And I didn't tell you then, either," Madhu said.

They both knew they were talking about this to avoid dwelling on whether their surrogate was pregnant or not. They had chosen this particular woman over two others. Madhu had been drawn to her because of her age. She was twenty-five and had two children. This would be her first time as a surrogate. She came from a good family and had a sister-in-law who had also been a surrogate. Her husband was a house painter, and they lived in a village close to Srirampuram.

The other two women were slightly older than this one and had been surrogates before. For some reason, the fact that they had done this before made Madhu and Priya wary. They should've felt surer because the women were experienced, but they still wanted this woman.

And then there was the name.

Priya was immediately attracted to Asha because her name meant "hope," just as her own name, Priyasha, did. One hope was giving hope to another hope; there was something inevitable about it, as if the universe had planned it.

Swati Gudla, their doctor and the owner of the Happy Mothers clinic, a fertility and surrogacy clinic close to Hyderabad, had been delighted with their choice, assuring them that Asha would make a wonderful surrogate.

Both Madhu and Priya had gotten to know Doctor Swati quite well over the phone during the past few months. There were many, many conversations to be had: about money, legalities, medical conditions, and more. They liked her instantly, from the very first time they had Skyped. She was down-to-earth and talked sensibly about the process, warning them about the emotional and financial toll. Financially, this was a lot cheaper than having three IVFs. Emotionally, they crossed their fingers that it would be less harrowing.

"You know I'd tell you if I had to use porn," Priya told Madhu in a serious tone. "I wish it were that easy for women. My stomach is still churning, thanks to that extraction business."

Madhu reached out his hand and touched hers.

"I wish you could've used porn, too," he said. "I know it was painful."

"But worth it, right?"

Madhu shrugged. He didn't say it because it

would hurt Priya, but she knew that he didn't want a baby "at any cost," like she did. He would've been plenty happy to live their lives without a child. He would've been happier in some ways if they had adopted. It wasn't like Priya was against adopting, but she looked at it as a last resort. And, as yet, there was this one avenue that was still available to them. If this didn't work out, then maybe . . . *Oh God, please let this work.*

"Do you think the baby will learn Telugu?" Madhu asked.

"Well, if you speak to her in Telugu, she will learn Telugu. If I speak to her in Telugu, she'll learn crap Telugu."

Priya always referred to the baby as "she." She didn't know why but she was convinced that she was meant to have one.

"Your Telugu, considering the circumstances, is fabulous," Madhu said. "I still don't get why Sush didn't bother to teach it to you. It's such a waste. It is, after all, your mother tongue."

"I guess it wasn't important to her," Priya said.

Even though she had an Indian mother, Priya's connection with India had been a fragile one at best. She had visited once as a child but could hardly remember it. There was some Indian food at home, but not a lot and not every day. There was some Indian classical music mixed in with Mozart and Mahler. There were no Indian movies, really. Priya's uncle, who'd died years ago, had been Sush's only relative in India besides her parents. Priya's grandparents had not been gung ho about their daughter marrying a white man and had not visited very often. Priya vaguely remembered them and felt no connection to them.

Priya's Indian experience really began after she met Madhu. It was a delight to her that he was Telugu like Sush, who was also from Andhra Pradesh. He had indulged Priya by speaking to her in Telugu, helping her rudimentary language skills develop. Now she spoke it half-decently, albeit with a strong American accent.

Before meeting Madhu, Priya had always felt a part of her was missing. She was half-Indian, but there was nothing Indian about her. Having a completely Indian husband who helped her discover her Indianness had made her feel complete.

They fell silent as they neared the clinic, her prayers battling the insidious thought that maybe the surrogate hadn't gotten pregnant this first time after all and that they might have to try again in a few months, if they didn't give up altogether.

Madhu parked and they got out. Priya stood by the car, not wanting to walk in. There had been so much bad news for so long that she was terrified to believe that this time could be different.

Her hands started to shake.

Madhu put his arm around her and kissed her lightly. "You need to relax," he said quietly.

"I couldn't stand it if she isn't pregnant," Priya said with tears in her eyes. "I . . . I don't know what I'd do. I want a baby, Madhu."

"I know," Madhu said as Priya turned in to him.

When she lifted her head, she gave him a teary smile. "I'm such a shit," she said as she wiped her tears with a tissue from her purse.

He grinned as they started to walk toward the entrance. He leaned down slightly when they stepped into the reception area.

"I didn't use the porn," Madhu whispered into Priya's ear. "I thought of you in that blue Victoria's Secret number."

Transcript from message board
www.surrogacyforyou.org

NearlyMother: Our surrogate lost our baby. This is such a painful and horrible time. I hear about people who get pregnant the first time and then have a healthy pregnancy and I can't understand why this can't happen to us. This was our second time. I think my husband is ready to give up.

Mommy8774: I am so sorry to hear about your loss. It's terrible. With our first baby everything went well. With our second baby we had to try three different times to get pregnant. So hang in there.

Prietysmommy: We just got through the first trimester. I can only imagine how you feel. I was so scared. And it isn't easy with us here in Dallas and the baby in Gujarat. Torture.

NobuNobi: My MIL and FIL are against us getting an SM and have been so mean about the whole thing. They're visiting now and make me feel so bad. I mean they see this as my fault and that it has nothing to do with DH. I mean, DH gave his f****** sperm, didn't he? I have some uterine problems and that's why we had to go the SM way. This really hurts. Our SM is doing very well. She's nearly five months pregnant and we talk every week; I see her belly over the webcam. Anyone else having to deal with family disapproval?

UnoBaby: My friends have been very unsupportive. Now I don't even tell people. It's nobody's business anyway. One of my friends actually told me that I was exploiting this poor Indian woman.

But my SM wants to help us and to them the money we give can help change the lives of her children.

Trying1Time: My mother is not very supportive about this either and also accuses me of exploiting the poor people of India. But I agree with UnoBaby that this is a mutually beneficial thing. We're waiting to hear if our surrogate is pregnant. I have my fingers crossed.

Newbie1209: I'm so glad I found this message board. You all seem wonderful. I wish you the best, Trying1Time. And NobuNobi, I'm so sorry your in-laws are giving you a hard time. And NearlyMother . . . I am so so so so sorry. I really want to go the surrogate route. Any suggestions on how I can convince my husband?

CantConceive1970: My husband flat-out refused, but once I showed him pictures, testimonials, walked him through Dr. Patel's website, he was all for it. Now we're working on baby #2 and he's game for a third one if we want it. It's a great way to have your own baby when you can't do it yourself. It's a gift.

Mommy8774: Just be prepared with facts and proof. I made sure I had all the information when I sat down with my husband. Turns out I didn't need to, because he had been investigating it himself and was afraid to bring it up, thinking I would be against it! So it turned out really well. I hope it turns out well for you, too.

Chapter Two

Each time the bus jerked, Asha placed her hand on her belly, trying to nestle the life within. It was an instinctive reaction, not one she even noticed.

She knew she was pregnant. They hadn't done the blood test yet to confirm it, but she knew. It had been just three days since she had been through the procedure at Doctor Swati's clinic, and already she knew.

Just this morning when she brushed her teeth, there had been blood. That was how it had been with Manoj and Mohini. A woman knew her body.

The bus jerked again, and this time Asha felt her hand move to her stomach, but she balled it into a fist and let it lie on her lap. This would not be like the other times. This baby was not hers.

Pratap slept, his head resting against the dirty glass window of the bus. They'd had to wake up at four in the morning so that they could be at the hospital by nine o'clock. Asha had worn her best sari, even though she knew that it would get wrinkled in the time it took them to get to Doctor Swati's hospital. She had insisted that Pratap wear his nice pants and shirt and had painstakingly ironed the shirt to make sure there were no creases. It was now covered in wrinkles and sweat stains, his odor mingling with those of the other passengers.

Kantamma, the tailor in their village, had made the shirt. Asha had bought the cloth from Hyderabad when she had gone there for a wedding. It had blue and white stripes. It looked good on him. Pratap didn't care what he wore, but it was important to Asha that they look like a handsome couple today, well-to-do, even though she was selling her womb for money, *especially* because she was.

She was almost grateful that her parents were dead. Her mother had died nearly five years ago, right after Asha was married. She'd had pancreatic cancer, and as soon as she was diagnosed at the government hospital, the doctors had told them that she would have just a year or so to live. Asha's parents immediately started to look for a boy for her—her mother wanted to see her married before she died.

They didn't have enough saved up for a dowry, and they knew this meant that they couldn't find Asha a good match. Asha's brother, Venkat, was supposed to get married and receive a dowry, which would then be used to marry off Asha. But Venkat had fallen in love with another clerk in the bank he worked in. Asha's parents didn't like the idea of a love marriage, but Venkat had always been headstrong. No one could tell him what to do, and he had gone and married the woman he loved without taking any dowry, ruining Asha's chances of finding a good husband. The best they could've done was a painter. Pratap's family was not mercenary (after all, they had no daughters to marry off) and had asked only that the wedding be arranged well and that the girl come with the basic jewelry: gold bangles, a gold chain, and gold earrings.

Venkat and his wife, Prabha, now lived all the way in Vizag. Asha rarely saw them or their two daughters. She had visited them once for her father's funeral. Her father had moved in with Venkat after their mother died. He had not survived much longer; a heart attack claimed him just a year later.

It had been strange to meet the brother she had grown up with, with his own family. A family he cared more about than his own sister. But that's how it was supposed to be. They wrote letters once a year to each other for Ugadi, the Telugu New Year, but beyond that, Asha knew that Pratap's family was now her only family. Her relationship with her brother died alongside her parents. It was probably for the best, Asha thought. She doubted her brother would approve of her getting pregnant with another couple's baby for money. And she would be ashamed if he ever found out.

• • •

It was a strange day—a day of anticipation, a day where everything, their entire lives, would be altered completely. Asha and Pratap's neighbors, an elderly couple, were taking care of Manoj and Mohini for the day. They treated the children like their own grandchildren, and Asha knew they would be heartbroken when she and Pratap left the village.

Asha had kissed her sleeping children before leaving. Mohini was nearly two, a tiny princess, and the joy of Pratap's life. And Manoj, such a beautiful, smart boy—just five and he could already read. It was scary that he could, both in English and in Telugu! When his teacher told them that he was one of those *very intelligent* boys, Asha and Pratap had known that they had to do something. They couldn't give Manoj an education in a big-city school with what Pratap made as a painter.

Pratap made a sound and shifted in his sleep. He wasn't comfortable in the jerking bus—but he was sleeping. Here she was pregnant with some other man's child, and he was fast asleep, like a baby, Asha thought angrily. She wanted to wake him and make him see the atrocity she was committing.

This was his fault anyway. It was Pratap's brother, Raman, who had planted the idea. Last year, Kaveri, Asha's sister-in-law, had given birth to a bald, blue-eyed baby for a British couple living in Nottingham in England. Asha hadn't even heard of a place called Nottingham until Kaveri and Raman had told them. The parents had paid five lakh rupees to Kaveri for having their baby. Five lakh rupees! Pratap's eyes had almost fallen out. And when the teachers told them about Manoj and how he needed to go to a better school, Pratap had started to talk about it with Asha. She couldn't blame him entirely, not really, because five lakh rupees was a lot of money, and it had made her think as well. Could she? Could she do what Kaveri had done? And now she had done it, just like Kaveri.

Asha wondered if there had ever really been a choice for her. Could she have said no? Coul she have been selfish and said, "No, this is my body, I decide"?

And now? Now it was too late. The seed had taken hold, and she could feel her body already nourishing this child that was not hers.

Asha's mother-in-law, Puttamma, who now lived with Kaveri and Raman (they had a brick flat with an indoor bathroom), had also thought it was a great idea.

But to give birth to someone else's baby—a stranger's baby—how would that make her feel? Would this be an act of perversion, because it was perverse to deny nature her right to make someone barren and give that person a child anyway? Would this make Asha less of a mother to her own children? Could it somehow corrupt her mother-hood, taint her soul?

"Where are you going?" the woman sitting next to Asha on the bus asked. She was a fat woman who took up a lot of space. The seat was designed for three people, but with this woman's size, Asha was all but sitting on Pratap's lap. It didn't help that Pratap was a big man as well.

"Srirampuram," Asha said, looking at Pratap's hands, the nails always smeared on the edges with remnants of paint, this time white. "Our relatives are there. We're visiting." She felt compelled to embellish.

Their relatives did live there—Kaveri and Raman had bought their big flat in Srirampuram with their baby money. In any case, she couldn't tell anyone the truth. Society had its rules, and even though many women were now stealthily carrying other people's children in their wombs, it was all hush-hush, hidden, a dirty secret. The story they'd tell was that Asha became pregnant and then lost the baby. No one in her village would ever approve of this. Decent women didn't use their bodies to make money. Their family name would be ruined if anyone found out. Asha couldn't help but wonder what else would be ruined. Her heart, her mind, her body? What if this baby destroyed her womb? What if God struck her down for going against his wishes, giving birth to a child he didn't wish to see born?

"I'm going to Hyderabad," the woman said. "My daughter is about to deliver—any day now. I will be a grandmother for the first time. Do you have children?"

"Two," Asha said, and felt a pang. What would she say after this baby growing inside her came out? Would she still say two children, even though she had carried a third and given birth a third time?

Pratap changed sides to rest his head on Asha's shoulder, snoring softly. He was fast asleep, she marveled—fast asleep with the noise of the bus, the heat, the smell of sweat, let alone the life inside her womb.

The noise of the bus engine competed with that of chickens stuffed into baskets in the rear seats. People were talking, a radio was playing Telugu songs, there was the rustle of newspapers being opened, and babies were crying, making the crowded bus feel even more stifling. A woman sitting across from Asha had a basket of vegetables on her lap—tomatoes, coriander, cucumber, and bitter gourd. People were taking their wares to the bazaar in Srirampuram. Someone somewhere on the bus was eating *mirchi bajjis*, and Asha could smell the chili and the oil they were fried in. Pregnancy was already sharpening her sense of smell. They could do all the tests they wanted, Asha thought; she already knew she was pregnant.

"We have a boy and a girl," Asha said proudly. One of each, she liked to say—an accomplishment.

"We wanted to know if the baby was a boy or a girl, but they wouldn't tell us; you know how it is these days," the woman said. "A shame that people kill their baby in the belly because it's a girl."

"Yes," Asha said, and shifted to be comfortable in spite of Pratap's weight on her shoulder.

"That's your husband? What does he do?" the woman asked.

Asha told her and the woman smiled. "Handsome boy."

Asha smiled back and then looked fondly at Pratap. He was handsome—with his mustache and rugged features. He was tall and built well, like his father had been.

When she had first married him, two things had struck her: his size and the smell of turpentine and paint. The first day she saw him come back from work, spattered with paint from head to toe, she had been shocked. He had used turpentine to remove the paint while he bathed with water drawn from the well in the backyard that they shared with several of their neighbors. The well was a bone of contention, and people complained about how much water Pratap used to wash himself, especially in the summer, when the well was almost dry. So Asha had started to hide water, store some away each time she drew some from the well in a big white bucket with a lid she had bought for just this purpose.

Now she was used to the turpentine and the paint, and even his size.

The woman and Asha chatted all the way to Srirampuram, and Asha was grateful for the company. By the time they got off, Asha knew the woman and her three children's life stories. The woman knew nothing about Asha. There was nothing to tell. The most exciting thing that had ever happened to Asha was happening to her now, and this she could tell no one.

The waiting room at Happy Mothers was teeming with life. Besides Asha, there were three women there. One was about five months pregnant, and two looked like they were ready to pop any minute now. Each of them was carrying someone else's baby. Some would have white babies, some would have brown babies, and some would have half-white, half-brown babies. Asha had been happy to know that her baby would be mostly Indian. Not that it mattered, but a part of her felt that it made more sense for an Indian woman to push out an Indian baby from her womb.

Kaveri had not seen her white baby after he was born but had seen a photograph months later when the parents sent her a picture. They were standing in front of a decorated tree, two white parents with a smiling white baby. The card said HAPPY CHRISTMAS as if she were Christian and celebrated the holiday. It seemed impossible that the baby had come out of Kaveri, who was as dark as coal.

The parents and the baby boy all looked so joyous that Kaveri had had tears in her eyes. "I made them happy," she told Asha. "It makes it all worthwhile to know that I gave them so much happiness."

Asha had not said that the happiness had cost five lakh rupees plus whatever the parents had to pay Doctor Swati for her clinic and services, which was probably a lot more.

It seemed wrong to do this for money, but Asha wouldn't do it if their finances were better, would she? If Manoj had to go to a good school in the city, they needed money, and this was an easy— or, say, viable—way to earn it. That had been Asha's mother-in-law's argument. Puttamma had moved out of Asha and Pratap's house as soon as Kaveri and Raman bought their brick flat with a toilet, the kind with a flush that you could sit on like a chair. No more taking a mug of water and looking for a place to go in the bushes.

Puttamma had been all for Asha and Kaveri renting out their wombs. "It's for a good cause, and it's better than selling a kidney, isn't it?" *Easy for her to say,* Asha thought. *The old woman cannot have children anymore, so she thinks it's a picnic for us to have one.*

She looked at Pratap, the only man in the waiting room; he seemed incongruous with his tall, masculine frame against the pink and blue walls covered with baby pictures. He had said he didn't want to put pressure on Asha to do this, but he had put the pressure on all the same. She knew all he saw were rupees in the bank. She, on the other hand, had worried about it, worried and thought and cried about it . . . and then worried some more. She was still not sure they were doing the right thing. But there was no point broadcasting that fact. The baby was inside her. That was the end of the story.

When Asha had met Doctor Swati for the first time, she had been full of concerns, and the doctor had been kind and compassionate, speaking about the ease of the procedure, the gain for Asha and her family in the end, and the happiness she would give two people.

"Not many of us get a chance to give such a big gift," Doctor Swati said. "You have that opportunity. But if you have even a small rice grain's worth of doubt, you shouldn't do it."

Asha had had a handful of rice grains' worth of doubt, but she pretended and acted, and Doctor Swati had believed her. It helped that Pratap seemed so open to the idea. The only thing he had a problem with was that during her last four months of pregnancy, Asha would live at a house in Happy Mothers where all the surrogate mothers lived until they gave birth.

"So many months without seeing my husband and children?" Asha hadn't liked the idea at all.

"They can come and visit. You're lucky because you will be living in Srirampuram. We have women from Hyderabad, Vizag, Warangal, and they come to the house as soon as they conceive. They don't see their families until they give birth and go back home," Doctor Swati said. "Even for your own pregnancy, don't you go and stay with your mother during your last months?"

"My mother is dead," Asha told her.

"Pratap and the children can come and visit every day—unless they're sick; then we don't allow it to make sure you don't fall sick and the other women in the house don't, either," Doctor Swati continued. "But besides that, Pratap can come by every day after work and school to spend time with you, Asha. What do you think, Pratap?"

"Yes, yes," Pratap said. "It won't be a problem. My sister-in-law will help with the children when Asha is here."

Asha had done that for Kaveri, so it seemed natural she would do the same for Asha.

Kaveri had said that it had been fun to get away from her house, children, and husband for four full months. She had spent time with other women like her, and they had watched movies together, eaten food that was prepared by a maid, and had done no housework at all. Someone cooked and cleaned for them, even made their beds. She had felt like a queen for those months, and it had been a rude shock, Kaveri confessed, to come home and do everything herself again.

They'd thought about moving to Srirampuram after they had the baby and got all their money, anyway. They would buy a flat just like Kaveri and Raman had done, and enroll Manoj in a good school in town.

With this money, Manoj could become whatever he wanted, Asha thought. Maybe he would become a doctor, someone like Doctor Swati who could chatter away in English, so poised and confident. Maybe he would become an engineer, like those they showed on television, the ones who worked for big companies in America.

"Do you think it's a good idea to live with Kaveri and Raman? Their flat will become very crowded," Asha said as they waited to meet with the doctor.

"It will be good to live with family," Pratap said. "We will have help and they will have help. Raman is talking to his contractor to get me a job as well. Manoj can already start going to a good school with some of the money we get from Doctor Swati if you're pregnant."

Asha nodded, holding her tongue. He had

already decided. He wasn't asking her for her opinion; he was telling her he had made a decision and they would just have to do what he wanted. She had thought she would be able to exercise more decision-making power, since the money they would be enjoying would come from her labors, but Pratap didn't seem to see it that way. And what could she say, "It's my womb, so it's my money"? No. That wasn't like her. She had never countered any decision Pratap had ever made. Women like her didn't do that kind of thing. But it still chafed that he hadn't talked to her. It was as if she were just a body, not a person with feelings and a mind. It was as if she didn't exist.

"It will be nice to live here, in a city, instead of our village," Pratap continued. He had envied his brother's fortunes, Asha knew, and now felt eager to have the same advantages for both himself and his family.

Before Asha could answer, a nurse dressed in a white dress and a white bonnet called for them. "Pratap and Asha Vardhan?"

Asha stood up and checked her sari, making sure everything was draped just the way it should be. Pratap had already started to walk toward the doctor's office. She watched his back for a moment and then straightened her own and walked behind him.

Chapter Three

Priya had found out about surrogacy through Poonam, whom she had met at a South Indian cooking class. Priya had always prided herself on her cooking, but then she met Madhu's mother, Prasanna, who was like a South Indian Jamie Oliver. And Madhu loved his mother's cooking.

It wasn't really a competition, she knew—after all, could Prasanna whip up a coq au vin or bake a chocolate soufflé that melted in your mouth? But still, Priya couldn't help but want Madhu to drool over her *sambhar* and coconut chutney just as he did over his mother's.

It was a sponsored link on her Facebook page that led Priya to a cooking class at Restaurant Sakshi, owned by Mrs. Sachidanadan or, as she went by, Mrs. S, convenient for the non-Indians who found her last name to be a tongue twister.

And Mrs. S definitely delivered. She transformed Priya from an amateur South Indian cook to a decent one, and Priya knew that with four more months of classes to go, her chances of acing the *dosa*, the holy grail of South Indian cooking, were good.

Poonam took the classes mainly to get away from home.

"I have two kids and they're home all the time.

My husband travels nearly five days a week. By Friday night every week, I'm ready to slit a wrist. But with this class, every other Saturday at least, I feel like a normal person, not a mommy or a wife or a crazy lady who's running around her life like a chicken without a head," Poonam told Priya at their first class.

Poonam wasn't the type of woman Priya usually got along with. She was a stay-at-home mom who let her husband run her life. She got permission to go to a cooking class, the mall, the grocery store . . . everything. She would go to the salon and lie about how much it cost, as if her husband couldn't just check the bank statement. She was the kind of woman who bought something new and, if her husband noticed, said, "This old thing?"

But Poonam understood the tragedy of Priya's life. She herself had gone through five miscarriages and three failed IVF treatments before hiring a surrogate through Happy Mothers. Now she had two children who were driving her out of her mind.

Priya even invited Poonam and her husband, Ranbir, over for lunch one Saturday to help convince Madhu about using a surrogate.

Of course, Priya had not counted on Poonam's two kids being an unholy nightmare. Natasha was three and Tara was fourteen months old, and both were walking advertisements for contraception.

That lunch had been a turning point for Madhu.

"*Arrey yaar*! You can adopt, but God knows what you bring into the house," Ranbir began as they sat on the patio with drinks and snacks.

"I think adoption is a good thing," Madhu said as patiently as he could.

"Good for people like Angelina Jolie and Brad Pitt, but for people like us it's a nuisance," Ranbir continued. "It takes years. It costs so much money. And you don't know what blood you bring home."

"You bring home a kid," Madhu said, putting down his beer carefully on the wooden garden table. Priya knew his impulse was to throw that beer in Ranbir's face.

Poonam was holding Tara in one arm and put a hand on Ranbir's shoulder. "Come on, Ranbir, we might have adopted if we couldn't have had these two with a surrogate."

Ranbir shrugged. "I don't think so. My parents once brought this boy home . . . he was about ten or so. This was when we were living in Chandigarh. The boy came from a poor family. An orphan, I think, and we were going to have him do things at home. He turned out to be a total rascal. He stole from us and told stories about us to the neighbors. It was a disaster. We had to send him away."

This time it was Priya whose spine straightened a bit.

Ranbir looked at her and sighed. "I can just see the look on your face. You're thinking, how could they have a ten-year-old boy servant? Look, that kid would have had a better life with us than without us. Living on the street is not all *Slumdog Millionaire*; there is no game-show winner at the end of the dark pit their lives are," Ranbir said. "Those are the facts of India. Just like . . . *arrey*, Natasha, don't pull out those roses, *beta*."

Both Priya and Madhu noticed how his tone went from harsh, while talking about India, to honey-sweet when he addressed his errant daughter, who was busy plundering Priya's well-maintained garden.

"That's why surrogacy in India made sense to us," Ranbir continued. "Those people need the money. Our surrogate has two children and no husband. She lives with her parents. Her father is part of a cleaning crew for offices or some such thing. They have little money. This way she is able to give her children a better life." Ranbir smiled at his daughters. "And we get joy. Immense joy."

Ranbir and Poonam were regular people like them with regular incomes and lives. These were real people, not some couple on a television show talking about their experiences. These were everyday people. And if they could do it, how bad could this be? It was legal. If it were this horrible exploitation, someone would have a law against it, wouldn't they? It was safe. Thousands of couples around the world had had babies this way. It was affordable.

Priya didn't believe in the blood nonsense, but

she had heard horror stories about adoption. How you waited for years, and even then you might not get a baby. The heartbreak of thinking you had a child and then didn't. Or worse, you had to adopt a baby with special needs and the haunting burden of that. Adoption was an option, but less attractive than surrogacy for her.

With a surrogate they not only brought home their baby, but helped a poor woman lead a better life. Nine months of carrying a baby against a lifetime of *immense joy,* as Ranbir put it: it was no contest. By sundown, Madhu had agreed to talk to the doctor who ran Happy Mothers. Priya never invited Poonam's family over again, but she was happy to see her every other Saturday in class and discuss her surrogacy plans without worrying about being judged.

"Doesn't she look thinner than she did the last time we saw her?" Priya whispered into Madhu's ear as soon as the surrogate and her husband walked into Doctor Swati's office.

"You're imagining things," Madhu said, and held her hand tightly.

"Look at her; she's even thinner than me," Priya said, trying her best not to have a nervous breakdown right there.

Priya's whispers were louder than she had expected, and everyone in the room turned to look at her.

Both Priya and Madhu smiled sheepishly.

Namaskaram, they greeted Asha. It seemed inappropriate somehow to stand as strangers when this woman could now be carrying their child, Priya thought.

"Well, the blood test is here and Asha is pregnant," Doctor Swati said with a smile.

The air whooshed out of Priya and she gasped. "Thank God."

Madhu grabbed her hand and they hugged. He kissed her on the mouth, and they both laughed softly. Magic had happened. When they pulled apart, their act of joy seemed almost vulgar. The surrogate and her husband sat quietly, displaying no emotion at all.

"Congratulations," Doctor Swati said.

Maybe the woman was being forced to have the baby, Priya thought. Maybe that was why she wasn't happy. But why should she be happy? she thought again. This was just a paycheck baby.

"This is a very special moment," Doctor Swati continued. "And I'm sure you have a hundred questions . . . both of you." She looked first to Priya, then Asha.

Priya gathered her wits and leaned over to touch the surrogate's hand. "Thank you so much," she said in English. Priya understood Telugu fairly well and had agreed to have the proceedings in the clinic conducted in Madhu's mother tongue, but she felt lost, unable to find the words that conveyed her joy and gratitude in her adopted language.

"You are welcome," the woman responded shyly in heavily accented English, and Priya thought then, happily, that the woman wasn't really that thin. She could see a nice strip of firm belly exposed through her sari.

"What happens next?" Madhu asked.

"Well, in two weeks we do an ultrasound. When we see a heartbeat we know it's going to be OK," Doctor Swati said. "I don't foresee a miscarriage, but you never know."

Priya knew all about not foreseeing miscarriages. She had not foreseen three of hers.

"We understand," Madhu said, and smiled at the woman carrying his child.

Priya wondered how he felt about the situation. What did he feel for this woman? Was he attracted to her on some primal level because she was going to give birth to his baby? No. Priya shook her head. These were crazy thoughts. She had no reason to be jealous of this woman. Asha was a surrogate baby maker, not a surrogate wife.

"Can we be in the room when you do the ultrasound?" Priya asked.

Doctor Swati nodded. "I have already discussed this with Asha, and she will be happy to have you with her."

"Thank you," Priya said again to Asha. "Thank you." She knew she sounded silly repeating herself, but a mere thank-you and some money didn't quite show how grateful she was, not when what they were getting from Asha was so enormous, so life changing.

Asha just nodded and then stared at her hands that lay on her lap.

"Thank you," Priya repeated, this time to Asha's husband, and he flushed visibly and nodded hurriedly.

What was his name? Priya tried to recollect, but she kept drawing a blank.

"Asha, Pratap, do you have any questions for Madhu and Priya?" Doctor Swati asked, and when they shook their heads, she continued. "Then if you could please wait outside. I'll speak with them and then call you in."

Priya thanked the couple one more time before they stepped out of Doctor Swati's office, and Madhu held her hand a smidge tighter. What the hell were they doing? They were handing over a baby, a person, to this woman's womb, a woman whose husband's name she hadn't been able to remember this morning. They would leave for California in two weeks and leave their baby here with someone they didn't know at all. This was insanity.

"Priya, are you OK?" Madhu asked, seeing her pallor. He put his arm around her. "You should be happy; we're pregnant."

"I *am* happy," Priya said. "But this baby will

grow far away from me, and it's just . . . it's scary."

"Yes," Doctor Swati said sympathetically. "But Asha and Pratap are part of a warm and loving family. They will take very good care of your baby."

"He doesn't beat her, does he?" The words sprang out of Priya.

Madhu gave her a quizzical look.

"No," Doctor Swati said, looking amused.

"Sorry, I feel so stupid," Priya said.

"Don't. You're not the first mother to have these questions and this reaction. It's a lot of stress to have someone else, someone you don't see every day, carry your child," Doctor Swati said. "But I promise you, this baby will be monitored and so will Asha. And you have nothing to worry about with Pratap. He's a kind and gentle man."

When they had first met them, spoken to them, Priya had felt that this was a good couple even though she had no reason to think so. It was a gut feeling, an instinct. And they were such a sweet-looking couple. She was almost petite in front of her husband's tall and broad frame. He was built like a quarterback. Asha seemed like a good mother who talked fondly about her children and her hopes for them. She seemed sincere when she told them that she wanted to help other people and that was why she had decided to be a surrogate. Still, Priya had felt a slight pinch of worry that this woman was not fully on board. But the husband, the kind husband, the one who didn't beat his wife, had been convincing.

"Her first two pregnancies were so easy. Even the births and deliveries were easy," he had said. He told them that he had been in the room with her when their babies were born. This was not the typical Indian husband waiting outside, avoiding the blood and mess with cigars or whatever it was that Indian men gave each other to celebrate the birth of a child.

Priya picked up the blood-test results that were in front of her on the doctor's table and traced her fingers over the strange numbers and figures and the line that read PREGNANCY = POSITIVE.

"You will make sure she takes her vitamins and all that?" Priya asked, even though she knew the answer. When Doctor Swati nodded, she nodded as well. "And you will see her once every two weeks?"

"Yes, and then every week during her second trimester, and when she is in the third trimester, I will see her every day," Doctor Swati said. "We have state-of-the-art prenatal care; you don't have anything to worry about on that account."

"I know you are very professional. I don't mean to doubt your expertise," Priya said apologetically, then jumped to another question before she forgot to ask it. "Do you think it will be OK for us to talk to Asha once in a while?"

"Yes, yes," Doctor Swati said. "We can set it up so that you can call on the days she comes for her checkup. The nurse will give you an update, and you can talk to Asha as well."

"Can . . . I don't mean to be rude, but can we send her some things that she might need? They would be gifts, not part of the payment," Priya said.

Doctor Swati seemed to think about it a moment and then said, "Some parents have no connection with the surrogate and that is their choice. If you choose to have a relationship with her, that is entirely up to you. I know some parents who send care packages once a month, something for the children and the mother. Things like moisturizer, shampoo, and underwear . . . small basic items. And I also know some parents who don't want to know their surrogate at all. Sometimes that is easier."

Priya knew she wasn't one of those mothers. She needed to know this woman. She needed to have a connection with her. A woman who was a complete stranger had transformed into one of the most important people in Priya's life, at least for the next thirty-seven weeks. How could she not know her?

"What are you smiling about?" Madhu asked as they drove back to Hyderabad.

"I saw this very, very cute crib the other day at

Babies 'R' Us . . . I went shopping with Nina—her sister's having a baby—and I thought that if we ever did have a baby I'd get that bed," Priya said. "How long do we have to wait, you think, before we can start buying stuff?"

"Ah. My capitalist consumer American wife," Madhu said cheerfully, but then suddenly became serious. "I'd rather we didn't buy anything until the baby is born."

"But then we'll have nothing when we come home," Priya objected.

Madhu shrugged. "I . . . I don't want . . . it's too hard, Priya. Remember that cricket uniform I bought when you were first pregnant? It killed me to throw it out, but I couldn't keep it, either. I just don't want to do that again."

"So, where will the baby sleep when we get home?" Priya asked.

"Ask Nina or Krysta or one of your friends to start shopping for you after the baby is born. You've helped Krysta move, like, a million times, and you've spent God knows how much money on Nina's kids—they owe you, and if not, I'll get Athar to buy what we need. Farah will probably jump at the idea," Madhu said.

"No way. I'll ask Krysta. I don't want Farah anywhere near my baby's room," Priya said. Her friends she loved and trusted implicitly to know her taste, but not Madhu's. And besides, she couldn't stand his best friend, Athar, and his wife, Farah.

"As you wish—and I don't think I'd want Farah decorating any room in our house," Madhu said. "She has a distinct style."

"You mean gaudy?" Priya suggested.

Madhu laughed. "I was thinking vulgar, but yeah, same ballpark."

They drove silently for a while.

"There's no guarantee, is there?" Priya asked quietly.

"No," Madhu said, and put his hand on hers. "But I have a good feeling about this."

"I'm scared, Madhu," Priya told him.

Madhu didn't say anything for a long while, and then as he pulled his hand away from hers to shift gears, he said, "I'm scared, too."

Prasanna was waiting with an open box of *ladoos* at home. Madhu had called his parents from the road to give them the good news. Prasanna confessed she had bought the sweets the day before and hidden them, just in case. Priya decided to call Poonam before she called her parents.

"See, it happened just like I told you it would," Poonam said, her voice loud against the screaming sounds of her girls. "Ranbir, I'm on the phone; can you get Tara? Natasha, stop pulling your sister's hair." Then there was a pause, and she said, "No, she's not a doll. Ranbir, can you please deal with this? I'm on the phone.

"Sorry," Poonam said. "I'm back and now have found sanctuary in the bathroom. Some days these girls drive me crazy."

"I can't wait to feel like you," Priya said, unable to contain her excitement. Usually she would have made a mental promise not to raise her kids like Poonam, but right then she would have given anything to be able to say that her kid was driving her crazy.

"It's going to happen sooner than you think," Poonam said.

"But what if she loses the baby? We've got no guarantees yet." Priya voiced her concerns.

First they had needed to get through conception, then the two-week check, then the twelve-week check, then the twenty-week check, then the twenty-five-week check, then . . .

"Indian women are tough; she won't lose the baby," Poonam assured her.

After hanging up with Poonam, Priya called Krysta, her closest friend, and then, begrudgingly, her parents. Talking to her mother when she was this happy was never a good idea; Sush could only ruin it. But Priya had to tell them. They were the grandparents, after all. *Still,* Priya thought, *better to call Dad's cell phone.*

"She's pregnant, Dad," Priya said as soon as he said hello. "We're pregnant. We're going to have a baby."

"That's great news," her father said. They

chatted for a while before he asked if she wanted to talk to her mother.

"No," Priya said.

"Why not?"

"Because she'll be difficult about the whole adoption-versus-surrogate thing again," Priya said. "And I'm too happy to be brought down by—"

"Come on, Priya," Andrew interrupted. "Sush is happy for you."

"No, she isn't," Priya said, frustrated. She knew what Sush would say, and she prepared herself for the soapbox speech.

"Yes, yes, she is. Here . . ." Her father handed the phone to Priya's mother despite her protests. He did this all the time, had done it all her life. Andrew was an absent parent—a present husband but an absent parent. He loved Priya, she had no doubt about that, but he had always kept himself out of her relationship with Sush.

"I can have a relationship with you and with your mother, but I can't broker a relationship between the two of you," he would say.

Priya had long given up on getting support from her father if her mother was against something. His parenting style was simple: *if your mother is OK with it, then OK.*

"Congratulations, my dear," her mother said stiffly. "But you know you have to wait to celebrate for a few weeks to make sure there isn't going to be a miscarriage."

"Mum, why would you even say that word?" Priya demanded. "Think positive. No negative vibes, please."

"It isn't about positive or negative. I'm being practical here. Miscarriages happen in the first trimester; you know that better than anyone. I just want you to be prepared," her mother responded.

"I don't want to be prepared for the worst situation all the time," Priya all but yelled. "I don't want to think about the bad things that can happen. Can't you talk about the baby? Can't you talk about how wonderful it's going to be to be a grandmother?"

"There isn't going to be a baby if there's a miscarriage, sweetie," her mother said calmly. "I just don't want you to get your hopes up too much yet."

"So, I should just wait to hear the worst for the next nine months?" Priya asked.

She heard her mother sigh across thousands of miles from Seattle. "You're misunderstanding me and twisting my words, as you always do. All I'm saying is that you need to prepare yourself in these early days of a pregnancy. It's just like when you were pregnant and you wouldn't listen—"

"Just because I miscarried doesn't mean she will," Priya snapped. "I have to go. Bye." She hung up before her mother could say one more word.

• • •

"Sush was her usual wonderful self, I see," Madhu said when Priya stormed into the TV room where the sweets were spread out along with some fried savory snacks. Just looking at the food made Priya crave a fresh salad with a simple dressing of lemon juice.

"Sush wanted me to be prepared for a miscarriage," Priya said, and flopped on a chair beside Madhu.

Prasanna offered a plate with a *ladoo*, and Priya took one to avoid another "eat something, you're too thin" scene.

"Your mother is not a bad person. She's difficult at times, I agree, and this was inappropriate, but you have to let it go," Prasanna said, and Priya's eyebrows went flying up.

Madhu cleared his throat. There were rules. Priya could bitch about her mother, but no one else was allowed to say anything about her.

"She just sees things differently than you do," Prasanna said, and Priya shoved the *ladoo* in her mouth to keep from saying something rude and unforgivable.

"She doesn't mean to hurt your feelings," Prasanna continued.

"She knows, Amma," Madhu said. "I just called Mayuri and told her."

Mayuri was Madhu's only sibling. Two years younger than Madhu, Mayuri was single, lived in

58

London, and didn't seem to care at all about the rules her parents lived by. Prasanna and Sairam didn't speak much about Mayuri—they didn't say it, but it was obvious that they were embarrassed about their thirty-two-year-old single daughter.

"Can't find a man and don't have time to have a baby, so maybe this could be an option for me as well. Need to find a sperm donor, though," Mayuri had said when Priya told her about their last-ditch effort.

Mayuri had struggled in India, wanting to be a fashion designer back when everyone wanted to be a doctor or an engineer. Her parents had been appalled. Not only was she saying no to an arranged marriage, she was also saying no to a dignified career.

But she had made it. Tough as it had been, Mayuri was now working for an international retail chain and thought of herself as a testament to how Indians could have careers outside engineering and medicine.

"How is your sister? She never calls us," Prasanna said, her attention quickly diverted from evil Sush to evil Mayuri.

"Mayuri is busy, Amma," Madhu said.

"You're all so busy. Busy all the time. Just work, work, work," Prasanna said, and then looked at her husband. "Why don't you ever say anything?"

Sairam, as always, had his nose in the news-paper and looked up, dazed. He wasn't following the conversation. He never did. Priya often thought that Madhu's absentmindedness came from Sairam. As for the rest of him, God knew where that came from. Looking at Mayuri and Madhu, it was amazing that they even had parents like Prasanna and Sairam. They were a relatively conservative Indian couple and had raised their children in this very house with their morals and values: duty was important; happiness was not. Yet both Madhu and Mayuri were seeking their own happiness seemingly without being affected by their childhood. Priya, on the other hand, was bogged down by her childhood and mother. Whether about her career choices or her family planning, Priya had always felt burdened by her mother's rejection.

"It's like this," Mayuri had once explained, citing the several thousand pounds and five years in therapy she had spent to find herself. "You keep going to a bookstore and asking for a dozen red roses. They obviously don't have red roses and you come home disappointed. That's what's going on with your mother. You keep expecting roses and keep getting disappointed. I know not to ask for roses at a bookstore. That's why I have no issues with my amma."

"You make it sound so easy," Priya said.

"I didn't say it was easy," Mayuri said. "It took me a long time and a lot of effort. There were a lot of tequila shots, irresponsible one-night stands, and shrinks involved."

• • •

Whenever they came to India, Madhu and Priya always stayed for two weeks at least; their trips were packed with visits to relatives and friends of Madhu's from college days. Tonight they were off to see Madhu's friend Jeevan and his girlfriend, Rosie. Jeevan and Rosie were defying convention and living together without the benefit of marriage. His parents were not happy about him living with a Christian girl, and her parents had disowned her for wanting to be with a non-Christian, and that, too, without marrying him. They intended to get married eventually, but for now they were too busy with their careers. Jeevan was a partner in a software consulting firm, and Rosie had her own advertising agency.

They met for drinks at Jeevan and Rosie's house in Banjara Hills. A mammoth mansion, the home was designed to cause envy. Jeevan and Rosie liked to throw parties that were legendary. Their New Year's Eve party was one of the best Madhu and Priya had attended, by far.

Jeevan and Rosie had decided not to have any children. It didn't suit their lifestyle.

"We like to travel," Jeevan told them. "We like to socialize and we have busy work lives. We don't have time for children."

Priya could imagine a man saying that—hell, she could even imagine Madhu saying that—but she couldn't understand how Rosie felt the same way. But for her persistence, Madhu would have been fine without a child. Disappointed, but he would have gotten over it, unlike Priya.

"Don't you want to feel life inside you? Don't you want to hold a baby, be a mother?" Priya asked, and Rosie shrugged as she smoked a cigarette.

"And give all this up?" she said, moving her hands over her body.

"You can always get your body back," Priya said. "I know plenty of women who have children and look amazing."

"Honey, I can buy my body back if need be," Rosie said with a laugh. "I just can't see how a child will fit into our lives. Just last week Jeev had to go to Paris for a conference, and I took a couple of days off and went with him. We had the best time. We couldn't do that with a child hanging on to my tit."

Priya wished then that she were more like Rosie, wished that she hadn't had this burning desire to be a mother that kept her and Madhu from jetting off to exotic destinations.

When Madhu had first told Jeevan about their plan to get a surrogate and asked him to check up on Happy Mothers for him, he and Rosie had thought it was a fabulous idea.

"The only way to do it," Rosie said now as she served mojitos on the patio with a view over their swimming pool. "Let someone else grow fat."

"Oh God, that's not why we're doing this," Priya said.

"I know, honey," Rosie said as she sat down next to Jeevan and lit another cigarette. "But you have to admit it's a nice way of doing it. If I wanted children, I'd do it that way. Someone else can deal with the blood and gore."

"But if you don't like the blood and gore, then what will you do once you take the baby home? There will be poop and gore," Jeevan said, and Rosie made a gagging sound.

Priya and Madhu looked at each other, thinking the same thing—these two *so* needed to grow up.

"Ten lakhs doesn't sound like that much money to us," Rosie said. "But to them it's probably a lot."

"Ten lakhs is a fair amount of money," Madhu protested.

"A hundred years ago, maybe," Jeevan said. "Remember the days when being a *lakhpati* was a big deal? It was like being a millionaire in the United States. Now neither seems to have much weight. A million dollars just doesn't cut it anymore, and a lakh is nothing. I paid ten lakhs for my car, and you're paying that much for a baby. It's ironic."

One of Priya's single colleagues who had no desire to have children used to joke about how in eighteen years Priya would introduce him to her child and he'd introduce her to his yacht.

"How are things in the United States?" Jeevan asked Madhu, and when he made a noncommittal sound, Jeevan laughed out loud. "How many times do I have to ask you to move back here, man? Hyderabad is as sexy as San Francisco, and there's so much money to be made here. You move here and I'll take you on as a partner. Your kind of sales experience will be great for my company."

Jeevan was constantly trying to recruit Madhu, but there was no way he would move to India, not as long as he was married to Priya. Vacations were one thing, but to live in India—to see this level of poverty every day, to see the dirt and dust, the desperate lives, the human suffering—it would be too difficult.

India was tough on the nerves if you hadn't grown up there. The abject desperation of people living on the streets; the children who grabbed your clothes, begging for money; the thin and dark woman who moaned while she held out her hand; a baby suckling on the nipple of her dried-up breast . . . it was a far cry from the States, where poverty had a very different meaning than it did here. Madhu tried to stop Priya when she gave money to every hand that begged for it, but she couldn't help it. A few rupees didn't amount to much for her, but for the person who was begging for it, it was a gift, a need fulfilled.

"Don't encourage the beggars," Madhu would say.

"I'm not the one encouraging them," Priya would respond. "If you guys cleaned up your country and gave these people a decent life . . . they wouldn't be here."

Each time she left India, Priya went back feeling so fortunate, so lucky to have the privileges and the luxuries she did. If she had a baby, that baby would have everything she needed and wanted; there would be no need to beg on the streets. But for these women, there was no choice. Just like Asha, who had to grow someone else's baby in her womb so that she could give her family a better life. It wasn't exactly charity, but Priya really did believe that by using a surrogate, she was helping a woman who could end up on the streets. Someone would have a better life while she got a baby. Really, how could her mother think that there was anything wrong with that bargain?

"Priya would learn to enjoy India, trust me," Rosie said.

"No, I wouldn't," Priya said, sipping her mojito. "Wild dogs couldn't drag me here. Not for love, not for money. California is home."

"What if Madhu insisted on moving?" Jeevan asked; it was a challenge.

Priya looked at Madhu and he smiled at her— that warm smile that told her he loved her and there was nothing he wouldn't do for her.

"He won't," Priya said confidently.

"So, he has to make sacrifices for you to live in California?" Jeevan attacked.

"*Arrey*! Let's not make a drama out of this. I love California a lot better than Hyderabad," Madhu said, interrupting Jeevan. "I couldn't imagine living elsewhere."

Priya knew this was true. Madhu had himself become too American to live in India. He might have grown up here, but he wouldn't fit in anymore.

They made love almost desperately when they got back to Madhu's childhood bedroom that night, thanks to the excitement of Asha being pregnant and three strong mojitos. Between giggles and loud whispers of telling each other to shush, they groped and touched and enjoyed having sex like they hadn't in a very long time. The pressure was off. Sex had nothing to do with making babies this time—sex was for fun.

"Do you think your parents heard?" Priya asked when they finished, sweaty and breathless.

"The whole neighborhood heard," Madhu said, and they both burst into laughter. "And this bed creaks like a son of a bitch."

"You think they knew what the creaking was about?" Priya asked, the rum in the mojitos still running through her blood, making her giggle.

"Probably," Madhu said.

"You think if they heard it again they'd be offended?" she asked.

Madhu started to move back and forth while he lay on his back, making the creaking sound, and Priya laughed hysterically, lying next to him.

"Our bed doesn't make such a ruckus, does it?" she asked.

"I don't think so, but it's been so long since you and I had some quality sex, I may have forgotten," he said. "Let's make sure when we get back we do this on an experimental basis, you know, to make sure the bed doesn't creak when there's a baby in the next room."

"Yes, it wouldn't do to wake up the baby," Priya said, and leaned back against the pillow, content. "We're going to have a baby," she said, still in awe.

"Yes," Madhu said. He moved his pillow up the headboard and leaned against it. "We need to think of names. We need some good names."

"I don't think we can name the baby before we see it," Priya said.

"True. But we can have a short list," Madhu said.

They'd had this discussion once before when Priya had been pregnant the first time. The second time they had been too scared.

Priya felt some of that old fear again. What if there was another miscarriage? She felt it was bad luck to talk about baby names. But she also wanted to talk about them, because that made the baby real. She felt the fears and conflicts of being pregnant once again, even though she wasn't the one who was pregnant this time; it was another woman, from another world.

"I like the name Abhay for a boy," Madhu continued.

"Americans can't pronounce Abhay; they will say *Abby,*" Priya said, pushing the fears aside. "My dad will say *Abby.* I think we need to find a name that everyone can pronounce.

"I still like the name Ayesha," Priya said. That was the name they had picked for the girl they were both convinced they would have when she had been pregnant that first, beautiful, carefree time.

"Me, too," Madhu said. "But I thought you liked Anastasia."

Priya shook her head. "Krysta told me she had a cousin called Anastasia, and everyone called her Nasty Girl."

"Great. That name is ruined," Madhu said.

"We don't have any boy names," Priya said thoughtfully. "How about . . ." She sighed. "I have no boy names."

Madhu put his arm around Priya and pulled her close. "We have plenty of time to come up with the right name."

Priya moved toward Madhu and nuzzled his chest. "And decorate the baby room. We'll need a rocking chair to feed the baby. I'm going to miss breast-feeding."

"Doctor Swati said that could be made to happen," Madhu said.

Priya shook her head. "It won't feel natural. And it's OK; it'll mean that you can also wake up to feed the baby at night."

They held each other as they fell asleep, Priya's thoughts on the baby that was growing in Asha's womb.

Transcript from message board
www.surrogacyforyou.org

Trying1Time: We have wonderful news. Our surrogate is pregnant, and on the first try. We will go for an ultrasound in two weeks and then back home to California. I'm so thrilled but also scared to leave my baby thousands of miles away.

Mommy8774: Congratulations. And I know what you mean. My heart broke in a million pieces to leave. I couldn't stand the idea of someone else having my baby. But at the end, when I held my child, it made it all worth it. With the second baby it was much easier. I knew what I was doing and in the end it's easier to do it this way than have more miscarriages.

LastHope77: Congrats! I know how you feel; I cried all the way back to the States. But Mommy8774 is right; holding the baby in your arms, you forget about the bad times. It's like women who forget how tough the labor and delivery was—this is our labor and delivery, this is our pain and suffering. No one said it was going to be easy, but it is beautiful in the end.

UnoBaby: Absolutely right. I love my baby. I don't even remember the sleepless nights of worrying. I am ready to do it again. LOL.

NearlyMother: We're going to try again. Our SM lost the baby—so now it's back to the drawing board, so to speak. It's going to be so much tougher this time. But congratulations, Trying1Time, on your pregnancy. XOXO.

Chapter Four

Asha glared at Pratap as she threw up for the second time that morning.

"This didn't happen with Mohini or Manoj," he said, concerned. "Are you sure everything is OK?"

"Yes," Asha said, wanting to scream at him. Now he acted concerned. Now that he had already forced her into this. He had used Manoj's future to blackmail her, and she had nausea from the pits of hell. If she had known it would be like this, there was no way she would have agreed to have another woman's baby.

"Doctor Swati says that it's a sign that everything is good with the baby," Asha said, annoyed with herself for comforting her husband while she could still taste the vomit in her mouth. Why didn't he have to suffer? He should have to feel this same swirl in his stomach—it had been his idea, after all.

The nausea started a week after they saw the baby's heartbeat in Doctor Swati's clinic.

The parents had been there. Asha knew their names, but she preferred to think of them as the parents, the mother and the father.

The mother was rail thin. She wore pants and a shirt, and you could see her collarbones. She had bright blue eyes and dark hair—she looked like Aishwarya Rai, the Bollywood actress, only not as pretty. The father was not as tall as Pratap, and he was thin, but not as thin as his wife. He wore sunglasses that he put into his shirt pocket every time he came inside a building. Asha wondered if the glasses would fall if he leaned over to pick something up. They both smelled expensive, and even though they were Indian, she felt they were foreigners, so different from anyone she had ever come in close contact with.

When Doctor Swati had pointed to the heartbeat, the father and mother had pointed as well and looked at the monitor as if it were a precious thing. Asha had felt neglected, like who she was and how she felt didn't matter; all that mattered to the parents was the baby, and that was the truth.

She was just a vessel, not a human being. Their relationship, if it could be called one, was about the baby inside Asha. Once the baby was born, there would be no relationship. They would not care about her. She would stop existing for them. There was no reason to feel bad about this; Asha had known it going in, but lying there with the cool gel on her belly, she felt a strange sense of injustice, of unfairness, that for nine months she would be very well taken care of, and after that, nothing except the money.

Before they left, they shook her hand; the

mother even hugged her, as if overwhelmed. She had said thank you again and again in English. *Thank you, sorry, please, I love you*—these were English phrases everyone was familiar with, even poor nobodies like Asha and Pratap.

The father spoke only in Telugu, clear and perfect, but the mother spoke a mixture of Telugu and English. Her Telugu was heavily accented, like when a foreigner spoke it, and she peppered it with many English words, not all of which Asha understood.

There had been no ultrasound when she'd been pregnant with her children. The *dai*, the village midwife, had checked her once in a while and had deemed everything OK. But this was different. Doctor Swati had prescribed her vitamin pills and instructed her on how much she could physically exert herself, especially when it came to cooking and cleaning and taking care of the family. No one had done that for her before. She couldn't help but feel that her children were not as important as the child inside her now.

"*Please* take good care of our baby," the mother had said as she left. She had said *Please* in English and the rest in Telugu.

"I'll take good care of the baby," Asha had responded.

"We'll send a device for you so that the baby can hear us," the mother said. "Will you play our voices for the baby?"

Doctor Swati had told Asha that some parents did this.

"Yes," she had said when they gave her a white device with their voices on it. But the baby would hear her voice, too, and Pratap's and Manoj's and Mohini's, Asha thought. Would their child seek them out after birth?

"We will come in the last month and stay until the baby is born," the father told her. "If you need anything, just let Doctor Swati know."

Asha couldn't imagine what she could want, but she said yes.

"If you ever feel anything is wrong, go straight to Doctor Swati," the mother said. "*Please,* just go to her."

Asha felt the mother's panic; it was just like hers when she was pregnant with Manoj. That had been her first pregnancy, and she had been certain that she would hurt him somehow.

"Don't worry," Asha said to the mother. "I promise I will take very good care."

The mother stared at her, as if checking to make sure she was telling the truth. Without thinking, Asha took the woman's hand in hers and put it on her belly. "I will think of this child as a gift for you. I promise."

Asha was surprised by her own words and actions, but the woman's agony had been compelling, and she found herself reacting.

Doctor Swati would send the parents reports

about Asha's health and the baby's and that would have to suffice. Asha couldn't imagine how hard that would be. She remembered the first time she'd had to leave Manoj as a five-month-old with her mother-in-law. She had been gone for just two hours for her puja, her prayers, at a neighbor's house, and she'd been worried the whole time. She at least knew her mother-in-law and trusted her, but these people were leaving their baby inside a stranger. They just had to take it on faith and on Doctor Swati's word that everything would be OK.

"If you need anything at all, please let Doctor Swati know," the father said to her again. "Thank you very much for helping us."

"You're helping me, too," Asha said, and for the first time since all of this had begun, she felt a modicum of rightness about what she was doing.

This couple would be overjoyed when she delivered. She would never make anyone as happy as she would make these two people.

"I wonder what else is going to be different about this pregnancy," Asha muttered as she walked out of the bathroom.

They had moved in with Kaveri, Raman, their boys, and Puttamma. Pratap's brother's *big* flat with its two bedrooms, one TV room, and small kitchen was filled to the brim.

Doctor Swati had warned her that every

pregnancy was different. So far, this one was sucking the energy out of her.

Asha took her weary body to a chair in the TV room and sank into its cushions.

The others had gone for a wedding in Hyderabad and would not come back for another two days. Kaveri had cooked enough food and put it all in the fridge. All Asha had to do was heat it up. Asha had had to get used to the fridge. She'd never had one before, but Kaveri had assured her that it was really very easy to use.

"Once you drink cold water from the fridge, you'll not want to drink any other water," Kaveri had promised her.

Manoj was doing his homework at the dining table. Pratap sat next to him, watching over his work. He couldn't understand the English words but felt it was his duty to sit with his son.

"Are you going to have a baby, Amma?" Manoj asked. His maturity was beyond his five years— they'd discovered that early on—so it wasn't a surprise that he understood Asha was pregnant.

"We'll talk about it later," Asha said, and then sighed. "Don't tell anyone about this."

"It's a secret?" Manoj asked.

"Yes," Asha said.

"Why?" Manoj persisted.

"It's just the way it is. So don't tell anyone anything in school, OK?" Asha said.

Manoj thought about it and shook his head. "I

don't understand. If I'm going to have a brother or a sister, why shouldn't I tell anyone?"

"Because we say so," Pratap interrupted. The problem with Manoj's extraordinary intelligence and maturity meant that he questioned more than his parents could answer.

Mohini woke up at that moment, and Pratap hurried to the children's room to pick her up. All four children were to sleep in one bedroom. Kaveri's boys were six and eight years old and had always been good to Manoj and Mohini. But Asha worried about the sleeping arrangement. For a few days anything could be tolerated, but for nine months?

Asha, Kaveri, and Puttamma slept in the other bedroom, while the men slept in the TV room. Kaveri and Raman had been very generous with their space and had even declined Asha and Pratap's offer to pay some form of rent while they stayed there.

"We're family; that won't be necessary," Kaveri had said. "You took care of my family when I was away having a baby, and now it's my turn to take care of you and your family."

Asha touched her jittery stomach; there was no bulge yet. Nothing indicated the change she was going through. She stroked her belly and then stopped; it was a futile gesture. This wasn't hers. She couldn't fall in love with this baby as she had with her own. She just had to let it grow. She wouldn't be picking names or thinking of what she would do once it was born, if it would be a boy or a girl.

It didn't matter this time.

As soon as the baby came out, it wouldn't be hers. She wouldn't even have to see it. Surrogates could if they wanted to, she'd been told, and she wanted to, just one glance before she sent it to its rightful parents. But after even a single glance, would she be able to give the baby away? Of course she would. She shook the silly thought from her head.

Pratap brought a sleepy Mohini to Asha. "Hold her; I'll get her milk ready."

Asha hugged Mohini, smelled her special smell, and kissed a plump cheek. "Did you sleep well?"

Mohini nodded. "Sleep," she said, and then laughed as Asha tickled her soft feet.

"Kiss," Asha said, and held out her cheek, and Mohini half licked it and half kissed it, a real kiss still not part of her repertoire.

Asha kissed her daughter on the nose. "You're such a pretty girl. Such a pretty girl."

Mohini turned away from Asha, grabbed the steel tumbler containing milk that Pratap held out, and guzzled it down.

Asha watched her daughter drink with gusto and felt relief. In the past, there were some days when they didn't have enough milk. But those days were over. They would now always have enough money to buy milk.

The poverty of their past would stay behind them. Each day would no longer be a struggle. They would be able to buy rice and sugar, the vegetables they wanted, and not just potatoes.

Asha used to count the money she hid in an empty steel container in their hut's small cramped kitchen to make sure there was enough to buy food for the coming day. It was a ritual on the weeks when Pratap didn't have work, weeks when they had to survive on the meager money they were able to save when Pratap did have work.

Pratap would feel guilty for sitting around the house, so he'd walk around the village, talking to people, seeing if he could find work in neighboring villages or in Srirampuram.

"We can always borrow some money from the village food store," Pratap had suggested more than once.

Afraid of owing money and being under anyone's thumb, Asha had always asked him not to do so. It wasn't as if Pratap listened to her, but he didn't want to be burdened by debt, either. He had seen his father work his entire life to pay off debt he had taken on as a young man, and that had been a lesson to both Pratap and Raman.

"We'll make do with what we have," Asha would say. "There's enough for the children to eat." But even as she spoke, Asha would worry about having enough for rent at the end of the month. Manoj went to a government-run school. It wasn't a good school, but it was a school and it was free. However, there were other expenses, and she knew that at this rate they would never have enough money to pay for a good school for Manoj.

"As long as there is food for the children," Pratap would repeat, "then we're OK."

Those had been difficult days. Impossible days. And there had been no end in sight. But now they would have a home, their own home, and they wouldn't have to worry about rent every month. They would have savings, so when things got tough they could still survive. She wouldn't have to go to bed hungry because she had given all the food to the children and Pratap. Manoj could become the man he was destined to be.

Thinking of the benefits this baby would bring calmed her upset stomach, helped the nausea subside. But it was a short respite, and before long she was running to the bathroom again, her stomach churning.

"You should have come to the wedding," Kaveri said to Asha the night they got back from Hyderabad. "You can't hide for the next nine months. We'll just tell everyone you lost the baby, like I did."

Puttamma was already asleep in the bed while

Kaveri and Asha lay on coconut straw mats on the floor, their heads resting on fluffy pillows.

"I'm just not feeling so good," Asha confessed. "All this nausea. I never had this with Manoj or Mohini."

"I was also tired a lot more," Kaveri admitted. "Do you think our bodies behave differently because the baby is not ours?"

Asha thought about it for a moment. "Maybe," she said. "You really didn't feel anything, giving the baby away?"

"It wasn't mine," Kaveri said. "It was someone else's. I always knew that. In the last months when I lived in the house, there was one woman who was very upset. She felt the baby was hers and that she would be cutting off a part of her soul. But we sign a contract; it's our job to be smart and not get attached to what's not ours."

Asha hoped she wouldn't be like that woman when the time came to give up her newborn. She hoped that she would be detached and not feel anything. But as she put a hand on her stomach, she wondered how a woman could not be attached to the life growing inside her.

"But you grow this life in your stomach; don't you feel it's your own?" Asha asked.

"You don't let yourself feel like that," Kaveri said. "Promise me, Asha, that you won't. It's a stupid thing to do. This is not yours. They put it inside you and you're like a machine; you're just growing it; you're not a mother to this one."

Asha didn't think it would be that simple. When the baby kicked and she soothed it by stroking her stomach, wouldn't she feel like a mother?

"Tell me about the surrogate house," Asha said instead.

Kaveri laughed softly. "It's hard in the beginning to be away from the children and home, but after a week I didn't want to come back. Gauri used to take care of us; she herself had been like us, twice before, and now she takes care of the pregnant women. We had a cook, a maid—we didn't do one thing. We went to this computer room for two hours every day to learn to use the computer. I didn't learn anything. But this other woman . . . I can't remember her name, but she did, and they say she got a job in some call center in Hyderabad because of it."

"Really?" Asha said. Everyone knew that you got paid well when you worked in a call center.

"And they also teach you English," Kaveri said. "I didn't learn much. But I can say, 'Hello, how are you this morning?' "

"What does that mean?" Asha said.

"It's just asking someone how they are," Kaveri said. "And you get back massages if your back hurts. Mine didn't, but I lied and got a massage every day. It was great."

"And when the baby came out?"

Before Kaveri could answer, Puttamma snapped, "Can you both stop the chitchat and go to sleep?" Kaveri and Asha fell silent.

Asha closed her eyes and tried to sleep, but it was elusive, like trying to catch soap bubbles when she washed the clothes.

She could remember when Kaveri had left the village; she was just six months pregnant. And then she came back and told everyone she had lost the pregnancy. Everyone had been very sympathetic, and no one had guessed what she had really done.

The next morning, Asha awoke with a flurry of emotions. Raw and confusing. She had dreamed of the baby that night. One with blue eyes and dark hair. For a moment she was holding it, and the next she wasn't. She had screamed in her dream and had kept shaking her head when a woman in a starchy white nurse's uniform like the ones they wore at Happy Mothers told her that there was no baby, there had never been one. She had dissolved into tears, and her dream had ended. But the burst of fear still ached within her.

As the dream dissipated, leaving behind the slightest bitter tingle in her heart, Asha rubbed her eyes and rolled her neck in a circle. She was just about to get up when she overheard Raman and Pratap, as always, talking about the money. How to spend the money? What to do with the money?

They were so preoccupied with it that they didn't notice her turmoil.

"Just buy a flat," Raman was saying.

Of course he was, Asha thought angrily as she got up.

"This is my money," she muttered as she straightened her sari that had come untangled while she slept. "I'm earning it with sweat and blood and pain and nausea," she added as she pulled her hair together and rolled it with a rubber band into a bun.

Being able to talk about such large sums of money was such a novelty that Pratap couldn't stop himself. Raman, for his part, felt that since he'd made such wise financial decisions with the money his wife had earned, he was the best person to offer Pratap guidance.

Guidance, my foot, Asha thought, her hand at the doorknob.

Puttamma and Kaveri had let Asha sleep in because the pregnancy was making her tired. Usually, she woke up early to get the children ready for school. She and Kaveri would pack small tiffin boxes, which they'd stuff into the bags the children carried on their shoulders, and run out to catch the green-and-yellow school bus.

But today was a Sunday. Everyone was home except Puttamma, who went to the temple for a good part of the day. She said she went there to pray, but Kaveri suspected that she couldn't stand having so many people in the house and left to gossip with the other old biddies on the street.

Asha was happy that the children were going to a better school than they had in Srirampuram, where they had just a thatched roof, a blackboard, and a teacher who struggled to teach all the classes.

Asha had been surprised to learn that Raman and Kaveri had none of their money left. They had spent more than two lakhs on buying their flat and had splurged with the rest on buying this and that. Now Kaveri was planning to be a surrogate again so they could save some money for Girish and Sirish's education.

Asha wanted to save the money for Manoj's and Mohini's education first, and once that was settled then they could start to worry about a house. They could stay in a rented place, something small in Srirampuram, or maybe buy something small if there was money left over. She could go back to sewing blouses for women and earn a small living on the side to help Pratap. In Srirampuram there would be more opportunities for tailoring, and she was a good tailor. She made all of their clothes, even Pratap's shirts, and everyone knew that sewing shirts was not easy.

"Yes, I agree that we should buy a flat. It gives us stability and it's an investment. That money is only going to grow. You bought a flat a year ago, and it has already appreciated," she heard Pratap say. She decided to open the door of the small bedroom with as much noise as she could.

They both stopped talking and smiled at her.

"You slept OK?" Pratap asked almost sheepishly.

Asha nodded and walked past them to where Kaveri was sitting.

She wanted to scream, but she knew better than to contradict her proud husband in front of his brother.

"I know," Kaveri whispered knowingly.

Kaveri was peeling potatoes at the dining table they had gotten for free from Raman's boss, who had bought a new one. The men were in the adjoining TV room. It was a small flat with thin walls; the two small bedrooms opened into the TV room and the adjoining dining space. Any conversation, even whispered, could hardly be private.

"You know what?" Asha asked icily.

"I know what you're thinking: that this is your money, and he should at least ask you how he should spend it," Kaveri said.

Asha didn't say anything, because no matter what she said it would sound like she was speaking ill of Pratap, and a good wife didn't speak ill of her husband to her sister-in-law, or anyone else for that matter.

"I felt the same way," Kaveri said. "Now we have no money left. He spent it all on this flat and on other nonsense. The flat is a good thing. We will always have a home. But we should have been smart about the boys' education."

"He bought you that beautiful necklace," Asha said.

Kaveri shrugged. "Good thing it's gold; I can at least sell it if I need to."

"Will you do it again?" Asha asked.

"I don't know. Maybe."

"Amma, when will the food be ready?" Girish cried out from the TV room. All the children were watching a Telugu movie. It was eleven in the morning and the children had had a light breakfast as they did on Sundays and were now waiting for a full and big early lunch.

"It'll be ready when it'll be ready," Kaveri yelled back. "You'd think we were maids."

"We are," Asha said.

"One day we should go on strike," Kaveri suggested. "Just sit down with our feet up, watching TV all day. That's what living in the surrogate house was like. I felt like I was on holiday."

Thanks to Kaveri, Asha was actually starting to look forward to moving into the surrogate house. She'd miss her children, but didn't she deserve to not take care of anyone for a few months? Imagine having someone to cook, clean, and give massages—what a life!

Due to the cramped housing situation, Asha and Pratap had not spent much time together. Not that they were allowed to do anything even if they could be together. Doctor Swati had asked them to not have sex three months before and during Asha's entire pregnancy.

Pratap had seemed embarrassed to hear a woman discuss such intimate things, but Asha had been relieved. She didn't like doing it when she was pregnant. In fact, she didn't like doing it at all, but then again, not many women she knew liked it. Kaveri was different. She said she had fun, which sounded like complete nonsense to Asha.

Asha wanted to talk to Pratap alone about the money and had planned for them to go and see the latest Chiranjeevi movie, *Shankar Dada Zindabad*, which was a remake of a hit Hindi movie. Asha had preferred the Hindi version to the Telugu one. She had seen it the year before with Kaveri and the children. Mohini had fallen asleep in the middle, but Manoj had enjoyed it very much, as had Kaveri's boys. Kaveri had just given birth to the white baby at the time, and she and Raman had just bought their new flat. Strange to think that it was just a year ago that Asha had judged Kaveri for getting pregnant with a white baby, and now here she was, also having to submit to her circumstance.

"What a bundle, complete *bakwaas* movie," Pratap said on their way back home. "Chiru is getting too old, and the story was a total waste."

"Well, he's what, sixty years old?" Asha said.

"And he's still playing a thirty-year-old hero," Pratap said. "I think there comes a point when you have to move on and do father roles like Nageswara Rao did."

"Ah, look . . . ," Asha began, and then faltered a little before she spoke in a small voice, her words rushed because of her fear. She had never questioned Pratap before. How would he respond? "Are you going to spend all the money on a flat?"

Asha had been just eighteen when she married Pratap, who was two years older. She had been so afraid when she'd met him that first time, during the bride-seeing ceremony, when he and his parents had come to her father's house. They had not talked at all before they had been married. All she had said to him was *namaskaram*, and he had nodded.

Now she had two children with him. She'd slept with him. She'd had sex with him. And yet, Asha was still afraid of Pratap. It wasn't *fear* fear— he had never hit her—it was just not being completely comfortable. It was the small things and the big things. Like when she was having her monthly, she would be too shy to tell him why she couldn't have sex with him; she would let him know with sign language, with a look in her eye and a shake of her head because she couldn't say it aloud.

She wasn't like Kaveri, who yelled and

screamed at Raman, even in front of their children. Kaveri did it with such ease, like it was nothing. She didn't seem to think it was strange that she called her husband by his name—"Raman, you whore's son . . . ," she'd begin. Asha always called Pratap *"yenvandi,"* the universal "dear husband."

So it took an immense amount of courage for Asha to ask Pratap if he was going to use the baby money to buy an apartment. She expected him to get angry about her interfering in money matters, but he surprised her; he didn't seem to mind at all.

"I don't know. That's what Raman wants us to do. But I don't know what's right for us. We have Manoj," he said.

Asha wanted to dance in relief. "And his education is so important."

"Yes," Pratap said. "We need to send him to a better place. There is a good boarding school in Hyderabad. He could go there."

A boarding school?

"But that would mean we won't see him every day," Pratap continued. "I don't know if that will work. Maybe we can find a nice one in Srirampuram. Chinna, this guy I work with, was talking about the one his boss's son goes to, which is supposed to be very good. They wear uniforms with ties and everything."

"Yes, it would be better if he stayed home with

us," Asha agreed, feeling a load lift off of her. He was thinking about Manoj when he thought about the money. He wasn't planning to barter his children's future away to buy them a house.

They walked silently for a while; then suddenly Pratap asked, "Do you think it's strange that you're carrying these people's baby for money?"

"Yes," Asha said. "Very strange."

"You know, it seemed OK when we all talked about it, but now that you're pregnant, it feels . . . it just feels odd," Pratap said. "Remember how much I touched your belly when you were pregnant with Manoj and Mohini? Now I can't do any of that."

"I can't do any of that, either," Asha said.

"I don't know if I'd want you to do this again," Pratap said. "So I want to be careful with the money we get and make some correct decisions. Raman wants Kaveri to do it again."

"Kaveri said she wasn't sure," Asha said.

Pratap nodded. "Raman told me that after the baby was born, Kaveri cried all the time for a couple of months. They never told anyone about it. But she was very upset."

Asha felt a shiver creep up her spine. That woman in the surrogate house who got attached to the baby, the one Kaveri warned her not to be like, what if that woman was Kaveri herself? Was that why Kaveri warned her not to get attached? Because she knew how hard it was to let go?

"Do you think it'll be hard on me to give it up?" Asha asked Pratap.

"I hope not," Pratap said. "And if we're careful from the start and make sure that we both know that it is not ours, it should be fine."

If only he could hear himself, Asha thought. Like it was that simple.

"Yes, we'll be careful," she said.

Pratap smiled and put his arm around her, and for that moment, Asha felt safe, forgetting for a few breaths her problems and the strange life inside her.

PART 11:
First Trimester

Chapter Five

The conception date was January 10, 2013, which meant the due date was October 3, 2013. Asha was now, based on the pregnancy calculator, five weeks pregnant.

According to the website Priya was consulting, the embryo was in three layers. The outer layer would become the brain, nerves, and skin. The placenta was fully functional.

She and Madhu lay in bed. "You know, no matter how many times you look at that website, the baby's size remains the same," Madhu said as he flipped channels.

Priya had lost the battle regarding having a television in the bedroom, and Madhu had lost the battle of having a laptop in bed. They both had sound arguments that each had chosen to agree to disagree about. Priya believed that when you went to bed, it was time to read, have sex, or sleep. Madhu, on the other hand, didn't read (Sush could still not believe that Priya had married a nonreader; it was a scandal) and liked to catch a cozy rerun while in bed. They had come to terms with this arrangement, and neither was bothered by it anymore.

"I don't think you appreciate the amount of pressure I'm under here," Priya said.

"Well, don't kill yourself," Madhu said, and leaned to kiss her. "I need to get some sleep."

"Aren't you jet-lagged?" Priya demanded. She had been cranky and drowsy at work the entire day and was now wide awake.

"Jet lag is for sissies," Madhu said, and within ten seconds she could see the gentle rise and fall of his chest.

She smiled, watching him sleep. He fell asleep so easily and peacefully.

Instead of reading on her iPad, she browsed the Internet, garnering unnecessary information about surrogacy and its emotional toll, reading arguments again and again about how it was actually a good thing to impregnate a poor Indian woman with your embryo.

"Madhu?" Priya nudged him. "Madhu?" she called out a little louder.

"What?" Madhu asked, burying his face in the pillow.

"Do you think we did the right thing?"

Madhu turned and looked at her in what she could plainly see was disbelief peppered with irritation.

"You've got to be kidding me," he said. "You woke me up to ask me . . . what?"

Priya bit her lower lip. Maybe waking him up wasn't such a good idea.

"Go back to sleep," Priya suggested.

Madhu groaned. He sat up and looked at her

pointedly. "You need to calm down. You need to drink some wine or take a pill or something."

"Oh for God's sake, I just woke you up because I was upset. *Soooorrrry*. It won't happen again, Mr. Grumpy," Priya said as she closed her iPad and put it on the bedside table.

"You wake me up in the dead of the night and you're angry with me?" Madhu demanded. "Are you fucking nuts?"

"You know what, you keep using that f-word all the time—but once the baby is here, you'll need to rein that in. Maybe you should start now," Priya said.

Madhu shook his head. "You need to see a shrink . . . no, not one shrink, you need a team of *fucking* shrinks."

"Such colorful language," Priya said. "Our daughter is going to look so cute using the f-word when she's three."

They looked at each other; Madhu was still baffled and Priya sighed. "So I'm upset and I'm trying to pick a fight."

"As long as we agree on that," Madhu said. "I'm going back to sleep. Do not wake me up unless there's an earthquake . . . over six point zero on the Richter scale, and only if someone dies."

He kissed her on the nose. "You're crazy, but I love you," he said, and rolled over and went right back to sleep.

"I love you, too," she whispered back.

Priya counted leaping sheep, keeping time with each snore.

They had met outside the library on a hot August afternoon. They were both in the second year of their master's programs. He was studying computer engineering, while she was getting a degree in environmental studies. She had been sitting on a bench under one of the trees, looking at her class schedule for the coming semester, and he had just walked out of the library. Their paths had never crossed before. He hung out with other Indians like himself who had come to the United States to pursue graduate school, while Priya belonged to a different crowd, one that had nothing to do with engineering or Indians.

He dropped a book as he was walking past her. It was more clichéd than a bad Hindi movie because the way Madhu told it, as he picked up his book and looked at her through his sunglasses, he fell in love. "Love at first sight," he would always say.

"Hi," he said to her as he straightened, picking up a book entitled *C++ Programming for Advanced Users.*

"Hi," Priya said, not particularly looking at him.

"Are you Indian?" he asked, and Priya snapped up her head. Only Indians asked a question like that, and only before proceeding to hit on her. She was nearly Indian, what they called an ABCD, an "American-Born Confused *Desi*," with *Desi* meaning "Country Person" in Hindi.

"Half," she said, because she noticed he was good-looking. Usually, she would've said something about being busy and walked away.

"What's the other half?" he asked.

"American," she said. "But . . . I'm completely American. Just ethnically half-Indian. How about you?"

"I've been in the United States for a year, so I feel completely American, too," he responded, and sat down next to her, which Priya had thought was optimistic of him. "But I'm ethnically fully Indian."

"Oh," she'd said, and started to put her books in her bag. It was time to leave.

"Can I buy you a cup of chai?" he asked. If he had said coffee, she would have left, but he'd said chai, and for some strange reason it had been charming.

"They don't serve chai at the canteen," Priya said.

"In that case, I can make you a cup of chai. I live just . . ." He stopped when he saw her lift both her eyebrows. Did he really think she'd go to his place after meeting him two minutes ago?

"On the other hand, I could just buy you a cup of coffee," he said with a broad grin.

It hadn't been love at first sight for Priya, but

she had spent that entire day with him and then had ended up in his room for the night in the apartment he shared with a friend.

Priya had never slept with someone on the first date. She generally believed in the third-date rule, but something about Madhu had made her lie down with him. Their lovemaking had been just as charming as their impromptu date had been. He had been careful, kind, and gentle.

"Is this OK? Are you OK?" he said so many times that she'd had to tell him, "You're not performing torturous surgery, you know."

He'd laughed then. "What can I say, I'm new to this."

"To sex?"

"Well, that, too, but I've never had sex with someone as beautiful as you," he said, and winked at her.

And after they'd made love, Madhu had heated bowls of rice with dal and brought them to his room. They had eaten the Indian leftovers and drunk white wine from a bottle, and sometime during that night, Priya fell in love with him.

They were inseparable after that. Desperate for each other. There had been no doubt within Priya; she knew Madhu was the one. There was a clarity about this relationship that had never been there for any other. And even now, years later, she still knew that this was the only man she had ever met who could make her as happy as she was.

But she wondered at times if he regretted their rushed courtship. Did he wish he had waited, married a fertile woman? Or a woman who wasn't "baby crazy" like she was?

She knew Madhu didn't want to hurt her when he called her that, but it wounded Priya all the same. He probably had no idea. By and large, Madhu and Priya shared a relatively dry, dark sense of humor and thick skins. But something about the phrase "baby crazy" got under Priya's skin. It was probably like calling a lunatic a lunatic to his face—the truth stung.

"You hit thirty and suddenly everything is getting wider and going south," Krysta complained as she and Priya got together for a coffee after they had sweated it out in a spinning class. They went spinning three times a week and, after some time in the sauna and a shower, ended up at the Starbucks on Castro Street, close to their gym.

"You hit thirty several years ago, and so did I," Priya said to Krysta. They were the same age, and the big three-O had passed them half a decade ago.

"You're married; you don't count. You can have hairy legs," Krysta said.

"So can you."

"No. I have to be prepared at all times, because you never know when the opportunity will hit. I may meet a guy at Whole Foods, and then maybe we'll end up at my place and . . . I'd need to have smooth legs for that," Krysta said.

"You pick up men at Whole Foods?"

"That's not the point, and yes, I once picked up a very nice BCG consultant at Whole Foods. He was cute, Romanian or Bulgarian or something, obviously didn't go very far," Krysta said.

It wasn't like Krysta slept around a lot, but compared to Priya, who had been with one guy for an eternity, she seemed like a sexual superhero. Krysta could pick up men anywhere she went. Priya didn't think she could pick up men quite that easily, even if she were single, but then again, being blonde, tall, and skinny probably helped Krysta a little as well.

"You can let your ass grow—and it probably will, considering your Indian genes—but I have to stay in shape," Krysta said.

Among all her friends, Krysta was the only one who talked nonstop about meeting men, sleeping with men, and weight control. It wasn't like Krysta was a ditzy blonde. She was a vice president at a big hotel chain, responsible for their sustainability department. It was her department that made sure everyone got those nice signs in the bathroom that talked about reusing towels to save water.

"My butt isn't going to grow," Priya said petulantly. "I spin."

"Yeah, but you can't fight genetics. And who

says a big butt is bad? JLo seems to be doing just fine with the junk in her trunk," Krysta said. "And speaking of JLo, I'm going to Rome next month for a conference."

"JLo? Rome?"

"Didn't she get married in Rome?"

Sometimes Priya wondered how Krysta's mind worked.

"Who cares," Krysta said. "Anyway, I'm going to Rome. You wanna join? Maybe Nina, too? I just have the conference for a day when I present, and then I'm all yours. We can, I'm told, find some excellent rooms at our five-star hotel."

"I can't just take off for Rome; I'm going to have a baby," Priya said without thinking. As the words came out, she realized how foolish it sounded. She wasn't even pregnant, for God's sake.

"I'll ask Nina," Priya offered as apology. "But she may pull the whole my-children-I'll-miss-them excuse."

"Are you going to become like that, too?" Krysta asked.

Priya shrugged. "I don't know. I don't know what kind of parent I'll be. I'm just relieved at the possibility of getting a chance . . . you know?"

Krysta nodded, and Priya felt that weight she always did when she thought about the baby.

"You'll be a good mother," Krysta said.

"How do you know?"

"Instinct," she said.

Priya shook her head. "Madhu says that I always need to have something to worry about. If it isn't getting pregnant, it's *Will the surrogate keep the baby?*, and if it isn't that, it's *Will I be a good mother?* I want to be a good mother. I want to be miles away from my own mother."

"Hey, everyone has issues with his or her parents, but it doesn't mean they didn't do anything right," Krysta said. "Your father is a good guy. I know, I know, he's always on your mother's side, but he's been there for you. Your mother is batshit crazy, but she's still in your life—she visits and makes you miserable, but she's there. I hardly talk to my parents. They have no idea what life I live. I see them once a year and . . . frankly, they're relatives but not family."

Priya smiled at Krysta. "I'm going to be the *Woe is me* routine, aren't I?"

"You sure are, but that's what friends are for— to tell you the truth when you're being a whiny little twit," Krysta said, drinking her coffee.

Priya met her friends alone in cafés and restaurants, but Madhu tended to meet his with their wives and children in tow, which meant, unfortunately, that she had to endure them as well. If it were just the men, friends mostly from Madhu's engineering-college days in India, she would probably be fine, despite their right-wing politics. But their wives? No one should have to endure these women.

"You know, I never ask you to spend time with Nina and Jordan, do I?" Priya used the line as an opening salvo.

"You don't have to come," Madhu said. "I'd like for you to; otherwise they'll gossip that we've gone splitsville. But besides that . . ."

Ugh. Priya could hear them loud and clear.

"Maybe they're splitting up, *yaar*," Aditi would say in her deeply accented English.

"Yes, yes, she never comes with him for our parties, like she doesn't care about his friends," Farah, who was married to Madhu's best friend, Athar, would say as she nodded, the way Indians did when they spoke, and then she'd stroke her belly. The woman was perpetually pregnant. She was on baby three or four now; Priya had lost count.

"I never liked her, Miss ABCD, always thinking she is better than us," Priya mimicked Simran, Brijesh's wife.

Madhu grinned. No one liked Simran. Brijesh used to be a normal guy, but then he met Simran and became this weird, money-obsessed, ball-less husband. Madhu's friends talked about Brijesh as BS, Before Simran, and AS, After Simran.

"You know, you might actually have fun," Madhu said as he slipped into a half-sleeve white shirt.

"Do we even have a present for JoJo?" Priya asked. JoJo was short for Jasmeet, who was celebrating her fifth birthday.

"I picked up a Barbie something that Brijesh suggested at Toys 'R' Us. It's in the car already," Madhu said.

"Well, aren't you Mr. Super Prepared?" Priya said.

"At your service, babe."

Priya narrowed her eyes.

"I promise wet, wild monkey sex if you come," Madhu offered.

Hmm. "Fine, but no baby talk," she forewarned him. She didn't want to discuss her surrogate with the very fertile wives of Madhu's friends.

"Of course."

"What? Have you told any of them?" Priya demanded.

When she told something to her friends, they kept it to themselves. When Madhu said something to his friends, they told their wives, and the wives made sure Priya knew that they knew.

Madhu had once made the stupid mistake of telling Athar about the problems they were having with fertility treatments, and wouldn't you have it, at Karthik and Latha's tenth wedding anniversary party, everyone told her how sorry they were before moving on to discuss fertility horror stories they had garnered from other friends and social media. If it wasn't infertility stories, then there was the whole, *Children are great, but if you don't have any, it doesn't mean your life is any less.* Only people with children said that. People who'd already had their biological fix could say that this wasn't so important, and you could be happy even if you didn't have a family.

Priya had been embarrassed and had felt inadequate.

"I don't need to see this on Facebook, OK?" Priya said.

"Just relax, no one cares that we're using a surrogate," he said, not looking at her.

"Have you told Athar?" Priya asked point-blank.

"No," he replied right back.

Priya didn't believe him.

Brijesh and Simran's lovely house in Milpitas was decorated up the wazoo for JoJo's birthday. Priya made a gagging sound when she saw the pink flowers, pink balloons, and general pink décor of the front garden.

"Jesus, it looks like someone threw up Pepto-Bismol all over the place," Madhu said.

"Why do adults have to be invited to a child's birthday party? I'd never invite JoJo to my birthday party," Priya said, stepping to the side to avoid being crashed into by JoJo and her posse.

"And who the hell calls their kid JoJo?" Priya demanded as they stepped into the doorway, fake smiles plastered on their faces.

"Celebrities and weirdos," Madhu whispered in her ear, and Priya had to control her laughter.

"Oh, you came," Simran said, like she was actually surprised, even though Madhu had said they would a month ago when the invitations had been sent out via mail, e-mail, and as an event invitation on Facebook. "You can put the present on that table." Simran pointed to a table that was piling up with gifts. "She's going to be so spoiled with all these presents, but you only turn five once."

"Right," Priya said.

"And you look so lovely, Priya," Simran said, her hands on Priya's shoulders. "What I wouldn't give to have that pre-mama body. Once you have children, everything goes to hell—the tits, the stomach, everything."

Well, then, good thing I can't have any, Priya thought to say, but only smiled and nodded and glared at Madhu, who put his arm around his wife.

"How about a drink, Simran? I could really do with a cold beer," he said, propelling Priya out of Simran's zone of attack and into the living room, which was decorated with pink balloon animals hanging from the ceiling.

"We almost decided not to serve beer . . . it is, after all, a children's party," Simran said, and then smiled. "But Brijesh put his foot down. You know how he loves his Sam Adams."

Madhu and Priya nodded and made the right

sounds as they sat down on a sofa, crushed between the armrest and Farah.

"How are you, Priya?" Farah asked, giving her a hug, her huge belly between them. "And Madhu, you look wonderful. Here Athar keeps growing wider; at least I have an excuse," she said, stroking her belly, "but you look tip-top."

Madhu looked bashful. Athar was slightly overweight. He was fine except for that protruding belly, which had, in all honesty, always been there, even ten years ago when Farah had married him.

"*Arrey yaar*, Madhu, you go to India, you come back and no call, no hello. What's up, man?" Brijesh cried out from behind them.

"Just been busy with work," Madhu said, shaking Brijesh's hand.

"*Kya*, work-*shurk*," Brijesh said. His voice was slightly slurred; as Simran had said, Brijesh did love his beer. It was five in the evening and the man was already a six-pack down, from what Priya could tell. Simran had managed to change a lot about Brijesh, but she couldn't quite get the frat boy out of him. He still drank like a fish, went out with the boys, and wasn't all that involved in his children's lives.

"Raising the children is Simran's business. Bringing home the bread is mine," Brijesh was fond of saying. Priya found that insulting, but Simran didn't seem to mind. Who knew, if Madhu had been a partner in a software company that went IPO in the nineties and avoided the Internet bust, maybe Priya would be too busy admiring her Chanel tennis bracelet to mind.

Priya knew that Madhu sometimes felt like the failure among his friends. They had taken advantage of the booming nineties, made money and built businesses or cashed in stock options, while Madhu steadily advanced at Oracle. He had a stable job, a decent career, but he wasn't about to become a millionaire. Even Karthik, who had a regular job like Madhu, had cashed in well when the start-up company he was working for was bought by Microsoft. Now he and his wife, Latha, had the money to buy a beautiful house in Los Gatos and invest in real estate back in India.

Madhu cared about these things. She didn't. Success was measured in dollars for him. It was an Indian thing, Priya had realized. She would always ask Madhu if he was happy and challenged in his job—the rest, she believed, would follow.

"I'm still waiting for the big payday," Madhu liked to say. "But I don't think it's coming. You don't become rich working your way up in a multinational. You become rich by starting a company and taking it IPO."

Priya wasn't part of that Silicon Valley crowd. She had a different academic and professional background. Even Latha, Karthik's mostly dim wife, could talk fairly intelligently about the

Internet boom, the Internet doom, and the stock market.

"I got him to get our money out, and it was the right time," she said. "You should've seen him then, screaming at me, but now he appreciates what I did. If we'd left the money there longer, we'd have lost fifty percent of it. Right, Karthik?"

"Right," Karthik said. "My wife is a financial genius."

"So when's the baby due, Farah?" Aditi asked.

Aditi and Tarun had one son, Dhruv, a five-year-old, and they had decided not to have any more. Dhruv had had many medical problems, and now he was finally getting better and not falling as sick. It had meant that Aditi, who used to be a consultant with Ernst & Young, had had to give up her career—and Priya felt she was bitter about it.

"April," Farah said. "And I can't wait. And this is it, *bhai*. No more children. Three is more than enough."

"Come on, *memsaab*, how can I have a cricket team if you stop at three?" Athar joked.

"You'll have to have the rest with your other wives," Farah quipped.

The conversation was cut short when seven children came into the dining room adjoining them, and the cake cutting and song singing began.

"Promise me we won't have parties like this when our kid turns five," Priya whispered into Madhu's ear.

"Promise," Madhu said, his eyes widening when JoJo shoved her little sister away as she clamored to have a piece of cake.

"It's my birthday," JoJo cried.

"Bebe just wants a slice of cake, *beta*," Simran said patiently.

"She should stay away from my cake. It's my birthday," JoJo yelled defiantly.

"And promise me that our children will be nicer than theirs," Madhu said, and Priya nodded, her eyes wide, as well, as JoJo pushed Bebe away again. Her parents didn't reprimand her but just carried her screaming younger sister away.

Everyone got cake in the end, even Bebe. They had samosas and *pakoras*, mutton *biriyani*, and plenty of candy for the kids to devour.

Except, of course, for Dhruv, Aditi's son.

"*Arrey*, Aditi, a little chocolate won't hurt him," Simran said.

"No," Aditi said, taking a mini Mars bar away from her son's hand. "You know, Dhruv—no candy."

Aditi then looked at Simran, her eyes angry. "Simran, he's only allowed candy on Fridays, and one piece at that. In this day and age, we can't take chances with our children eating all this processed sugar and . . . well, there is the weight issue."

She looked pointedly at JoJo then, who, for her age, was probably carrying more baby fat than she needed to.

"I can't stand her," Aditi said to Priya when Simran walked away, angry at the backhanded comment Aditi had made about her daughter being fat.

Priya only nodded. She wasn't about to say anything about anyone to anyone in this crowd. They might bitch and moan about one another, but they were best friends in the end. She, on the other hand, was an outsider.

"I'm so sick of these stupid parties," Aditi said. "I'm so sick of staying at home. You're lucky, Priya, no children, no nothing. You can actually have a social life, a career, and sex with your husband without worrying about who comes into the bedroom."

"Well . . . ," Priya began, and then shut up. She would trade all of that for a baby, she wanted to say, but she realized that Aditi wasn't talking about Priya; she was venting.

"My first job at Ernst and Young, in two years I was a manager, pulling six figures," she said. "Now, I spend my time worrying about when Dhruv will fall sick and when I need to clean up vomit. His life"—she nodded toward her husband—"on the other hand, hasn't changed. Tarun has a career, the six-figure salary, and a social life. He could even be having sex with someone on the side, and then life would really be perfect for him, wouldn't it?"

Priya put an arm around Aditi and led her onto

the patio out back, away from the kids eating inside.

"What happened?" Priya asked. It was obvious that this level of outburst was new.

"I started to apply for jobs," she said with a rueful smile. "I thought it would be easy. But damn it, it isn't. They wanted to hire mc as a program manager at Sun for fifty thousand a year. Fifty? I made more when I came out of business school. Now I'm worth fifty."

"Maybe you need to work your way up again," Priya said.

"I'm nearly forty, Priya; there isn't any work your way up. It's fucking over," she said, and then put her hand on Priya's. "Don't give up your job. No matter what. Keep your career. You give it up, you'll be fucked, like me."

"Did you take the job at Sun?"

Aditi shook her head. "You know Tarun got promoted? Vice president of business development. His travel days have gone up; he's gone now three days out of the week plus more weekends. I can't have a full-time job with his schedule. I mean, someone has to pick up and drop off Dhruv at preschool. Goddamn it," she said, choking up. "Even at fifty grand, I was ready to take that job. Why does he get to have a career and I don't?"

"Get a nanny," Priya said. "If he's making so much money, that shouldn't be a problem."

Aditi shook her head again. "Tarun doesn't think that's good for Dhruv."

"Tell him to stay at home, then," Priya said.

Aditi laughed. "I can't. He makes so much more than I ever did or could. We have the life we have because of him. I drive a Lexus, Priya. I should be happy."

"Is that what Tarun said?"

Aditi nodded and picked up a napkin from the patio table, wiping the tears off her cheeks.

"None of them gets it," Aditi said, pointing her chin to the house. "They think I hit the jackpot. Tarun has a great job, and I have the luxury of sitting at home, turning into a fucking vegetable."

"What are you girls talking about?" Tarun said as he walked in, a glass of scotch in his hand. "About your virile men?"

Madhu followed Tarun and came to stand beside Priya. He immediately put his arm around her.

"You know, you guys have been together as long as any of us have, and you're so lovey-dovey still," Tarun said. "The man can't keep his hands off of you, Priya. *Kya magic hai?*"

"Maybe because they still love each other," Aditi said.

"I still love you, *jaaneman*, my life," Tarun said, and dramatically pulled Aditi into his arms. She flinched and pushed him away.

"You smell of whiskey," she said.

"Well, that's what happens when you drink single malt, baby," Tarun said.

"I guess I'm driving, then," Aditi muttered. "I'll get Dhruv; it's time to go home."

"Yes, madam," Tarun said, and saluted. "She's a tyrant," he said to Madhu and Priya. "We should hook up for dinner sometime."

"Sure," Priya said.

"Wow," Madhu said as the unhappy couple left the patio. "Do you think we'll ever end up like them?"

"No," Priya said. *God, I hope not.*

"Are you sure?"

"Yes."

"Time to go home?" Madhu said.

"Sure," Priya said.

But they stayed for another drink while Simran's housekeeper, a Mexican woman named Maria, cleaned up.

They sat on the patio, the light breeze soothing. This was the best thing about living in California, Priya thought: even in February they could sit outside in nothing but a light jacket. Priya cuddled against Madhu, feeling secure in her marriage. Nothing made you feel lucky in your relationship like seeing someone else's crappy one.

"So, Priya, now that we have some quiet, tell us about this surrogate," Farah said, and Priya stiffened, feeling the squeeze of Madhu's restraining arm.

"Surrogate?" Simran asked. "What is this, *bhai*? No one tells us anything."

"When Athar told me, I couldn't believe it, but considering all your problems, this is a great solution, *nahi*?" Farah said. "So, this woman is in India? How much does it cost?"

Priya didn't look at Madhu because she wasn't sure she could stay calm if she saw his face.

Athar looked just as embarrassed as Madhu. "Farah, I'm sure this isn't something they want to talk about."

Farah waved a hand. "*Arrey*, having a baby is good news. So tell us, Priya, how does the process work?"

Priya took a deep breath. "Like Athar said, we don't want to talk about this. It's still early days."

"So there's a risk of losing the baby?" Latha asked.

"No," Madhu said immediately. "We just don't feel comfortable talking about it."

"That's the way to have a baby, though," Farah said, stroking her big belly. "I mean, you don't have to get fat or go through labor and delivery. Athar, we can have a cricket team if we can have the rest of the babies that way."

Priya wanted to scream. How dare Farah make light of this? Priya could hardly sleep. She was so scared about her baby growing up thousands of miles away in a stranger's belly. And this woman was making a joke about it?

Silence fell over the small crowd of people, and relief came in the form of Latha's daughter Noma, who stepped onto the patio wailing. "JoJo hit me," she said, rubbing her shoulder. Noma was seven and slight and couldn't quite compete with the full-bodied JoJo.

Nikhil, their five-year-old son, followed, eating a bar of unidentified chocolate. "My belly hurts, Mama," he said, and sat down on Latha's lap.

"We should go," Priya said then, and stood up.

They were in their car when Athar came running out. Madhu rolled down his side of the window, but Athar spoke to Priya.

"I'm so sorry, Priya. I know you wanted to keep this a secret . . ."

"It's OK, Athar," Priya said without looking at him, and turned the key in the ignition.

"*Yaar*, I'm really sorry," Athar said to Madhu, who just nodded. "Call me, OK?"

Madhu waved to Athar and rolled up the window.

They drove home in silence. Priya was the designated driver, but whatever buzz Madhu had acquired had quickly disappeared.

"I'm so sorry," Madhu said as soon as they were inside their house. "Priya, I'm really sorry."

"You lied to me, Madhu, to my face," she said. "How the hell am I supposed to trust you?"

"I should've told you that I had talked to him. I made a mistake, and you're saying that you don't trust me anymore?" Madhu asked. "I needed to talk to someone, and I did. You don't have to insult me. I said I was sorry."

"And that's supposed to make it all OK?" Priya demanded.

"No, but you're supposed to let things go once in a while. Life isn't supposed to be so damned serious," Madhu said.

"Serious? You told him and he told her and she told everyone. I asked you, I pleaded that we keep this quiet, but you just don't have any common sense," Priya said, and regretted it immediately. Calling him stupid wasn't fair, she knew, but she didn't feel like giving an inch or even half an inch.

"You know, we are just where Tarun and Aditi are. They're just more honest than we are," Madhu said once they were in their living room.

"You're kidding, right?"

Madhu didn't say anything and went into the bedroom.

Priya followed him, now ready for a good fight.

"I love you," she said. "But you don't really love me, do you? Otherwise—"

"So now I'm untrustworthy, without common sense, and I don't love you. Anything else?" he demanded.

Priya took a deep breath.

"No, that's it for now," she said, and slammed the bathroom door shut as she went in.

He was sitting on the bed in his underwear when she came out brushed and scrubbed. She was still wearing the dress she had gone to the party in.

"Can we make up now?" Madhu asked.

Priya looked at him. "Are you offering monkey sex?"

Madhu smiled and then nodded. "I did promise that, and a promise is, after all, a promise."

"Oh, please," Priya said, and pushed him onto his back to straddle him.

"We're nothing like Tarun and Aditi," Madhu said, and pulled the zipper of her dress down.

"No," Priya said, kissing him on the mouth. "I love you too much."

"Just so we have no misunderstandings and we're on the same page on this," Madhu said, "can you tell me what your definition of monkey sex is?"

Transcript from message board
www.surrogacyforyou.org

Trying1Time: I am so scared about having left the baby there. I feel so anxious. What am I supposed to do?

Prietysmommy: First thing, take a deep breath. This is very normal. I didn't start sleeping until a week ago. We just got through the first trimester, and it has been rough. But my DH has been very supportive and that has helped a lot.

NobuNobi: I have to say having DH's unstinting support (despite his horrible parents) has been so great. I don't think I could get through this without him.

Mommy8774: My DH was also wonderful. I cried and cried and cried the first time when we came home. But he was a rock; he told me everything would be fine. My advice: Talk to your husband. You'll feel much better.

MummiBest24: I don't understand what the big worry is really. I mean someone is taking care of your child there; it isn't like you left it on the street. I believe that when women use surrogates they feel the need to be extra hysterical because they don't have the baby growing inside them.

Mommy8774: That is a horrible thing to say. We are genuinely upset about not being able to see our babies grow. Why are you even on this message board? This is a supportive board and if you can't be supportive, please don't participate.

LastHope77: MummiBest24, I'm sure you didn't mean to hurt anyone's feelings, but to call women who use a surrogate hysterical is truly unfair.

MummiBest24: I have had two children through surrogates and I know exactly how it feels. I was worried but not crying and crying all the time. That's just insane and this is obviously not the right message board for people with a brain and a strong disposition. You losers can all sit and cry. It's best for you.

Prietysmommy: OMG, what a bitch! Can we block this person from using our message board?

Mommy8774: I'll check with the moderator. BRB.

Trying1Time: One more question. What kind of presents can I send to the SM? Should I also send something for the father?

CantConceive1970: I sent big boxes with

stuff. Clean underwear. It doesn't have to be Victoria's Secret, just good stuff from Target or Walmart. Toys for the children. Nothing too expensive, simple stuff. Things like that. I never sent anything for the husband, but it's a good idea. It'll mean he feels good about the whole thing, too—if he doesn't already, that is.

NobuNobi: My in-laws think we shouldn't send the SM anything. After all, we're paying her already. But I think we should send something. But it's just so hard with my husband saying no all the time.

UnoBaby: My friends said the same thing, but really, can we pay a woman enough for carrying our baby? I sent perfume, silly woman stuff that she can't even dream of buying and yes, underwear, too.

Prietysmommy: My SM keeps asking for stuff. I worry that if we say no she might hurt the baby. Next time we want another SM; this one is just too mercenary. We send whatever she asks for but nothing extra.

Chapter Six

Doctor Swati had a box waiting for Asha when she came for her regular biweekly checkup.

"Priya and Madhu have sent this for you. They have called every week since they left to check up on you," Doctor Swati said. "They have asked if you wouldn't mind talking to them once in a while. I can set it up so that they will call here after your next checkup."

Asha licked her lips. She didn't have a problem speaking with the parents, but she didn't know what she would say to them.

"You don't have to talk to them if you don't want to," Doctor Swati said when she saw Asha's reluctance.

"No, no, I'll talk to them," Asha said, and then paused. "But what will we talk about?"

"They might just want to say hello and ask you how you're doing," Doctor Swati said. "They won't interrogate you. They're just worried about their baby."

Asha nodded. "I don't have to talk to them now, do I?" She needed to prepare herself to speak to the parents. It would probably be the mother who would talk to her. She had seemed so worried when they had met.

"For now, just take this home with you and open it with your husband and children," Doctor Swati suggested. "It's gifts for all of you."

"But they're already giving us money," Asha said. "Why should they send us gifts?"

"Let them," Doctor Swati said. "It makes them feel like they're taking care of their baby as they take care of you. And it's also a way for them to say thank you."

Asha felt uneasy taking the box home, but she was also curious to see what was inside. Something from America, obviously, and that was exciting.

The box wasn't heavy, and in any case, Asha wasn't pregnant enough to feel any pressure at carrying things, not yet.

Pratap was painting a house that Raman was doing electrical work for, and the children were in school, so only Mohini, Puttamma, and Kaveri were at home.

Kaveri was sitting at her sewing machine, her feet moving as her hands maneuvered the blouse she was working on. Both Kaveri and Asha continued to sew for the local women. It wasn't a lot of money, but it was a little extra.

There was a letter in the box. It was written in Telugu. Asha would read it later, after the box had been emptied and everyone had oohed and aahed over the gifts.

"Underwear?" Kaveri said, holding a packet

with six panties. "They sent you underwear. And look, a watch! This must be for Pratap."

Puttamma looked at the clothes sent for the children. "Oh, just touch this material, so soft, so nice. And this pretty frock for Mohini! She will look like a princess."

They had also sent some toys. A few cars, a truck, a fake telephone that made sounds. Since they had sent nothing for Kaveri or her children, Asha divided the toys among Girish, Sirish, and her own children.

For Asha, they had sent a beautiful silk shawl. It was blue with a delicate design in silver and white. Asha draped it around her shoulder as she sat down to read the letter.

Dear Asha,

We hope that this letter finds you in the best of health. We are so grateful to you for carrying our baby and we hope that you are taking good care of yourself.

As promised, we have sent our taped voices by e-mail to Doctor Swati, and she will put them on the iPod we gave to you. I hope you can operate it without too much trouble.

We're also sending some gifts for you and your family. We hope that you like them. If there is anything else you need, please let us know.

You are free to write to us (you can find our address on the back of the envelope) if you wish. We would very much like to be able to talk to you and have asked Doctor Swati if this will be possible. We know that you do not have a phone in your house, but if you wish we could get you a mobile telephone so that you can keep in touch with us as well as Happy Mothers if you need to.

Thank you and all our best wishes,
Priya and Madhu

Asha knew the father had written the letter, as she didn't think the mother's Telugu was this good, but the sentiments were definitely the mother's, even though the letter was signed by both of them.

Were they trying to buy her good behavior by sending her presents? Or were they genuinely just saying thank you?

They had said that Asha could ask them for anything else she needed, and Asha thought about that as she stroked the soft shawl. She was already feeling too warm under it. She saw Kaveri eye it with envy and wondered if she should just give it to her. But it was such a beautiful shawl, almost like a silk sari, and Asha didn't want to part with it; it was the nicest thing she had, certainly the nicest thing anyone had ever given her. If they sent something in the next box, she thought, she would give it to Kaveri.

"The parents of my baby sent a box now and then, too," Kaveri said. "But nothing like this. It was more like vitamin tablets and a belt for my stomach and things like that. They never sent anything for the boys. Your parents are different. Good."

There was envy, but Kaveri had no malice. She was grateful and happy for Asha's good fortune.

"You can have the shawl if you want," Asha said suddenly. She hadn't intended to, but the words spilled out.

"No, no," Kaveri said, even though Asha could see she was tempted to take it. "You keep it. Next time if they send something, you can give it to me."

"They want to talk to me on the phone," Asha said. "And they want to buy me a mobile phone."

Puttamma shrugged. "These foreign people think we don't have phones in our country. Today, everyone has one."

Asha ignored Puttamma. Yes, everyone had a phone these days. The vegetable seller, the auto rickshaw driver, Raman, all did . . . but she and Pratap didn't.

"Did your parents want to talk to you?" Asha asked Kaveri, ignoring her mother-in-law.

Kaveri nodded. "Yes. I talked to them whenever I went for my checkup. But it was difficult. They didn't speak any Telugu like your parents do. So one of the nurses translated. They just asked me if I needed anything, if I felt OK. They always started crying when I told them the baby was kicking."

Asha smiled. "I think my mother will cry, too. She seems very emotional."

"We Indian women are," Kaveri said.

That night Pratap wore his watch and was impressed by its sophisticated look. It was silver in color with a chain band, and the dial was white with hour, minute, and second needles. There was a small box at the bottom of the dial that showed the date.

"Why did they send something for me?" he wondered.

"Next time we want parents like yours," Raman said. "It's good that they want to get you a mobile phone. In construction, you know, you can't do business without it." He held up his black phone wrapped in plastic to prevent scratching.

"You should be careful, though," Kaveri said. "Don't get too excited about presents from the parents. You know how it is; they take their baby and don't look back until they want another."

It was Mohini's second birthday, and for it she wore the pretty dress from America. Last year they had gone to the temple, and Asha had made a meal of the kids' favorite foods: mango dal, potato fry, and yogurt with thick slices of mangoes. Kaveri, Raman, their kids, and Puttamma had come to their hut. It wasn't a sumptuous meal, but Asha had had to save money to buy the mangoes, which were becoming more expensive by the season.

This year, since they had the money, Asha and Kaveri decided to have a big lunch with fried okra curry, *sambhar*, *pulao* rice, *payasam*, and even a cake that they had ordered at the nearby bakery. Cakes weren't part of Asha's childhood, but she wanted them to be part of her children's. She had ordered a pink cake with Mohini's name written on it in English.

It felt good to be in the kitchen with Kaveri. Her nausea had now passed, and she felt she had more energy. She wasn't tired all the time, holding her belly, feeling her insides swirl. She could play with her children, go to the market to shop—and best of all, make food for her family. Kaveri was a decent cook, but Pratap liked his wife's food, so he was pleased to see Asha back in the kitchen.

With the price of vegetables going up, especially basics like tomatoes, it used to be difficult to manage within their small budget. But since the parents were giving them ample money every month to buy food, Asha didn't think twice before buying a dozen tomatoes, though she still bargained with the woman selling them to get the price down, out of habit.

The morning of Mohini's birthday, they followed all the rituals. She was given a bath, and then the whole family went to the nearby temple. The pundit did the birthday puja in Mohini's name, and Pratap and Asha held hands, pleased with their family and what they knew the future now held for them.

At the end of the puja, Pratap broke open a coconut by smashing it on the floor. The water poured out, and Asha felt it was washing away their past and laying out a new tomorrow before them. The coconut was offered to Lord Venkateshwara Swami, whose temple this was.

Mohini held out her little hand, as they all did, to receive the holy water, tinged with mint. They drank the water with their right hand and wiped their hand by rubbing it over their foreheads and into their hair. Mohini followed suit, and Asha prevented her from drying her hands on her new dress by giving her a white handkerchief.

They all sat down on the floor, facing the god as they ate their *prasad*, white sugar candies that were said to be blessings from God.

"So many things have changed since her last birthday," Pratap said.

"All for the better, *Anna*," Raman said to his brother. "All our lives have been made better. I never thought we'd own our own house, a *pukka* brick house, but we do. And even though it is just a flat, it is ours and that makes me so proud." He looked lovingly at his wife then, and Kaveri smiled back at him.

"Lord Venkateshwara Swami has provided for us," Kaveri said, and put her arms around her sons, who were sitting on either side of her. They squirmed a little but allowed Kaveri to kiss them on their cheeks.

Manoj sat next to his father and looked speculatively at the white candy in his hand, melting slowly, making his right hand sticky. He then put the candy in his mouth and chewed thoughtfully. "Why does God give us sweets?" he asked no one in particular.

"Because whatever God gives us is sweet," Asha said, reaching out and wiping his hand with the same handkerchief she had used to dry Mohini's.

"God gives us floods and earthquakes, too, but those are not sweet," Manoj said.

Puttamma sighed. "Today is Mohini's birthday and not a day to talk about floods and nonsense."

"Next year you will start going to a special school, Manoj, and there you can ask all about such things," Asha said.

"I like my school," Manoj protested. "The teachers are nice to me."

"In this special school the teachers will be nicer," Asha promised. "And you will learn a lot more than you do now."

Manoj shrugged, his gesture strikingly adult on

his little body. "I learn enough now. I learned about the solar system yesterday."

As Manoj talked about the sun and the planets, Asha watched him with delight. She touched her stomach and thanked God for bringing her this opportunity. Manoj would learn bigger and better things. He would have more education than Asha and Pratap had ever dreamed of. He wouldn't end up painting houses; he'd end up *living* in those big houses, having a big job, being a big man.

Puttamma talked about how pleased she was that both her sons had found such wonderful and sacrificing wives. It was a day of celebration, of being positive. She knew that unpleasantness lay ahead—but for now, they should enjoy their good fortune.

In the afternoon, Srinivas, Pratap's cousin, joined them, along with his wife and parents. His wife, Nayantara, was from Hyderabad and was a little snobbish. She hated living in Srirampuram and constantly talked about how her husband and she were working on moving to Hyderabad as soon as possible. If anyone could do it, though, they could; Nayantara and Srinivas were the most educated people Asha knew.

"Another baby?" Nayantara asked when she noticed Asha's belly. "In India the way things are, no one should have more than one child. You already have two. Do you know that in China for

133

the longest time people could have only one child? If they had another, it was a crime. Now they can have only two and no more."

Srinivas looked apologetically at Asha and was about to say something when Nayantara shushed him. "I don't mean to be rude, but can you even afford to have a third child? I mean . . . you're living with Kaveri and Raman."

"We're going to buy our own flat very soon," Pratap said defensively. "This is just temporary until we find our feet. We just moved from the village."

"But still, three children?" Nayantara wouldn't let the matter go.

"Children are Lord Venkateshwara Swami's blessing," Srinivas's mother, Tarla Devi, said. "And I think Asha is doing a wonderful thing by having one more child. He might be like Manoj, another gem of a boy, or like Mohini, such a beautiful girl."

"God doesn't provide for children; money does," Nayantara said.

"Money isn't a problem." Raman spoke this time to defend his older brother and his wife.

"Please," Asha protested. "This is not an appropriate conversation in front of the children."

Even though the children were sitting in another circle in the TV room, Asha used them as an excuse. She could hardly explain to Nayantara that the child she was having wasn't hers. That all her concerns were meaningless.

"Oh," Nayantara said, immediately looking guilty. "I guess they're happy about having another brother or sister."

There won't be a brother or sister, Asha wanted to tell the stupid, arrogant girl. But she nodded and smiled and asked if anyone wanted more *sambhar.*

"Don't listen to her," Srinivas's mother said to Asha after dinner when they were alone in the kitchen making tea. "She is a she-devil who doesn't want children. You have the children you want. You are a wonderful mother, and your children are such a pleasure. I would love to have grandchildren like them. But I doubt sweet children will ever come out of my daughter-in-law's acid womb."

Asha quietly stirred the tea, adding the right amount of milk and sugar to the pot.

"And Mohini's dress . . . it's so beautiful," Tarla Devi said. "Where did you buy it?"

"A gift from friends," Asha said, and couldn't resist adding, "from America."

"You have friends in America," Tarla Devi said admiringly.

"Yes," Asha said, and didn't even flinch as she lied.

Chapter Seven

"Do we fight too much?" Priya asked the next morning.

Madhu had made an elaborate breakfast: a Spanish omelet with a spicy tomato salsa, yogurt with muesli, and a fruit salad. It was their Saturday-morning ritual. They woke up late, and one of them cooked a big brunch that they ate while they leisurely read the paper in the dining room.

"The fight wasn't my fault," Priya added as she put a triangle of Spanish omelet on her plate.

"I said I was sorry," Madhu said. "I know women think it's their exclusive, God-given right to talk to their friends about their problems, but men do it, too, you know."

"You bet I know," Priya said. "But Athar tells Farah everything, and she tells everybody, so that's probably not the right friend to confide in."

"Got it. Can we move on?"

Priya looked at him while she chewed on the omelet and nodded.

"Thank you," Madhu said sarcastically, and turned on the television, flipping channels until he found CNN.

"I think our Saturdays are going to be very different when the baby comes home," Priya said.

"Why? I think we can still have brunch with a baby in the house," Madhu said. "We shouldn't become the kind of parents who give up being a couple to become parents."

"I don't think it's a conscious thing," Priya said. "I think it's one of those things that just happens. Nina and Jordan were a normal couple until they had kids, and suddenly they had no time for anything. Either their kid is sick or she has a birthday party—something or other to keep her from seeing us on weekends."

Madhu stirred sugar into his filter coffee. "And look what happened? Jordan was sleeping with someone else, and Nina was having a nervous breakdown."

Priya grinned. "I don't think Jordan cheated on Nina because they became parents. Or is that something you intend to do?"

"No. But Nina won't even have a babysitter over so she and Jordan can go out. Hell, they've never spent a night away from their girls," Madhu said.

Priya wrinkled her nose. "I don't know if I will, either. Don't get me wrong, I understand that we have to be a couple as well as parents, but right now, as I wait for this baby, I can't imagine letting her out of my sight once I have her."

"But you will," Madhu said, looking her in the eye. "Just because it's been a long way to a baby doesn't mean we have to sacrifice our lives for it."

"But we do have to, Madhu," Priya said, licking

her lips. "A baby will change our lives. We will not be able to sit down and eat every meal in peace."

"As long as we can do it once in a while, that will be enough," Madhu said, reaching over to place his hand on his wife's.

Priya didn't think Madhu truly grasped the concept of what this baby would do to their lives. He was living with the idea that the baby would calmly follow his plans and agenda and not screw anything up. Nina told Priya how shocked she'd been at the loss of her freedom once she'd had Rebecca. It had been a huge blow to all of a sudden not even be able to go to the supermarket without having a baby hang about her. It had taken getting used to, but for the first few months she thought her life was over.

"Do you think we should shop a little this weekend? Buy something for Asha and her family?" Priya asked.

"Didn't we just buy them stuff?" Madhu said. "I think it can wait. Or do you just want to go baby shopping?"

"I always want to go baby shopping," Priya said, and then bit her lip. "But I think I'll wait. Just in case."

Madhu leaned and kissed her. "It's going to be fine."

"You promise?"

"I promise."

But Madhu couldn't quite keep his promise.

That night the phone rang and an old, familiar fear reared its ugly head.

"There is some bleeding," Doctor Swati said to Priya.

"What?" Priya could hardly form the word. Madhu had woken up as well, and they were huddled by Priya's phone, set on speaker.

"How much bleeding?" Madhu asked.

"Calm down. I suspect it's because of the examination we did yesterday," Doctor Swati said. "It happens; it's not a big deal."

Not a big deal? Priya wanted to scream. This is how her miscarriages had begun: a little bleeding here and there, and then one day the baby was gone.

"How's the baby?" Priya demanded.

"We did an ultrasound, and it looks just fine. The baby is under no distress; it's healthy and growing as it should," Doctor Swati said. "I sent some pictures by e-mail for you."

Madhu immediately pulled his iPad onto the bed to look at his e-mail.

"So what does this mean?" Priya asked.

"Well, bleeding is never a good thing. But it was just a small amount, and it's already stopped. However, since we want to be careful, I think it's best if we move Asha to the surrogate house now instead of in two more months," Doctor Swati said.

In the surrogate house, Asha would have twenty-four-hour care. There would be no accidents, no time lag from something going wrong to it being fixed. It was the best option, considering she was bleeding.

"But she will be away from her family then," Madhu said.

"Just for two months more than planned," Priya interjected before Doctor Swati said anything. "I understand it isn't easy but . . . it's our baby, Madhu."

"Asha's family lives close by, so she will be able to see them every day," Doctor Swati said. "They will come and visit, and on weekends she can even go see them for a few hours if she wishes to. But from now on she will live and sleep in the surrogate house."

Priya and Madhu had had a tour of the surrogate house. It was a clean and cozy place with room for about sixteen women in eight bedrooms. There were a couple of living rooms with televisions and sofas, a big garden, a spacious veranda, an oversize kitchen with a dining table, and a computer room where they were given computer classes. One of the living rooms was used for yoga lessons that the women were expected to take every day for fifteen minutes to a half hour.

The house had a full-time nurse, a den mother who used to be a surrogate herself, and two maids who cooked and cleaned. It was nice, halfway between a house and a hospital.

"Will Asha have a problem with this?" Priya asked.

"I have already spoken with her, and I think she understands the importance of her being taken care of," Doctor Swati said.

"But is she happy about this?" Madhu asked.

There was a pause before Doctor Swati said, "Well, she isn't happy about leaving her family, but it's for a short time, and she will be in the company of several other women like her. It's a place where she can bond and learn some new skills. And she will get better care than at home. She won't have to cook or clean or anything. We have help to do that. All she will have to do is relax and be taken care of. A lot of women love staying at the house and actually miss it when they leave. It's like being on vacation."

Madhu and Priya both had doubts that being away from one's family could ever be like a vacation, but it was their baby and they wanted what was best for their child.

"When will she move into the surrogate house?" Priya asked.

"Tomorrow, if you agree with me that it's a good idea," Doctor Swati said. "It's my professional opinion that she should. It's the best way to keep your baby and Asha healthy."

"Then let's do it," Madhu said, looking for confirmation at Priya, who nodded.

• • •

They couldn't sleep after the phone call. They lay in bed, just staring at the ceiling.

"My heart is still pounding," Priya said.

"Mine, too," Madhu admitted.

"Arc we being selfish, Madhu?" Priya asked.

"It's a bit late, don't you think, to worry about that?"

"What does that mean?" Priya demanded.

"Just that our baby will always come first, and Asha knew what she was doing when she signed the contract," Madhu said.

"Still makes me feel guilty," Priya said.

"Me, too."

Priya turned to Madhu, tears in her eyes.

"But you know what, I'm not just scared about the baby," Priya said.

Madhu turned to face her. "What else are you scared about?"

"Losing you," Priya said. "I'm scared that if something happens to the baby, you'll leave . . . again."

Madhu sighed and turned so he was once again staring at the ceiling. "Priya, it was a mistake. I thought we moved past this."

"We did," Priya said. "But that doesn't mean a part of me . . . I still have this niggling fear that . . . Forget it. You're getting angry."

Madhu sat up. "I'm not angry. I'm frustrated that you bring it up again and again."

"That's not fair," Priya said, sitting up as well. "I hardly ever bring it up."

"I said I was sorry and I was. I still am. But I can't take back what I did. It was stupid, but . . . why can't you just let it go?"

Priya wiped the tears off her cheek. "I have let it go. But it comes back. Come on, Madhu, you left me while I was bleeding. You left. You were gone for three weeks."

"And I came back," Madhu said. "I came back. That was three fucking years ago, Priya."

"I know," Priya said. "I'm being unfair."

Madhu hugged her. "I'm not going anywhere. I promise. I have no life without you. I love you."

"I'm being silly," Priya said, resting her head on his chest.

"No. I'm at fault here. I fucked up. I was . . . I fucked up, and there's nothing I can do to take it back, but it'll never happen again. You know that, don't you?" Madhu asked.

Priya nodded, not lifting her head.

"I'm sorry I brought it up. I don't think about it all the time or anything. I'm not upset about it, but . . . it comes back, that fear. Losing you, losing a baby, it's all mixed up in my head," she said.

"I know," he said, and stroked her hair. "I know. And I'm with you all the way. I'll never leave you again."

"And I'll never push you away as I had, either," Priya said.

They held each other for a long time, not wanting to let go. They were the only two people in the world who knew how they felt, knew enough to comfort each other.

"Will this baby be OK, Madhu?" Priya asked, sobbing.

"Yes," Madhu said, but Priya could hear the uncertainty in his voice.

The whole thing had been so out of character for Madhu that sometimes Priya wondered if it had actually happened. It was after her second miscarriage, and it seemed at the time like they were beginning to fall apart. The cracks in their marriage were starting to show. The stress of losing yet another baby and the doctor telling them that there could be more miscarriages had devastated both of them. They didn't officially decide to stop trying to have a baby, because they never used any protection anyway. Instead, their sex life had gone from prolific to once in a while. Depression was hell on the libido.

When Priya got pregnant for the third time, she didn't tell Madhu about it right away. And that had been the sledgehammer that devastated their already cracked marriage. Priya always felt that what really broke Madhu's heart was not losing another baby, but that she hadn't trusted him to be supportive enough to tell him as soon as she knew.

She waited nearly six weeks. They had started

spending less and less time together by that point. Both were busy with their work, and Madhu had been traveling a lot. Like the sex, they hadn't deliberately set about distancing from each other; it had just happened.

They were watching television late one night, sprawled on the couch, when Priya told him.

"What?" Madhu asked.

"You didn't hear me the first time?" Priya demanded, irritated by his tone.

"I heard you fine," Madhu said, turning off the television. "Pregnant? Again?"

"Madhu, we have unprotected sex; there is a chance we can get pregnant," Priya said.

"I know that, but . . . I just didn't expect it," Madhu said, slowly grasping the meaning of what Priya had told him. "When did you find out?"

Priya paused, contemplated whether to lie, and then told him the truth.

"You waited six weeks?"

"Well . . . yes."

"Why?"

Priya shrugged.

"That's not an answer," Madhu said, his voice getting hard.

"Well, this isn't exactly the warm response I expected," Priya said, getting defensive, standing up to leave the living room.

"You waited six whole fucking weeks to tell me that we're going to have a baby. Why?"

Priya had tears in her eyes. "Just because. You've been traveling and . . ."

Madhu shook his head. "You wanted to wait and see if you'd lose it. And then what was your plan? Not to tell me at all?"

Priya stared at him in disbelief. "How can you say that? Of course I'd tell you."

"I don't know, Priya. Right now I don't know what the hell is going on. Why the hell are we even still getting pregnant? Why the hell are we trying again and again? I don't want children. Can't you understand that?" Madhu yelled.

"I didn't trick you into getting pregnant. You could've worn a condom if the idea is so repulsive," Priya yelled back.

"Why did you tell me today?" Madhu asked.

"I thought it was time," Priya said.

"So you decide when it's time?" Madhu said, nodding. "Right, because this is your baby. I'm just the fucking sperm donor."

"That's not true, Madhu," Priya said, exasperated. "I didn't tell anyone I was pregnant. I'm scared of losing the baby. I just didn't want to say anything."

Madhu looked her in the eye and softly said, "I'm scared of losing the baby, too. We could've been scared together. But I think you should be scared alone this time. I'm done worrying about this shit."

They were still angry with each other the next

morning, and Priya had used that as an excuse not to ask Madhu to come to the ultrasound with her.

But she should've called him when the doctor told her there was no heartbeat and recommended a DNC. She should've called and asked him to hold her hand. By not calling him, she had wounded their marriage more. On the other hand, he packed up and left when she told him she had lost the baby again, so in retrospect they were even.

Krysta had driven Priya home. Madhu wasn't there. Krysta had stayed for a while, but Priya had wanted to be alone; it hurt too much—her body, her heart, everything—and it hurt more to have a witness to her pain, her grief, her ultimate inadequacy as a woman.

"You OK?" Madhu had asked when he got home, coming into the bedroom, his hand on his tie. He usually didn't wear a suit, which meant he'd probably been meeting clients that day.

"No," Priya told him. Did he think she was OK? Couldn't he see the tears? The pain? Couldn't he see anything?

"You lost the baby," he said matter-of-factly, like he was telling her that she had burned the rice again.

"Yes," Priya said, her face cracking, her arms lifting ineffectually like she wanted a hug but didn't know how to ask, knew that he wouldn't give her one.

He shook his head. "I knew it."

"You knew it?" she demanded, dropping her hands on her lap. "You didn't think the baby could survive?" She wanted to blame someone, and here he was. He didn't believe it would last, and now she'd lost the baby.

He shook his head again. He didn't come near her. He stood by the door like she had a plague, a horrible, contagious disease he was afraid of catching.

"Yes, I knew it and so did you," he said. "That's why you waited to tell me you were pregnant. You were waiting for the miscarriage to happen so that you never had to tell me."

"No, that's not why I waited. But is that what you wished for? That I never told you?" Priya demanded.

"Yes," he said, and surprised her. "Yes. I wish you didn't tell me you were pregnant so that I didn't have to know that we lost yet another baby. I wish . . . you'd stop getting pregnant altogether so that we can stop losing babies."

"How can you say that? Don't you want a child as much as I do?" Priya asked.

"No," Madhu said. "No. I don't want a child. I don't want a dead baby. I don't want any of this. I just want us to have a normal fucking life where we can go for a movie, go out, laugh a little, enjoy life. When was the last time we had a good time as two people?"

"We've had plenty of good times," Priya said, her insides churning because he was telling the truth. The past year had been a nightmare. She had been depressed, disinterested in everything and everyone. But it wasn't like he had tried to cheer her up or get her out of her rut.

"There have been no fucking good times since you got on the damned mommy bandwagon," Madhu said, screaming now, tears rolling down his cheeks. "Why the hell can't you just give it up? Just give up. We can't have children. Now let's get on with our lives. OK?"

"No," Priya screamed in response. "I want a baby. I don't want a life without a baby."

"You have me," Madhu said. "Or is that not as important?"

Priya waited a long second before saying the worst thing she could have. Looking back, she couldn't really be blamed, not when her hormones were running crazy and her head wasn't screwed on straight.

"No, you're not as important as a baby to me," she told him calmly. "Nothing is more important to me than having a baby. I want a child."

"Well, then, have your baby. You'll just have to do it without me," Madhu said.

He had packed his travel suitcase then, right in front of her while she lay in bed, seething, still bleeding, unable to believe that he was leaving.

He couldn't be leaving, could he?

No. He was just being stupid.

Well, then, let him be stupid.

"I'll pick up the rest of my stuff later," Madhu said, and left.

Priya heard the door shut, heard his car roar away. And then she was alone.

She was alone for three weeks.

Priya hadn't been able to find him. He hadn't answered her calls and she had too much pride to start calling his friends or show up at his work to look for him. If he wanted to be gone, then so be it, she had told herself. She was the injured party here. She was the one who'd had a miscarriage— how dare he have a temper tantrum while she was bleeding and weak?

But after the first two nights of his absence, Priya worried that this wasn't a temper tantrum. He was gone, probably for good.

"Go to his office, corner him, and ask him what he wants," Krysta had suggested when she came to check on Priya over the weekend.

"I can't go to his office," Priya said. "I . . . do you think my marriage is over?"

"He did pack his bags and leave," Krysta said thoughtfully, and then, seeing the devastated look on Priya's face, patted her hand. "But marriages go through stuff like this. He just needs to get some distance. And so do you, Priya. It's not all him. You need to think things through, and so does he."

"And then he'll come back?" Priya asked, terrified that he wouldn't. She didn't know how to go about her life without Madhu. She didn't know how to wake up and live her life without him. She couldn't sleep well when he traveled. She didn't cook if he wasn't at home. She didn't laugh without him.

"Sure, he'll be back," Krysta said. "But . . . just in case, you do have your own bank account, right?"

Priya shook her head. "No, we have a joint account."

Krysta's eyebrows rose into her hairline.

"Come on, we've had a joint bank account since we moved in together in school," Priya said. "He isn't going anywhere with our money."

"Go to the bank and set up your own bank account, and then transfer half your savings there," Krysta recommended.

Priya couldn't fathom separating their finances like this. It would be a signal to Madhu that she didn't have faith in them.

"Don't be stupid, Priya," Krysta warned her. "Those women on *Oprah* are just like you and me."

"Madhu isn't a thief, Krysta," Priya said.

"This isn't about moral values or what you believe in. Divorce brings out the worst in people. At least you guys don't have children to fight over," Krysta said pragmatically, unaware of how insensitive that sounded.

Priya had not gone to the bank. She refused to give up hope. But she had also stopped calling Madhu's cell phone. If he was going to come back, then he was going to come back, but not because she called him five times a day.

She told no one about his leaving. He was on a business trip, she told her parents when she spoke to them, and she had the same answer for their friends who called. She would lie: "I'm not sure where he is. Dallas, or was it LA?"

She said it to so many people in such a short period of time that she started to believe it herself. Madhu was on a business trip; he hadn't walked out on her.

The loneliness was bitter. It was acidic, this feeling of being just one person in mind and body. There was no one to reach out to in the night, no one to turn to and comment about the news, no one to share a joke with or bitch about traffic. She was alone. *This is what it means to be divorced and single,* she thought. It was one thing to have always been single—then you didn't know what you were missing—but it was another to have been so deep into a marriage, into a relationship, and then find that part of your soul ripped out.

She lost weight, nearly eight pounds in two weeks. She couldn't eat, couldn't sleep, couldn't feel. She checked her messages, her cell phone, her e-mail, incessantly. He would be back, wouldn't he? Yes, he would. It was a mantra she repeated.

In the evenings, she picked up takeout for herself from the Indian place or the Chinese place or KFC. One takeout meal lasted two evenings. She sat in front of the TV and ate, unable to sit alone at the dining table. It felt like a farce to sit there. There was no one to eat with, no one to light candles for. She thought less about her miscarriage this time around. She worried about Madhu.

He came back on a Sunday, nearly three and a half weeks after he had left. She didn't even hear the car in the driveway, though she had been listening for it for days now. She had been working, trying to keep herself busy with a design project she'd acquired the previous week.

She'd had her iPhone earbuds jammed in her ears. She didn't hear the door open over Maria Callas's voice.

She'd been in the study, deep in concentration, her fingers tapping on the keyboard, moving the mouse, her eyes scanning the InDesign file open on her laptop screen. And then she'd smelled him.

Afraid she was finally losing it enough to imagine things, she turned and saw him standing at the doorstep.

She wanted to run to him, jump up and down, and cry with joy, "You're back, you're back, you're back!" But she wasn't sure if he was back to be back with her or just to pick up the rest of his stuff, as he had promised.

"Hi," he said. Priya only nodded, unable to get words out of her throat.

"I'm sorry," he said.

Priya nodded again, and when he held his arms open, she walked into them and they both wept for the baby they had lost and for the way they had almost lost each other.

He apologized for his desertion. He said he would make it up to her with vacations, flowers, presents . . . anything she wanted. He was sorry and Priya had forgiven him. She understood when he told her that he had been frightened. She believed him when he promised he'd never leave again.

"This baby is important to me, too. So we'll work on this together. But you have to promise to make room for me, and I'll promise to make room for the baby," he had said.

"When you left, I didn't even think about the baby," Priya confessed. "I only worried about you. Without you, there's no me and there's no baby."

It was the worst thing that had happened in their marriage, and the best thing. The lessons learned were important ones. They didn't leave things unsaid. They didn't shrink away from telling each other how they really felt. They didn't mind disagreeing. They had become a closer team than they'd been before—more honest, more comfortable with the truth. They had seen what life could be like without each other, and they had both recognized how much they loved each other. Maybe Priya wanted a baby more than Madhu did, but he was by her side all the way. And maybe Priya was baby crazy as he accused, but she wasn't giving up on their marriage or making the baby more important than him, than them. They had gotten better at balancing themselves and accommodating each other. They felt they were on their second marriage, and this time around they were smarter and wiser, healthier and happier.

Priya had always believed happy couples agreed on everything, but now she realized that healthy couples learned to respect even when they disagreed. It wasn't how much you fought; it was about how good you were at making up. It was about trusting each other and the relationship to have that fight, to get it out there and have the love to heal the wound, temper the argument, and laugh about it. And they both learned that makeup sex could be an awesome healing thing.

Transcript from message board
www.surrogacyforyou.org

Trying1Time: My SM has been moved to the surrogate house. She had some bleeding after an exam. It stopped after

155

a day, thank God. The doctor says this is common. Do you have any experience with this?

NearlyMother: I'm so sorry to hear about this. This is how it started with my SM. We had crossed the twelve-week barrier so I felt quite safe. But then suddenly bleeding began and she had a miscarriage. It was horrible.

UnoBaby: I'm sorry that this happened to you, NearlyMother, but bleeding doesn't mean a definite miscarriage. I have friends who have had spotting after a regular exam. It's supposed to be quite common. Trying1Time, is this bleeding or spotting?

Trying1Time: It is spotting and it has stopped. But I'm so worried.

Mommy8774: I don't know how common it is. When my SM had bleeding it was the bloody show and she went into labor a couple of days later. But I agree with UnoBaby, this doesn't mean a miscarriage and it's a good thing she was moved to the surrogate house; they're safe there. She should've been there from the start and most women are, so this is a good thing.

NobuNobi: I say relax. I don't have experience with this, but if you think positive then everything will work out. Good luck.

LastHope77: If my SM had spotting I'd freak out, too. I'd be on the next plane to India. Have you thought about going there and staying for the rest of the pregnancy? I want to, but I can't quit my job; we need the money. We're saving up to hire a nanny so that I can continue to work after the measly twelve weeks maternity leave I get.

CantConceive1970: My SM had all sorts of spotting and the babies came out just fine. So I say relax as NobuNobi says. Be positive. No point killing yourself over this. And I think it's a bad idea to move to India at this point. You'll be isolated there, away from your husband. It'll just make things very hard for you.

Prietysmommy: Why did your doctor even do an exam like this? How pregnant is your SM? Some of these doctors are just bad. I hope you chose yours carefully.

Trying1Time: I trust the doctor. She's very experienced and has a sophisticated clinic. We did our research very thoroughly before choosing her.

Prietysmommy: I'm sure your doctor is great; I didn't mean to say she isn't, just that sometimes these doctors are just not very good and it ends up becoming a tragedy for us.

Chapter Eight

Asha missed Mohini and Manoj. She missed Pratap. She missed her life at Kaveri's house. She missed her life back in the village. She hated having this baby inside her.

There were fifteen of them at the Happy Mothers House, as they called it in English, in various stages of pregnancy. Fifteen women who carried the babies of other people. Fifteen women, and most of them didn't seem to get along that well with one another. It was understandable. Pregnant women are known to have a bad temper, and having so many of them together only resulted in squabbles, yelling and screaming, and general bitching.

On her first day at the Happy Mothers House, Asha sat in her room, the one she shared with Gangamma, a twenty-nine-year-old woman who was doing this for the second time. The room was small. It had two beds with thin mattresses and blue sheets that should be cleaned every week but, as Gangamma told her, if it happened once a month that was a blessing, not that Asha cared. She slept on a mat at home, and there were no sheets to clean. There was a small dirty window that didn't open, making the room stuffy when there was no electricity and the rattling ceiling fan didn't move the air. If this were her home, Asha would have cleaned the window, done something about the dark patches of dirt in the corners, and she would have asked Pratap to paint over the hideous patch of dampness on the wall by the window. But it was a brick house with two toilets, one with a chair toilet, one with a regular toilet where you had to squat to go. There was one bathroom to get a bath. The house had its own water tank, so the taps worked. The women brought their own soap and towels to the bathroom to bathe. There was a metal stool where the women could sit and take mugs of water from a bucket to wash themselves. It was much better than many of them had at home, where they might have a hut or shack to bathe in.

There was a sink outside the toilet, and all women had been instructed to wash their hands after they went. It was a rule, and if you didn't wash your hands, you'd hear about it from Doctor Swati. Hygiene was important in the house. You had to take a bath every day; you had to wash your hands before and after a meal and after you used the toilet. With one bathroom and fifteen women, there were invariably arguments about who should go before whom, and how much time one woman spent in the bathroom over another.

Gangamma was the gregarious sort and told Asha about all the house rules. She talked and talked until Asha ached for silence. After just an hour, Asha knew the woman's entire life story.

"We're from Mehdipatnam in Hyderabad, so I don't even get to see my children," she told Asha, who was desperately waiting that first day for the clock to strike four in the evening, when Pratap would come with Mohini and Manoj.

"You get used to being without them," Gangamma told her. "I have two sons and they are wonderful boys. Jaya is eight and Sri is five." She had pictures on the floor by her bed, which she showed to Asha.

"They look like good boys," Asha said, and then sighed. "I miss my children."

"But you'll see them every day, and once you get settled here, you'll start having fun," Gangamma said, and laughed. "You'll have a lot of fun here."

Asha wasn't sure what Gangamma meant by "fun."

The housemother, Revati, was kind and treated all the women like daughters, but she could also be strict, as Asha had already seen. Revati had admonished one of the mothers for not cleaning up the shells of the freshly boiled peanuts she had eaten as she watched TV in the common hall.

You had to clean up after yourself. You had to eat the meals. If you didn't like something specifically, you had to tell Revati. You had to attend either the English class or the computer class every day except Sunday, because "you can't just sit around all day; this isn't your mother's house."

You had to attend the daily thirty-minute yoga class that was given in the common hall at nine in the morning. If you couldn't do the exercises, it was OK, but you had to show up unless Doctor Swati said otherwise. In the Happy Mothers House, Doctor Swati's word was the word of God.

Asha was also starting to dislike Doctor Swati. A small bleeding that Doctor Swati herself agreed had happened because of the examination that she'd insisted on, and Asha had been asked to move here earlier than planned.

"For the safety of the baby," Doctor Swati had said.

And what about her children? Who would take care of them?

True, it wasn't like Asha had left her children on the street. Kaveri was there, and so were Raman, Puttamma, and Pratap. Asha knew she was being unreasonable, but somehow her heart could not follow her mind's lead on this matter.

"Trust me, once you get used to someone else cooking and cleaning for you, you won't want to come back," Kaveri had told her.

Asha didn't believe it. Home was home. No matter what palace you went to, if it wasn't yours, if your family wasn't there, it wasn't better than home.

Pratap and the children came five minutes after four that first evening. She would have an hour with them. Those were the rules.

Mohini ran into her arms, and Manoj gave her a hug and a kiss. He looked around at the women in the big hall and then looked carefully at his mother. "Is this a hospital for women who're going to have babies?"

"Yes," Asha said. "The baby will be safer here."

"Why? You had both of us and never stayed in a place like this," Manoj said.

Asha looked in panic at Pratap.

"Did you see the ducks in the pond outside?" Pratap asked Manoj, who looked briefly at his mother and then, with childish abandon, ran outside with his father to investigate the pond and the ducks in it.

"I miss you, Amma," Mohini said, and slobbered over Asha's cheek.

They sat outside on the terrace with a view over a yard where there was a large patch of grass and, in between, a small pond with three ducks. Two steps from the terrace was a tulasi plant, standing almost chest high in a square cement pot attached to the ground. The pot was freshly painted, and the yellow-and-red paint that swirled around the pot gleamed. Revati did her puja, her prayers, there every morning.

"I read the *Gayatri Mantram* here every day, six in the morning," she had told Asha.

"Can I join you?" Asha had asked. She had always done puja in the morning in her village. She hadn't had such a nice tulasi plant as this but had shared a small one in an earthen pot right in front of the well with several neighbors.

"If you wake up that early," Revati had said. "I don't wait for anyone."

The terrace had several pieces of furniture, chairs, tables, and even a ceiling fan. The walls had recently been whitewashed, Asha had seen when she'd first received her tour of the house.

The furniture was typical of many Andhra homes. Two plastic lounge chairs. The plastic fabric that went over the chairs was weathered and slightly worn. Once a bright blue with sunny yellow stripes, it was now dull, faded under the sun and with repeated use.

There was a swing—one of those two-person wooden swings that you saw in the movies that was always used in romantic scenes. The swing was definitely old, maybe even a hand-me-down, Asha thought, because the varnish had chipped, revealing the wood beneath, and it creaked when you rocked it gently with your feet. But Asha liked the sound as it kept pace with the creaky fan attached to the ceiling—when the city didn't cut the power out, that is. When the electricity was out, everyone gathered outside, sitting on the furniture, the floor, and the two steps that led to the front yard.

While Manoj watched the ducks, Asha sat on the swing with Mohini. Pratap sat on one of the plastic lounge chairs, and when he realized that it wasn't quite stable, he got up and sat on one of the old wooden chairs pulled next to the swing.

Mohini disentangled herself from her mother and joined her brother by the small duck pond.

When she was out of earshot, Pratap leaned a little closer, inclining his head toward Asha. "I'm sorry," he said.

It was almost a whisper. A wisp of air. Asha felt her face burn. She couldn't look at him, so she stared after Mohini and Manoj. Had her husband just said "sorry" to her?

They had fought before she had left. They had *actually* fought. They never fought.

But she had been upset. After Doctor Swati told her that she had to move into the house two months early, Pratap seemed to think it was for the best. Kaveri kept on as if Asha were going away on holiday. It had infuriated her.

"No cooking, no cleaning," Pratap had teased as Asha packed a hard-top brown suitcase, the only one they had. It had belonged to Raman's boss. It was old and dull, the color faded almost to beige. There were two scratches on the top and a deep gash on the bottom that Pratap had closed with duct tape. But it was sturdy and big enough for Asha to pack her saris, blouses, and petticoats.

"You're going to live like a maharani," Kaveri said.

Asha had been sitting on the floor, folding and packing saris into her suitcase. Her back hurt. She would need help to stand up from the floor.

"And we'll be fine without you," Pratap continued. "We'll eat Kaveri's good food and get fat."

"Because my food isn't good enough?" Asha demanded tersely as she put her favorite pink sari with the green border into the suitcase.

Kaveri raised her eyebrows and left the bedroom, closing the door behind her.

"That's not what I meant," Pratap said.

"Then what did you mean?" Asha asked. "Everyone seems happy that I'm leaving."

"No one is happy, but we're trying to make the best of it," Pratap said.

"By eating Kaveri's good food? Maybe if I died while giving birth, no one would care," Asha said.

"Asha," Pratap said sternly.

"Don't yell at me," Asha said, her voice raised.

You didn't raise your voice at your husband. It wasn't done. But Asha couldn't help herself.

"I'm stuck here with someone else's baby in my stomach because you can't support us."

"No one forced you into this," Pratap said defensively. "You volunteered. I asked you a hundred times—"

"No, you didn't," Asha said. "You wanted me like this. You wanted the money. Counting money like an ugly businessman. And you know what you sold? Me. You sold me."

"Don't get all high and mighty, *madam*," Pratap said. "You're still my wife, and even if I asked you to do this, there's nothing wrong with it. Many women do this. It's you . . . *you* who are selfish. I work all day and night to make money for us, and you have to do one thing and you behave like you're carrying the world on your shoulders."

In other circumstances, Asha would have backed down. Apologized. But not this time. He would not make her do this and tell her it was nothing. No, he needed to be prostrate, on his belly, crawling on the floor, kissing her feet and thanking her.

"Get out," Asha said. "And ask Kaveri to bring the children to the hospital. I don't want to see your face."

Pratap bent and brought his face close to hers. "Don't think you run this place because you're making some money. I'll do what I feel like, and you'll see my face as many times as I want."

For a moment, a small moment, Asha thought he would slap her, and she was prepared for it. Another bruise on her martyred body. But he didn't. He walked away, slamming the door behind him.

Raman had carried her suitcase to the auto rickshaw, and Kaveri had come with Asha to the

167

Happy Mothers House. Asha hadn't seen Pratap since the fight. And even though Asha had been occupied with Revati, Gangamma, and the rules of the house, their fight, their first real fight where she had fought back, had been a worry that tore at her insides.

"I'm sorry, too," she said. She didn't want to be the kind of wife who raised her voice at her husband and fought with him. That was well and good in the movies and television shows, but in real life, Asha knew that it was important for her to listen to her husband. He knew more than she did; he was worldlier than she was.

"We're both worried and upset, and that's why we fought," Pratap said. "Are you feeling better now?"

Asha nodded.

"Doctor Swati is going to give us information about schools for Manoj, and once we know . . . once we know what that will cost . . ." She let her words trail away. She had never been the one to make decisions for her family. That was Pratap's job, but now she was talking like an equal, telling him what she thought they should do. It felt wrong, but it also felt exhilarating, like she had a say in her life.

Pratap nodded. "That's OK. We'll buy a flat when we have Manoj's school settled."

"Are you sure?" Asha asked.

"Well, I think we should have the security of a

home first, but the money is, as you say, also yours, Asha. So if you feel that the school is more important, then that's what we'll do," Pratap said.

He seemed submissive and Asha didn't like that. She felt ashamed of herself.

"I'm sure there will be money left for a flat," Asha said, even though she had no idea whether that would be possible. "And I didn't say the money is mine, Pratap; it's ours. It belongs to our family."

"OK," Pratap said, and smiled at her. "You look so beautiful when you're pregnant."

Asha smiled back shyly.

"I miss the children," Asha confessed, and stroked her belly. "I don't know how I'm going to get through the next months."

"We'll come every day, I promise. Just a few months here and you'll be home again," Pratap said, and Asha knew he was thinking that there was no home for her to go back to. If they didn't buy a flat, they had nothing. The owner had probably rented out the hut in the village to someone else by now. They couldn't just live with Kaveri and Raman forever. They had to buy a flat, buy something, or rent something as soon as the pregnancy ended and the baby was born.

Asha weakened then and wanted to tell Pratap that he should just go and put a deposit on a flat, but she didn't. Pratap might be worldly and smarter than she was, but he wasn't seeing the big picture here. Raman was influencing him; she had to be the sensible one. The strong one.

It took one week—just a week—for Asha to get adjusted to the Happy Mothers House. It was like Kaveri had said, "We've always had to work. Cook, clean, wipe someone's ass, something—this will be the first time when someone else will do all the work."

In addition to not having any housework, making a new friend had made the house inviting, almost cozy. Keertana was seven months pregnant, had three children of her own—ten, eight, and six—and was delighted to be away from her house and family.

"Once in a while, a woman needs her rest. The best part, my devil of a mother-in-law has to take care of the three brats and that son of hers," Keertana said, smiling.

This was her second time as a surrogate, and because pregnancy, labor, and delivery had always been easy for her, she thought she'd do it yet again if they'd let her.

"Now we have a house, a TV, a car—next time we can save for a dowry for our daughter," she said, rubbing her belly vigorously. "Look, this is a place of relaxation. You should think of it that way. You don't want to get all upset and hurt the baby or yourself."

"I miss my children," Asha had said to her stiffly when they first met in the TV room. They sat in the back while the others eagerly watched a Telugu evening soap opera, *Anandam* ("Happiness").

"We all miss our children," Keertana snapped at her. "You're not the only glowing example of motherhood here. *We all miss our children,* and we all deal with it. You've been sitting around crying your eyes out."

Asha wanted to snap back and say that maybe she was so upset because she was a better mother than Keertana, but she kept quiet. She realized soon enough that there was no malice behind Keertana's stern words. She was stating a fact, and maybe it was her directness that got Asha to stop feeling sorry for herself.

"I like this show," Keertana said. "That Tanushri is such a bitch."

Anandam was about a wealthy Telugu family living in Hyderabad. The father owned several factories, and his wife was a religious and pious homemaker. They had three grown sons, and the story circled around the lives of the sons and their wives, and their interactions with the factory owner and his wife. The whole family lived together in a massive and opulent house, and there were fights and over-the-top drama to keep everyone engaged every evening from seven to eight.

Tanushri was married to the youngest brother and was the vamp of the story, always up to no good. Every episode showed Tanushri making trouble for her family members.

"I'm telling you, once Manisha finds out that it's Tanushri who's secretly feeding her a contraceptive . . . all hell will break loose," Keertana said as she popped some roasted peanuts into her mouth.

Anandam had been a constant evening fixture at Kaveri's house, too. Kaveri and Asha had watched every episode with mounting tension and pleasure.

"Do you think they will introduce a surrogate in this story?" Keertana wondered. "That would be something. Manisha cannot have a baby and uses a surrogate. It could be like our story."

"Why would they do that?" Asha asked.

"Because it's a very special story," Keertana said. "We're giving a gift to someone—something they can't get themselves—and they give me the resources to build a better life. What do you plan to do with your money?"

Asha shrugged.

"Don't give it all to your husband and let him take care of it; that's a mistake you don't want to make. Charu . . . the one in the orange sari." Keertana pointed to a plump woman who was about nine months pregnant from the looks of it and resembled a very ripe orange. "She gave all the money the previous time to her husband. He took it and ran away with some bitch from their village. She was left alone with two kids and no money. This time she had Doctor Swati put it all in the bank—Doctor Swati is helping her buy a house."

Asha warmed up to Keertana as she told her about the other women at the surrogate house. There was Urmila; this was her first time, but she had tried twice before and lost the baby—though she had still made some money.

"Now she is fully pregnant, so this is the jackpot for her," Keertana told Asha.

Ragini was doing this for a third time and said she was tired of it. She was thirty-five years old and her body was beaten. But her husband was an alcoholic and she had three daughters. She was saving money for their dowries.

This was Gita's second time with the same parents. The parents had been really good to her with the first baby, buying her a TV and fridge and whatnot. They had even come and stayed in Srirampuram, visiting her every day in the last month of her pregnancy.

"My son, Manoj, he's very smart," Asha confided in Keertana. "I know all mothers say that, but he is. He's only five years old and he can already read and write, both in Telugu and English. I'm going to use the money to send him to a special school."

Keertana nodded thoughtfully. "Isn't there one here in Srirampuram? It's supposed to be a really good school. The chief minister's grandson goes there, I think."

"My husband wants to buy a flat," Asha said. "I don't know if we'll have money left for both the flat and Manoj's education."

"Education is very important in this day and age, and if your son is smart, that's what you should spend the money on," Keertana said. "Just do it again in two years or so and buy the flat, too. Doctor Swati won't let you do it more than three times anyway, and you have to be no more than thirty-five years old. So think about that and make your decisions."

"I won't do this again," Asha said firmly. "How was your first time?"

"Very, very easy," Keertana said. "The baby just popped out. I had about fifteen minutes of labor. But if you're in a lot of pain, Doctor Swati will give you medicine. It's safe for the baby and everything, so don't worry about that."

Doctor Swati had talked about the pain medicine with Asha. The parents had signed a release saying that Asha could use the medicine if she wanted or needed it during her labor. But Asha couldn't imagine putting any medicine in her body when giving birth. She knew that Doctor Swati was a really good doctor, but what if something happened? She couldn't ruin a baby's life just because she couldn't handle the pain of labor.

"Did you feel bad about giving the baby to the parents?" Asha asked.

"Not at all," Keertana said. "I know some of the mothers cry and nonsense, but I always knew this was a means to an end. I was relieved when it was born. Out with it and away with it. And frankly, I was glad to not be taking one home. No way was I cleaning up another baby's shit.

"I didn't even see it after it was born. I also told the parents not to send pictures and all that," Keertana continued. "I'm just a coolie; the suitcase belongs to someone else. And you'd better take that smile off your face when you stroke your belly, Asha. There's only hurt and pain if you forget this one is not yours to keep. It's a suitcase. The contents are valuable, but you give it away when you reach the destination."

Asha's hand froze midstroke and she put it next to her thigh. She leaned over and picked up a bowl of *chakli* that was in front of Keertana. There was nothing like eating fresh *chakli*— warm, savory treats made with graham flour and fried to a crisp in peanut oil—and there was extra pleasure in knowing that she hadn't been the one to make them.

Chakli in hand, Asha let out a sigh, leaning back on her chair to watch Tanushri cook up a new scheme on *Anandam*.

• • •

Asha took the computer class instead of the English one. She didn't need to learn English, she decided, or rather, Keertana decided for her.

"We're thinking of buying a computer with some of our money," Keertana told her. "It's good for the children to get familiar with computers at an early age. The future is all computers, so it's important they learn. You should think about it, too."

Manoj's school, Pratap's flat, and now a computer—five lakh rupees was dwindling quickly and they didn't even have the money yet. No wonder, Asha thought, women came back to be surrogates again and again.

The first computer class was all about how to turn on a computer and open something called the Internet. This was different from her life in the village, different from the day-to-day at Kaveri and Raman's flat. Asha had gone to school for a few years until she was ten, but after that she had helped around the house. School had never been important, not for girls. Their class had been a hut where their teacher, a retired schoolmaster, taught them the alphabet in Telugu. Asha had learned to read and write but hadn't aspired for more.

As a girl in her village, life was about taking care of the house, helping your mother, and then getting married and taking care of your husband, your children, and your mother-in-law. Asha spent her days sweeping their hut—Mohini never had to do that, and now if they would be able to buy a flat, she would never have to live in a hut again. Mohini would wear a white shirt and a blue skirt and go to a proper school. She would learn English. She would not look at a computer as if it were something special but see it as a normal thing, something she knew, understood.

The computer teacher was a young woman in her early twenties who was apparently Doctor Swati's niece. Her name was Divya, and she wore modern clothes—pants and a shirt and very pretty black shoes with a heel and a golden buckle on the side.

"You can even read the newspaper on the Internet," she told Asha. She sat next to her and took her to a page where the news was in Telugu.

"I can read Telugu," Asha said happily, because everything else was in English, and Asha was having a difficult time with that.

Divya taught Asha how to use the mouse and click on blue words to read more. Tentatively, Asha approached the news, but she couldn't figure out how to use the mouse. She didn't want to annoy Divya with too many questions in the first class, so she kept it to herself, reading what was on the page that Divya had conjured up for her.

Not that Asha was interested. Who cared if Narendra Modi became the prime minister or that Gandhi boy did? And the Telangana riots were what they were—if Andhra Pradesh was one state or two, how would her life change? And whether Aishwarya Rai lost all the weight she had put on with her precious baby or not—if she would make movies again or not—did it really matter? Who cared?

Kaveri loved the movies and was a great fan of Salman Khan. She watched all his movies even though she didn't understand much Hindi. Asha only liked to see Telugu movies or listen to Telugu movie songs on the radio and watch the songs on the many movie-song TV shows. But she didn't care enough to read about it on the computer; in fact, sitting here in front of the bright monitor was making her sleepy.

In the middle of class, Charu cried out as a gush of water came out of her where she stood.

"I think the baby is about to come," she said, panic in her voice.

Almost immediately, Revati, a maid, and one of the day nurses were by her side, walking her away from the computer class.

Another maid came to clean up the floor, and the class came to an end earlier than usual. Asha was grateful. She didn't know how she would spend a whole hour sitting there, trying to be enthusiastic about a computer.

"It's over for Charu," Gangamma said enviously when they sat in the TV room that night after dinner. "I have another two months to go, and I can't wait to be done with this."

"It's been six hours; we should have heard something by now," Keertana said, looking at her wristwatch.

"Remember that woman, what's her name . . . Meena," Gita said. "She was in labor for fifteen hours. I hope that doesn't happen to me. I can't do fifteen hours of pain for someone else's baby."

"You do what you have to do," Keertana said sternly.

"Easy for you to say," Gangamma said. "You were in labor for fifteen minutes the first time."

Keertana grinned proudly. "Some women are just lucky. I've never had a long labor, even with my own children."

"My back is killing me," Narthaki said. She was five months pregnant like Asha and had moved into the Happy Mothers House as soon as she got pregnant. Her family lived in Kavali, quite far from Srirampuram, so she hadn't had the choice of staying with her family until her last trimester.

"Sometimes I think this is not worth the money," Narthaki continued. It was her first time, too. "I've had my two children and now I'm doing this. It's madness."

"Can't Doctor Swati help with the back pain?" Asha asked.

"She gets a massage every day," Keertana piped in. "Narthaki just likes to complain. The food isn't good, the maid doesn't clean right, her clothes are never white enough . . . like she was living in a palace before this."

"I come from a decent family," Narthaki protested. "We just need some extra money."

"We all need some extra money," Gangamma said wearily. "You think that we'd be here if we didn't?"

"I just keep thinking how strange it will be to give birth to a white baby. They have no hair," Narthaki said. "My parents are from London. And they keep writing letters to me, and when they call, they want me to put the phone on my belly. They sent me this white machine, which Doctor Swati keeps here, and I have to play the machine—iPod, P-pod, something—with their voices close to my belly. They want to make sure the baby learns English in the womb itself. Crazy people."

"They gave me one, too," Asha said. "Doctor Swati plays it when I go for my checkup."

"What do they say?" Narthaki asked. "Mine say, hello, I love you, their names . . . whatever."

"The mother says things like that," Asha said, although she wasn't sure, because it was always in English. The father spoke in Telugu:

"We live in California, and both the ocean and the mountains are close by.

"My name is Madhu and I'm your father. I love you very much.

"Your room is next to ours, and we will decorate it with butterflies and flowers for you.

"Take care of yourself, little baby."

Asha liked to hear the father's voice. He would be a good parent, she was sure. The skinny mother, Asha wasn't so sure about. She couldn't even speak Telugu properly; what would she teach this child about where she came from? Nothing. That woman was all American, all foreign. But the father. He seemed like a nice man. A good man. A good Telugu man. And his Telugu was good and clean. He didn't insert English words in between like so many people had started to do.

"Mine sent CDs," Keertana said. "Doctor Swati keeps them here and plays them on her computer during my checkup. It's so stupid. The baby isn't going to remember anything when it comes out."

"What about your parents, Asha?" Gangamma asked. "How are they to you?"

"They're nice," Asha said. "They call every week and send presents. They even send toys for my children. The father is Telugu; the mother is half-Indian and half-American."

"At least your baby won't be white with blue eyes," Narthaki said.

"How does it matter what it looks like?" Keertana demanded. "It's not like we have anything to do with it."

"We're carrying them," Narthaki said.

Gangamma, like Asha, wondered if she was going against the wishes of God by giving a barren woman a baby.

"If she can't have a child, it's because God doesn't want her to have one," Gangamma said. "Don't you think we're doing something wrong here?"

"And if God gives us cancer, we still get treated, don't we? We don't sit around and think this is God's will," Keertana said. "This is the same thing."

Despite her harsh demeanor, Asha was starting to really like Keertana. She seemed not to have any moral or emotional issues with being a surrogate. She was doing it for the money, plain and simple, and she didn't think there was anything complicated about that.

Her philosophy was simple: she wasn't going to win the lottery—this was her lottery. So she had to put in a little effort to get the prize; it was worth it.

Revati announced that Charu had given birth to a healthy baby boy after seven hours of labor. Everyone clapped and Revati distributed *ladoos* to mark the occasion. Charu would come by the house to get her things in two to three days, after which she'd go back to her family and they would probably never see her again.

"Poor Charu," Gangamma said. "She really liked

being here. Someone to cook and clean, and now she has to do it all by herself."

"As we all will," Keertana said. "I say enjoy this time; it will be over soon enough."

"I like cooking and cleaning," Narthaki said. "And I at least do it better than that maid Rangamma."

This would become a pattern, Asha realized. She would make friends with these women, and one by one, they would leave and new women with new pregnancies would join them. And then it would be Asha's time to leave the house and go back to her life. And what would that be like?

Chapter Nine

"I miss my children. Every day I see them, I feel they have grown up," Asha had told her. "But I'm happy here. It's very nice."

Priya had put down the phone feeling like a monster.

"She misses her kids," Priya told Madhu unnecessarily. He had been part of the conversation over the speakerphone in their study.

Madhu sat down on the office chair and sighed.

"You feel bad, too," Priya said. She stood up and started to pace up and down the small study.

"But our baby needs to be safe, and it isn't for the rest of her life, just a few months," he said.

Priya nodded.

"And it's for her safety, too," Madhu added.

Priya nodded again.

"But I still feel like shit," Madhu admitted.

"I can just hear Sush say we're exploiting the poor." Priya stood in front of him for a moment and then started to pace again.

"We're helping her give her children a better life," Madhu said. "We're making sure her family has a better future."

Priya shook her head. "We're rationalizing. This pretty much sucks. All of it. Our baby is growing halfway around the world while we sit here. Every time I drink coffee or a glass of wine, I feel I shouldn't be doing it because we're pregnant."

No matter what she did, Priya couldn't shake a feeling of inadequacy—that she should be pregnant, that she was somehow a lesser woman because she wasn't. She had even considered buying a fake belly and putting it on . . . just around the house to feel some connection to the pregnancy that was going to result in her and Madhu's child.

Her back wasn't hurting. Her feet weren't swollen. She had no nausea, and she could drink like a fish if it pleased her.

"We *are* pregnant," Madhu said. "But I feel it, too, the strangeness of this."

"But I'm the one who would've been pregnant, who should've been pregnant," Priya said. "I'm the one who outsourced this."

"Not because you had a choice, and don't use that word," Madhu said. "Don't be so hard on yourself."

"Hard on myself? I think that I'm being way too easy on myself," she said.

They sat silent for a while, and then Priya gasped. "Oh my God! We're going to have a daughter."

Madhu grinned. "Yeah."

Doctor Swati had told them the sex before they had talked to Asha.

"Oh my God," Priya repeated and looked wide-eyed at Madhu. "What if I have the same relationship with my daughter as my mother has with me?"

Madhu sighed. "You are not your mother, sweetheart."

"No, seriously," Priya said.

"Yes, seriously," Madhu said. "You're not your mother, and our baby is not you. Whole different set of people, whole different chemistry."

"You know, I've been worried about the whole baby being a girl thing," Priya said. "I mean . . . a boy is never going to come home at age fifteen and say someone knocked him up."

"Woman, you need to calm down," Madhu said.

And I even know her name, Priya thought. *Ayesha—alive; she who lives.*

"Do you sometimes wish we'd adopted? Wouldn't that have been easier?" Priya wondered aloud.

"That isn't a picnic, either. I did the research and it's tough. Remember Sandeep, who went to New Jersey to work for Accenture? They went through the whole thing, even had a picture in hand and were then told the baby wasn't theirs. His wife was completely broken after that, and Sandeep swore never to try adoption again," Madhu said.

Priya took a deep breath.

"We'll get through this; you know that, right?" Madhu said. "As long as you and I are together, babe, we can move mountains. We just need to not lose our minds for the next few months."

But as the weeks progressed, that was exactly what they did. They did nothing on Friday nights but wait to call India and talk to Doctor Swati and then Asha. And then they spent Saturday and Sunday doing nothing but talk about the baby and how horrible it was that they were here and their baby somewhere else. They talked about the same things over and over again, going in circles.

Priya constantly worried the baby would die—and when she convinced herself the baby wouldn't die, she obsessed about everything from hygiene at the Happy Mothers House to the labor.

"What if something goes wrong during the birth?

"What if she gets toxemia?

"What if she gets ringworm?"

Madhu tried to calm her, but Priya was spinning. The absolute last thing she needed now was a visit from her mother.

"If it isn't French, sweetheart, it isn't really wine," Sush declared as she sipped a Napa Valley Merlot.

"That's not true, Sush," Madhu said. "Maybe we're not wine connoisseurs like Andrew and you, but California wine is as good as the wine you get in Europe."

"Not all European wine is good," Sush said. "I know people get all up in arms about the German Riesling, but I'm a red person—something bold, like Bourgogne."

"Italian reds are pretty good," Priya said, even though she knew this was not a discussion she could win. She wasn't a wine person. She didn't care if it cost five dollars or fifteen or fifty—some tasted good and some didn't.

She should've anticipated this and served French wine, Priya thought as she pushed a piece of duck around her plate.

Madhu had cooked dinner, because Priya was not able to figure out what to cook for Sush that wouldn't elicit toxic criticism. Indian? No, Sush would immediately launch into how she cooked Indian food much better. French? Hell, no. Sush would demolish the food. She was such a Francophile. Italian? That might be too simple. Sush might say something about carbs and pasta. It was always so complicated.

They had discussed whether the best recourse would be to take Sush out to a restaurant, but they knew she would complain about having to eat out yet again when she had been eating out for nearly a week during the conference she had been attending in San Francisco. After spending the week at the Hilton, she was going to stay the weekend with them.

They wished there were some way of getting out of it, but there had been no polite way of saying, "No, don't come, we're stressed enough as it is."

Both Priya and Madhu (and probably even Sush) knew that the wine talk was going to be short-lived. Sooner or later Sush was going to launch into a discussion about their baby. And after three glasses of even a substandard California Merlot, Sush would not hold back, or would, as she called it, speak from her heart.

"How was the conference?" Madhu asked as he attacked his duck breast. He had decided to stick with his specialty, duck à l'orange. He did it well, and the last time he had made it for Andrew and Sush, they had raved. Of course, then he had served it with a good French Bordeaux.

"These save-the-world conferences are a waste of time," Sush said, pushing her plate away. She had not complimented the food, but both Priya and Madhu noticed that she hadn't insulted it, either.

"Then why do you go?" Priya asked, and put her cutlery down. Sush killed her appetite, had been doing it since she was a child.

"Because in my position, I'm expected to," Sush said, and smiled. "When you reach my level in the NGO business, you have to show up for such conferences and speak; otherwise when you have something important to say, no one will listen."

Priya and Madhu quietly sipped their wine.

"And if I don't continue to network, I'll be out of a job," Sush said. "I've worked my entire life for nonprofits, and now as I turn sixty . . . anyway, you get older and people stop listening to you. You find that what you have to say is not as important. I feel like I'm being shoved aside. I'm not young enough to warrant attention. You have to be Angelina Jolie these days to get anywhere."

"No one is shoving you aside, Mama," Priya said, feeling sorry for her mother. Her career had been everything to her, and it wasn't easy to accept that she would soon have to retire, whether she was ready or not. And Sush wasn't exactly sixty, more like sixty-five. But Priya knew her mom liked to fudge her age here and there.

It always amazed Priya that despite working for NGOs—working for the poor, as her mother put it—Sush was steeped in vanity up to her ears. Someone who worked for the poor shouldn't be bitching about California wine! Someone who worked for the poor should be grateful that there was food *and* wine on the table.

"How are your jobs? Secure?" Sush asked.

Madhu shrugged. "As secure as can be."

"The economy is a disaster," Sush said, and emptied her glass of wine. Madhu promptly refilled it.

"It'll get better," Priya said.

"Layoffs in your company, Priya?" Sush asked.

Priya nodded. "We had a round, and we'll probably have another if business doesn't pick up."

"You should be careful, both of you. I don't know what you're thinking, having a baby in this economic climate," Sush said.

And here it came.

"If you were just having a baby yourself, that's one thing, but spending all this money to have one is insane. If you have so much money, you should give it away to charity."

Priya sighed.

Madhu took a deep breath, as if preparing himself for the argument that would probably follow.

Sush looked at both of them. "It's selfish to have a baby like this. I don't approve."

Priya rose and picked up her plate. "Guess what, we don't need your approval."

That led to another interminable discussion about Priya's lack of respect for her mother. If only she didn't get so riled up, Priya thought. If only she didn't turn into an angry teenager every time her mother came around, maybe then Sush's visits wouldn't be such a disaster.

They lay quietly in bed, listening to Sush putter around the guest room. When the room fell silent, Priya turned to face Madhu.

"Is your job secure?" she asked.

Madhu strangled another sigh. Sush had hit a home run. She planted these seeds of doubt, and they thrived.

"Like I said, as secure as it can be; the world economy is in the toilet."

"If both of us lost our jobs, how would we manage?"

"We have savings."

"And what would we do about health insurance?"

Madhu put a hand on Priya's cheek. "We'd get on COBRA. I can always find a job. Something, anything, to get us through. We'd manage, I promise."

Priya's eyes filled with tears. "I see these stories about people being homeless, and I get scared. What if it's us next? What if . . . what if our house got repossessed? What would we do?"

"Move in with Sush and Andrew?"

"Haha. Very funny," Priya said.

They were silent again and Priya said quietly, "Madhu, I'm scared."

"Don't be. I'll take care of you."

Madhu was old-fashioned when it came down to it. He believed that the man took care of the family. He never begrudged Priya her career, but Priya often wondered if he'd be one of those jealous husbands if she started to make more money than he did.

"In any case, Calvin has assured me that there will be no layoffs. We're still in the black. We're not going to lay people off," Madhu said.

"I'm just looping because of her," Priya said.

"She has it down to a science, she does," Madhu said. "The minute you're happy about something, Sush makes sure you have some reason to be down."

"But it's my fault. I let her," Priya said.

192

"A mother's voice is powerful," Madhu said. "You never had a choice, sweetheart."

"The hell with her," Priya said.

"That's the spirit," Madhu said. "I'd hoped we could have sex tonight, but I'm worried that if we do and she hears us, she may comment on my technique."

Priya laughed.

The next morning, they went to a nearby South Indian restaurant for breakfast. Sush had left behind most of her Indian ways, but she still enjoyed an *idli* with *sambhar* and coconut chutney on a Saturday morning.

"Do you want Madhu to drive you to Redwood City tonight?" Priya asked as they waited for their food to arrive.

Sush had been invited to dinner at a friend's house that night, and both Madhu and Priya were relieved that they didn't have to entertain her for yet another evening.

"If you don't mind," Sush said. "Actually, Heidi told me that you're both very welcome as well."

Heidi and Sush had gone to Berkeley together years ago. They had remained friends even though Heidi had gotten married to a heart surgeon and now spent her days worrying about her antique furniture pieces and her kids, in that order. When Priya was young, they had gone on family vacations together. But as Heidi's daughters and

Priya grew older, the joint family vacations were limited to the parents. Heidi's husband, Mike had died a few years ago. Sush and Heidi would now occasionally take a long weekend at a spa, getting facials and seaweed wraps. As a teenager, Priya could never understand how Sush and Heidi got along. Heidi had no career and talked mostly about her fitness trainer, while Sush talked about saving the world—but as she had grown up, Priya had figured it out: Heidi didn't threaten Sush. Heidi was just a housewife who looked up to Sush as some kind of superwoman. And Sush loved it.

"Like I said, Madhu and I have this thing . . . so . . . ," Priya said, kicking herself for not having planned a better excuse. *We have a thing? Could she have said anything lamer?*

Sush's eyebrows shot up.

"It's been tough for both of us at work lately," Madhu interjected. "And we were planning on a quiet romantic evening. At least, I have been planning an evening. I had it all set up before you said you were coming."

"So what are your plans?" Sush asked suspiciously.

Madhu grinned. "It's a surprise for Priya."

Sush nodded, but she didn't buy it, which resulted in her being in a crappy mood for the rest of the day. She even turned down Madhu's offer for a ride and instead got one of Heidi's sons-in-law to come all the way from Redwood City and pick her up.

"So what are the romantic plans?" Priya asked.

Madhu shrugged. "Being a vegetable in front of the television? And drinking some—pardon me—California wine. And if there's nothing good on TV, we can have sex without worrying about your mother commenting on my sack style. What do you think?"

Priya grinned. "It's a good plan. Can we wait with the sex? Krysta said she wanted to come see me."

"Bad breakup?" Madhu asked.

Priya nodded.

It was a pattern with Krysta. When she was dating, they didn't see her, but when she broke up she would come over for dinner regularly.

"But it's a good breakup this time. She was dating a married guy," Priya said.

Madhu shuddered. "Aren't you glad we have each other? It's a bloody jungle out there if you're single."

"Sometimes I feel like such a fraud when I talk to Krysta, handing out platitudes. What do I know? We've been together for so long that I can't even remember being single," Priya said. "And she's thirty-five. She's scared she won't meet someone."

Priya and Krysta watched *Pretty Woman* on TNT while Madhu holed up in the study, working.

"So where's my Richard Gere?" Krysta said.

"We should've watched *The Fast and the Furious*," Priya said, and sighed.

"I could do Vin Diesel," Krysta said, then shook her head. "You know what, though, I don't think I can do anyone anymore."

"Well, it's good to take a break sometimes," Priya said.

Krysta shook her head again and drank some wine. Suddenly tears were rolling down her face.

Priya consoled Krysta the best she could, but all she had were words and hugs. And Kleenex. Lots of Kleenex. Krysta was still there when Sush came back home, now convinced more than ever that Madhu had not planned a romantic evening, not when he was in the study and Priya was with Krysta in the living room.

"Hello, Krysta," Sush said when she came in with the spare key Madhu had given her. She looked at her wristwatch in a dramatic gesture and then at Priya. "If you didn't want to come to dinner at Heidi's house, you just had to say so, not make up lies."

"Hi, Sush," Krysta said, standing up. "I guess I'd better go home."

"Let me walk you out," Priya said, ignoring her mother.

By the time Priya came back inside the house, Sush was reading Madhu the riot act in the study.

"I come all the way and you treat me like this? I see how Heidi's daughters and sons-in-law take care of her, and I'm embarrassed because you two have no manners. You treat me—"

"Enough," Priya said. "Just enough."

"What?"

"Just stop, Mummy," Priya said. "You can't talk to Madhu like this. He isn't your child. And yes, we don't like having you over because you spend the entire time telling us what we're doing wrong. If it isn't the surrogate, it's the car I drive, or the condition of the house, or the garden, or my cooking. You never come here and say, 'Hey, your roses are blooming, that's nice.' Or that we bought a beautiful new couch. Or ask us how the baby is doing, how we're dealing with this surrogate situation. You just launch into a discussion about what terrible people we are."

Sush just stared at Priya and then marched out of the study.

She stopped and turned around. "Call me a cab; I'm leaving."

"No, you're not," Priya said wearily. "It's two in the morning, and you're not going anywhere at this hour but into the guest room to get some sleep."

This time even Madhu gaped at Priya.

"Priya, you don't tell me what to do and—"

"Mummy, for once, no drama. You have to admit that you treat us like garbage. And in return you want us to treat you like a queen. Only Dad can do that," Priya said.

"I treat neither you nor your father like garbage," Sush said angrily.

"Sure you do. Nothing he does is ever right. You're nice enough about it and you'll say, '*Darling,* you screwed up' or what have you, but you still say it," Priya said. "And I need you to stop, at least with me. We're going to have a baby soon. So if you can't change and can't start appreciating us, you can't see the baby. Especially if you intend to rant about us using a surrogate. I don't need that in my life. And our child definitely doesn't need that. You can't say anything negative to me anymore."

"Then I have nothing to say to you," Sush said. "I say what I see. I speak the truth, and I won't lie to soothe your feelings. I'll stay the night because, as you said, it is two in the morning, but I will leave tomorrow. I will never come back to your house. And I will never speak with you again."

Priya saw her retreating figure and lowered her head.

"And here I thought if I stood up to her, there would be this great moment between us," she said.

"Didn't work out like in the movies, did it?" Madhu said as he came toward her.

Priya shook her head, her eyes wet.

NobuNobi: The baby is due anytime and I'm sooooo nervous. We're in India now and I all but live in the hospital with my SM. She's great. And I can't wait to see our son.

Trying1Time: Good luck and congratulations. I look forward to seeing the pictures.

NearlyMother: Congratulations! I can't wait for when our SM delivers, now that we have one who is pregnant. But my husband just got laid off. Thank God I still have a job and it pays well. Hope I don't lose my job, too, because we'll be screwed then.

CantConceive1970: The economy is tough. My stepdaughter and son-in-law both got laid off last month. They're fine for now, and my son-in-law will hopefully find a job soon. But if they don't . . . I think they'll be moving in with us.

LastHope77: I'm so scared of losing my house. My husband is so annoyed with me because I keep asking him if his job is safe. I'm a stay-at-home mom so he's the only one putting bread on the table.

NobuNobi: I know I'm going to be laid off soon, especially because I'm in India now and then I take twelve weeks maternity leave. My in-laws keep telling us how stupid we are to do this. Like the baby is making me lose my job. I don't care about the job. I just want to bring my baby home.

Trying1Time: My mother is not very supportive, either. We got into it last night and I don't think she's ever going to speak to me again.

UnoBaby: So sorry to hear that. I've lost friends because we're using an SM and I say good riddance. But you can't say that about a parent. After all, you only have one mother. I hope she'll come around.

Trying1Time: I don't think she will. I raised my voice at her, which I've never done. But in some ways I'm OK with her not being in my life right now. She's too critical, not happy for us or the baby. Sometimes it's just easier to let it go rather than fight to keep the relationship going. It's just too painful.

PART III:
Second Trimester

Chapter Ten

The mother had cried when Asha had told them that she missed her children. She had told her that she liked living in the Happy Mothers House, but as the mother had prodded, Asha had also told her how much she missed Manoj and Mohini. And because the mother cried, Asha felt a little better, as if her sorrow were now shared.

The mother had asked her what she missed the most, and she had said that she missed dropping Manoj off at school. That, and bringing him back home. She loved to walk with him, his hand in hers and Mohini in her arms while he rattled on in the morning about what he would learn in school that day; and on their way back, he would tell her what happened during the day.

But the best part, the very best part, was when she would lean down at the gate of the school, Mohini standing next to her, and Manoj would hug her and kiss her on her mouth. And then Mohini would giggle and ask for a kiss, too. Manoj would sigh and kiss his sister's cheek. Then he would run inside and Asha would feel her heart swell. My God, her children were wonderful.

Asha counted the days.
She had another eighteen weeks to go.

She had to admit, the weeks went by faster in the Happy Mothers House than they had at home. Her days had a pattern here. She woke up and there was a yoga class. After that, they took a bath and ate a hearty breakfast of *idlis* or *dosas* or *vadas* with *sambhar*, fried curd rice, and fresh hot rice with a vegetable curry. The breakfast was the big meal at the house, which was different from how she did it at home. But apparently it was healthier to have a good breakfast and a light dinner. After breakfast, they had computer class. They took a break and watched television after that and had a snack of fruit and milk. Asha had to learn to eat fruits like apple and pineapple because she ate only bananas and mangoes during the season at home. Fruits had always been too expensive to eat every day.

After they snacked, some of them got massages or just sat around. Then there was lunch and more rest. Many of the women took naps. Some women read; others watched television in the TV room and chatted. Asha tried to nap, but she wasn't used to having time to rest. There had always been clothes to be washed, dinner to be made, home-work to do with Manoj, and Mohini to take care of.

Unable to nap, she would join her new friends, Narthaki, Keertana, Gangamma, and Gita, in the TV room. They'd play cards during the day and watch the serial *Anandam* in the evening. Mostly they talked.

Gita's parents, who were American, were now in Srirampuram, and they came to see her every day at four when Asha's children came to visit. Asha had seen the parents. They were generous, bringing gifts for Gita every day. One day it was a television for her room, another an empty photo album for pictures of her children, and just yesterday they had given her dried fruits.

"Gita knows how to get things," Keertana said as they played rummy.

"I don't know how to get things; my parents are just good people," Gita said.

"Oh come on, just the other day I heard you tell them, in English, too, 'My back hurts so much; the bed is so hard,' and *arrey*, they get you a new mattress," Keertana said, dropping a nine of hearts in the pile of cards among them.

"I wasn't asking them to bring me anything," Gita said angrily, and threw her cards facedown on the table. "I pack."

"You always pack," Narthaki complained. "Do you never have any good cards?"

"Maybe not, but she has a new Sony television in her room," Keertana said.

"You're just jealous that my parents are better than yours," Gita said.

Keertana's parents didn't want to have any contact with her. They didn't want to meet her or know her. They just wanted to take their baby and never deal with the woman who gave birth to it.

There were at least three other surrogates in the house whose parents didn't want contact with them. Doctor Swati said it was to not have an emotional attachment because it was so hard for parents to have a baby this way.

"My parents have had so much bad luck with other surrogates that they want to keep things simple. Which is fine by me," said Keertana. "Don't want to know strange people from Britain anyway. And I don't speak any English, so we'd have to talk through Nursamma, which is more trouble than I want in my life."

Nursamma, or Nurse Alice, was the live-in nurse. She was in her midfifties, a portly woman who wore a cross around her neck. She was a Christian and spoke English very well. She was nice to all the surrogates, and Asha liked to speak with her about her life in Kerala, which she had left behind after her husband had died. She had no children and no relatives. She thought of the surrogates as her family. She and Revati, the housemother, were good friends. These two lonely ladies had made their home here at Happy Mothers, and when she saw them, Asha was glad that she had a husband and children.

Nursamma spoke Telugu very well, now that she had lived in Andhra for nearly fifteen years, but her Malayalam accent was strong. She would still say *b* for *p*, especially when she spoke hurriedly.

She had very curly hair, which Asha associated with all Malayali women, and instead of a sari, she wore a kurta over a long skirt.

"In the old days, women used to have children before they turned twenty," she told Asha once while they sat out on the veranda stringing jasmine flowers for the women to wear in their hair.

"Even now in my village that's how it is," Asha said.

"And there, women don't have trouble having children. But in the city with women working and everything, they wait and wait to get married, and then they complain when they are thirty that they can't have babies," Nursamma said.

"Thirty and no children?" Asha asked.

"Yes, and they say in America women sometimes have children even when they're forty," she said. "It's not healthy."

"Have you always been a nurse?" Asha asked Nursamma.

Nursamma nodded, took a string of jasmine, and handed it to Asha. "You take the first one."

Asha took the flowers and secured them on her head by lacing the jasmine flowers through her hair, just like her mother used to do. Asha had always had long, black, flowing hair that she braided, and her mother would always say that a woman looked beautiful with long black hair crowned with sweet-smelling jasmine.

"I was a nurse in the Indian army," Nursamma said. "For seven years. From 1982 to 1989."

"Really?" Asha asked as she laced the jasmine flowers together with a white thread in a practiced motion. "Is that where you learned such good English?"

"Yes," Nursamma said, and laughed. "The stories I can tell you about those days. Oh my. But then my husband fell sick and I had to leave. You move around too much in the army, and that wasn't good for my husband. So I became a nurse in Kochi, and then after he died, I just couldn't live there anymore. Too many memories."

"Was your husband nice?"

Nursamma nodded, her eyes clear and bright, her face smiling as if thinking of something pleasant. "The nicest man in the world. Now let's finish this before *Anandam* starts."

Asha wondered if she would be so content with memories if Pratap died. She saw Puttamma and how bitter she was as a widow, but then, Puttamma probably had been no better when she was a married woman.

"How about your parents, Asha? Are they going to come here when the baby is due?" Narthaki asked now.

Asha shrugged. "I think so."

"They send you things, too. They must be wealthy," Narthaki said.

The surrogates competed with respect to how

nice their parents were, how much they sent, how often they called. White parents were more exotic than Indian parents. But the women agreed that it was strange to give birth to a white baby. A baby with marble-white skin, blond hair, and blue eyes—it was a sight to behold for the mothers when they gave birth.

"I have no idea if they're wealthy," Asha said. Fact was, she didn't know much about her parents at all, and she didn't feel loyalty toward them, as some of the other surrogates seemed to.

"They must be. Only rich people can afford to have children like this," Gita said.

Bored with the conversation, Keertana slammed her cards on the table. "Are we playing or not?" she demanded.

"I don't want to play anymore," Gita said.

"You packed already, so I wasn't talking to you," Keertana said as Gita stormed away.

"Why do you always pick on her?" Narthaki said as she piled the cards together and started to shuffle them.

"I don't pick on her," Keertana said, and then sighed. "She just annoys me, OK? She's such a beggar. At least I'm only taking the money they give me. I don't send letters saying I want this and that. That's what she does. 'My son needs spectacles and we don't have the money'—and then they send money for that, which she uses to buy herself a sari."

Narthaki shook her head. "She bought her son spectacles, too. Gita is a good mother. And she's right, you know, you do sound jealous. If your parents kept asking you what you wanted, wouldn't you tell them?"

Asha had had enough of the discussion and stood up, promising herself once again that she would try to take a nap or read a Telugu book in the afternoon instead of sitting with these women. They fought every day about one thing or another.

Even though they had all the creature comforts they could dream of, none of the women in the Happy Mothers House was happy. Asha saw it everywhere. The frustration of being away from their families, the humiliation of lying to everyone about their pregnancy, the conflict of having a baby inside them they mustn't bond with—these were definitely *not* Happy Mothers.

That evening, Doctor Swati came to speak with them after dinner, collecting all the surrogate mothers in the television room.

"A television news show from England is doing a program about mothers like you," Doctor Swati told them. "They are coming here in two weeks, and they will want to talk to some of you. Nursamma and I will select the women who will talk to the television crew. I know you're worried about being seen on television, but you can cover your face while you speak with them."

"What will they want to talk to us about?" Gita asked.

"Will they show the program in India?" someone else asked.

"Will they pay us for this?" Keertana asked.

Doctor Swati raised her hand to quiet the room.

"They will ask you what it means for you to be a surrogate," Doctor Swati said. "They will ask about your health and how you feel about living here at Happy Mothers. And no, they won't pay you, and the program will only be shown in England."

There were murmurs among the women, and Gangamma seemed more agitated than most, so Doctor Swati asked her if she had a specific question.

"What are we supposed to say to them when they ask us questions?" Gangamma asked. "What do you want us to tell them?"

Doctor Swati cleared her throat. "The truth. I think you're very comfortable here. This is a nice house and you're well taken care of. Tell them how you know what you're doing is a gift for these couples who cannot have children."

"Like that is the truth," Chitra whispered into Asha's ear.

Asha had not spoken much to Chitra, who had come to the surrogate house the previous week. She was barely four months pregnant and looked like she was already about fourteen months along.

Asha didn't like her, and it wasn't just her weight; she looked mean. She reminded Asha of an aunt who used to beat her when she was a little girl. She would twist her ears or give her a quick slap for no reason at all. Asha had been only ten then, but she figured that her aunt was one of those women who enjoyed beating children. She felt the same about Chitra. It was unreasonable, really—Chitra was probably nothing like her aunt, but Asha couldn't help the feeling.

Doctor Swati continued to talk about the filming details as Chitra babbled on.

"It's a business, you know. We just get five lakhs, but she . . . she gets fifteen. We carry the baby and she gets more money," Chitra said. And look at this house. The paint is peeling off, and they stuff as many of us here as they can."

Maybe Chitra came from a bigger house, Asha thought, because she didn't think the house was small. She had seen a program on television about a house like this for surrogate mothers in Mumbai, and in that house all the women slept in the same room. Here, Asha just shared a room with Gangamma. Sure, the room was small, with barely enough space for their beds; still, it was bigger than what she shared in Kaveri's flat with Kaveri and Puttamma.

"This is a baby business," Chitra continued, still whispering. "They sell our wombs to make money."

Asha wanted to ask her to shut up. Ask her why she had agreed to it if it was so terrible. But she didn't. Partly because it wasn't in Asha's nature, and partly because she had thought the very same things Chitra was saying.

Doctor Swati went into the computer room and asked some of the women to come and talk to her, one by one. Asha was one of those who was asked to come in. Chitra was not.

Asha knew why she had been chosen. She was the quiet one, polite.

"Do you think you could be on television?" Doctor Swati asked her.

Asha shook her head. "I don't think so," she said. "What if someone sees me? No, no."

"They will hide your face," Doctor Swati said. "They will make sure no one will recognize you."

"But they can recognize my voice," Asha said. There was no way she was doing this. There was, of course, the fear that someone she knew might recognize her, but beyond that, how could she tell the lies she'd have to? No, no, it was better not to be asked the questions in the first place.

Doctor Swati sighed as if disappointed in Asha.

"This is a big opportunity for Happy Mothers. And not just for the clinic but also for all the women who want to have babies like this, for women like you who want to give this gift and better your life," Doctor Swati said. "The more couples that come to Happy Mothers, the more we can help women like you. And this program will be shown in England, not here, so there will be no way anyone you know will watch it."

As much as Asha didn't want to get involved, she also felt an obligation to help Doctor Swati and Happy Mothers because of all that they had done for her family.

"What if I say the wrong thing?" Asha asked.

"Don't worry," Doctor Swati said, now smiling as she laid a hand on Asha's. "We will go through the possible questions with you beforehand and make sure you say the right thing. In any case, just be honest and tell them the truth."

"I will ask Pratap this evening," Asha said.

"Yes, yes, of course," Doctor Swati said. "Ask Pratap. I'm sure he'll be fine with it. I'll talk to him as well."

Asha nodded and got up.

"And Asha, I looked into that school for Manoj. It's a very good school, just outside Srirampuram. Very expensive if Manoj lives there, but if he lives at home and goes to school every day, it shouldn't be that bad. You'll be able to afford it with the money you get," Doctor Swati said.

Asha's face lit up. "Really? That's such good news. Thanks, Doctor Swati."

"Of course, it's very hard to get into the school, you know. It's where all the smart children go," Doctor Swati said, then paused before going on.

"You'll need some top recommendations to get Manoj in."

Asha stared at Doctor Swati. Recommendations? From whom?

"But you shouldn't worry about that. I can give Manoj a good recommendation. I know the local MP very well. Mr. Rajnish Reddy. And I'm sure Rajnish-*garu* will give a recommendation as well," she continued. "We'll take care of you and your son."

Asha felt her breath catch in her lungs.

"You just think about whether you want to be part of the program," Doctor Swati said with a broad smile. "Even though they'll talk to you for half an hour or so, you'll be on the program for just one or two minutes, not much. And think about it; you'll be on television and everyone wants that, right?"

Asha touched her swollen belly as she walked out of the computer room, feeling like something heavy had slammed into her and taken her breath away.

She felt disgust rise within her, for Doctor Swati, the parents, herself, the baby . . . everyone.

Chitra was right. This was a bazaar, a marketplace. First she had to sell her womb to get money. Now she had to sell her honesty to get Manoj into a good school.

Asha talked to Pratap about the television show when he came to see her that evening. Mohini sat in her lap on the swing on the veranda, falling asleep because she had missed her afternoon nap. Manoj was reading an English comic book, laughing to himself as he flipped the pages and read what most children his age were unable to read, what she herself was unable to read.

"I know," Pratap said. "Doctor Swati told me about the program. Do you want to do it?"

Usually, as soon as Pratap and the children came, someone let Asha know. But this time Asha had come looking because it had been twenty minutes past four and no one had said anything. Doctor Swati had been talking to Pratap.

Asha shrugged. "Not really. But I feel that after all they have done for us, we should do this for them. I mean, Kaveri has a flat now. And we will be able to send Manoj to a good school."

"As long as they hide your face," Pratap said. "If people find out, our reputation won't be worth anything. We'll lose face and we have a daughter to marry off. We have to remember that."

Asha kissed the sleeping Mohini's cheek and couldn't really imagine Mohini as a grown woman, ready to get married.

"Doctor Swati looked into the school for Manoj. She says it's affordable if he stays with us at home. You should talk to her more and find out how much it will cost exactly," Asha said. "But Manoj needs recommendations to get in. Doctor Swati said she will give one and also get one from the local MP. But she said I shouldn't worry about that; I should just think about the TV thing."

"I see," Pratap said.

Asha hugged Mohini closer, tighter. "She seems like a nice woman, doesn't she?"

"Who? Doctor Swati?" Pratap asked, and when Asha nodded, he sighed. "No one is nice without a reason, Asha. I say to hell with the school. Let's buy a flat . . ."

"Pratap, please, we've discussed this," Asha said.

"OK, OK," Pratap said. "So school is more important than a place to live. Fine, do the TV thing. Just make sure your face is hidden. And maybe you can hold your nose when you speak? So people won't recognize your voice."

Asha frowned. "You want me to hold my nose?"

Pratap grinned, pinched his nose, and said in a nasal tone, "It was a joke, dear wife."

Asha laughed. Manoj looked up from his comic. "Why are you laughing, Amma?"

"Your father is being silly," Asha said.

Manoj put down his comic book and came up to his mother. He kissed her on the cheek. "I like to see you laugh. You should do it more."

Asha's smile froze as she realized what Manoj was saying to her, that she seldom laughed. Her heart sank. Was she always sad? Was she never laughing or smiling? Asha had always been serious. Careful. Somber. She didn't laugh much, not loudly. She didn't express herself. She was the quiet one.

"Well, then, I'll laugh all the time," Asha said, hiding her dismay.

"Good," Manoj said as his father pulled him onto his lap.

"What about me? Do I look nice when I laugh?" Pratap asked.

Manoj shrugged. "Laughing doesn't make you look bad," he said, and Asha knew that she would do a hundred television shows, she would do them even if they didn't cover her face, just to give her boy a chance.

Divya, Doctor Swati's niece, was helping the three women chosen to participate in the TV program. They would be interviewed by a British person in English. A translator would accompany the interviewer.

Asha's roommate, Gangamma, was also chosen to participate in the TV program, as was Vinita, a woman who had just become pregnant. She had moved into the surrogate house as soon as she got pregnant because she lived far away from Srirampuram and couldn't come for regular checkups.

Asha couldn't help but notice that all three women were the quiet type, not vocal like Keertana or Chitra. They had been chosen, she thought, to say the right things. Doctor Swati didn't want anyone to say anything that would reflect poorly on her practice.

"Each of you will be interviewed in the TV room," Divya said. "And tomorrow we will have someone come and paint the room so that all those cracks are gone. They will also walk around the house so they can see that this is a clean building, as is the clinic."

Nursamma, who had joined them, was very enthusiastic about the British TV crew. "I saw this program about a house like this in Mumbai, was it? Old, dirty building. They didn't even have a kitchen. The women got food from some hotel or something in a big tiffin box."

"In that place, they had thirty women," Divya said. "We would also like Happy Mothers to grow. We have room for at least thirty women in this house, and with this program I think we'll have more couples coming here."

Asha didn't think they could fit thirty women in the house. What, would they put beds in one of the halls?

"So, I'm going to ask you a question as if I am the interviewer, and then you can each answer it," Divya said. "Ready? OK. Gangamma, you start first. How do you like being at Happy Mothers?"

Gangamma looked at Asha and Vinita, a little confused, and when they nodded with encouragement, she said, "It's nice."

Divya then looked at Asha, who mumbled it was nice, as did Vinita.

They went through twenty probable questions. For each question, Divya made them repeat the answer several times until she was satisfied.

"We're practicing to make sure that you're very clear in what you say," Divya said. Asha and the other mothers knew they were practicing to make sure they didn't say anything Doctor Swati didn't want them to say.

Vinita pulled Asha aside into the room she shared with another newly pregnant woman, Ratna. Vinita closed the door of her room and looked Asha in the eye.

"My husband will kill me if anyone finds out what I'm doing," she said. "Ratna told me that these TV people lie and that they will show our faces anyway. My husband's family will not stand for it."

Asha didn't know what to say. This was her fear as well.

"You can just cover your face with the *pallu* of your sari," Asha suggested. It was what she was planning to do. Pratap had been very clear: If anyone found out, it would bring shame to their family, and their lives would be made miserable.

Vinita sat down on her bed and looked at Ratna's empty bed. "They asked Ratna, but she just refused. She said she can't take that risk. Her family lives in Hyderabad. She comes from a good family. Not like mine. We live in a slum outside of Hyderabad. We have no money."

"No one here comes from a good family," Asha said. "We all come from nothing. Ratna can say what she wants, just like Narthaki. If they had any money, they wouldn't do this."

Vinita had tears in her eyes. "I have two daughters. My in-laws are so angry with me for not having a son. Then they heard about this, and they said that this was the least I could do to make sure my girls get married. It's my fault. If I had one boy, then we could take the dowry from marrying him as dowry for our daughter."

Asha knew how that felt. She had been relieved when her first child was a boy. Pratap was a good man, but if Asha had had two daughters, he would've been disappointed, too. That was the way it was. Kaveri had two boys, and she always talked about how she didn't have to worry about marrying off daughters. Boys were easy to marry. They brought home a dowry; they didn't take money away.

"I don't want to be part of this TV thing," Vinita said. "But I'm scared to say anything to Doctor Swati. Can you talk to her for me?"

Asha smiled. "If I could talk to Doctor Swati, I would've told her that I didn't want to do this."

"You don't?"

Asha shook her head. "My husband said it was OK as long as my face was covered."

Vinita nodded. "I'm not telling my husband or my in-laws. They'll kill me."

The mother talked about the television show as well the next time she called.

"Doctor Swati said that you volunteered," the mother said. "We think it's perfectly all right."

"Will the TV people talk to you, also?" Asha asked.

The mother was silent for a moment, then said, "I don't think so. The show is British, so they'll probably talk to a couple living there."

"Will they show this on TV in India?" Asha asked.

"No, I don't think so," the mother said. "But I don't know for sure. Are you worried . . . are you . . . I'm sorry, let me put my husband on the phone. My Telugu is not so good."

Asha heard the mother speak to the father in English, and then the father spoke.

"Hello, how are you feeling?" the father began. And after they exchanged the usual words, he asked, "If you don't feel comfortable being on TV, just tell us. We'll tell Doctor Swati not to have you as part of the program."

Asha thought about it for only a moment. She wanted Manoj to go to the good school, and Doctor Swati had pretty much told her that the price of a recommendation was her participation in the TV program.

"No, no, it's OK," Asha said. "My husband said it was OK, too."

"Do this only if you're sure," the father said. "Just because you're carrying our baby doesn't mean you have to talk to anyone you don't want to about it."

Asha almost told him then how she felt, but she held back. These people were not her family. They were no one. The only reason they called her was because she carried their baby.

"It will only be for a few minutes, they say. I don't think it will be a problem," Asha said.

Chapter Eleven

Her hands shook as she dialed Madhu from the car. *Just do it,* she told herself.

"I got laid off," Priya blurted out as soon as she heard his hello.

"Oh," Madhu said, and was then silent.

"Oh? Oh? I got laid off, Madhu," Priya said as she felt the panic rise. Her throat was already raspy, and hot tears were filling her eyes.

"I'm sorry," Madhu said, and he sounded genuinely sad. "Are you on your way home? Why don't you come to my office; we'll go for lunch."

Priya wiped the tears falling on her cheeks. \ "It's humiliating."

"No, it's humiliating to get fired. Getting laid off . . . that's just business," Madhu said.

"They didn't lay Angela off," Priya said.

"Angela gets paid about half what you do," Madhu said. "It happens. The economy is tough."

"What will we do, Madhu?" Priya asked.

"We'll be fine," Madhu said.

"Are you sure?" she asked.

"Of course," he said.

The good thing about Madhu was that he kept his cool, no matter the situation. The bad thing about Madhu was that he stayed so calm that he forgot to do anything to fix the bad situation.

Priya started to mentally calculate their bank balance and future expenses against, now, just Madhu's salary. Her boss had actually been quite generous, giving her four weeks' severance pay, while the others had received only a two-week package. But what happened after four weeks?

"Sorry to hear about your job, Priya. Madhu just told me," Calvin, Madhu's boss, said to her as she walked into the reception area of Madhu's office.

"Well, you know, it is what it is," Priya said, smiling. Worse than feeling like a loser after you lost your job was to let someone else see that you felt like a loser.

"Look at it positively: now you'll have time to get the house ready for the baby," Calvin said. He and his wife, Sandy, had three children. Sandy was a stay-at-home mom. She drove her kids everywhere and attended every parent-teacher thing, baked cookies, the whole nine yards. She was Supermom.

Of course, Priya fantasized about being a stay-at-home mom. But it had never been on the books as a thing she would ever actually do, baby or not. Now the choice might not be hers to make.

Madhu and Priya went for lunch at a small Indian place down the street that did the typical North Indian lunch buffet where all the curries tasted the same.

"I don't have a job. I don't want to spend too much money on going out," she told Madhu when he suggested another nearby restaurant instead of the Indian place he disliked.

"Do we have to eat total crap because you lost your job?" Madhu asked as they sat down with their food on wooden chairs upholstered in dark-purple fabric. It was an unwritten rule—almost all Indian restaurants used the same dark purple on chairs, curtains, tablecloths, and napkins.

"This isn't crap," Priya said as she broke off a piece of roti.

"This is complete crap," Madhu said. "The chicken tastes like the lamb, which tastes like the potatoes. And there is lard in everything. I guess now that you're jobless, it's OK if we get clogged arteries."

"Well, unless you start making twice as much as you do now, you'd better start liking this complete crap. Or maybe we can cook at home more often," Priya said, and shoved the roti into her mouth.

She had to keep perspective here. So, she'd lost her job. But she had a good husband and a baby on the way. As long as Madhu didn't lose his job (*please, God, Madhu can't lose his job*), it would be fine. They wouldn't be able to afford a vacation, but they would be able to take care of their baby.

"Worse comes to worst, we'll just move to India," Madhu said, half-jokingly.

"Why not just move in with my parents instead?" Priya retorted sarcastically.

Madhu bit into a piece of chicken and grimaced. He put his fork down. "So, what're your plans now?"

"Update my résumé and start looking for a job," Priya said.

"Or . . . you could take a break," Madhu suggested. "You've always worked. You got a job right out of school. You've never taken time off, not even a month here or there. Maybe you can see how it feels not to work."

"Can we afford that?" Priya asked.

Madhu nodded. "Within reason. We can't afford any big purchases, but for day-to-day expenses we should be fine."

"And the baby?"

"It's already in the budget," Madhu said.

"What if I can't get a job after the break?" Priya wondered.

"Why not see how it feels not to work? You were going to take maternity leave; think of this as an extended maternity leave, like they do in Scandinavia, where women get a year off," Madhu said.

"And what about my career?" Priya asked.

"You can go back to it."

"That's what a lot of women tell themselves,

and they end up never going back to work," Priya said. "I don't know if I want to be *that* woman. Look at Nina."

"Being a mommy might be so much fun that you might not want to work again," Madhu said. "And if you do, we'll make that happen, too."

Two days after she was laid off, Priya decided to take advantage of all the time she had now and do something meaningful with it.

"What're you doing?" Madhu asked as he stood outside the baby's room.

"Making beef bourguignon," Priya said as she dipped a paint roller in a paint tray.

"Right," Madhu said. "So, we're going with . . . pink?"

"Sherman Williams calls it 'Coming Up Roses,' " Priya said, looking up. "I'm going out of my mind. I had to do something."

"OK," Madhu said.

"The paint was on sale," Priya added, in case he thought she was spending too much money.

"Can I help?" Madhu asked. "I just need to change."

Priya shook her head. "Nope. This is my project. And once I'm done with the walls, I'm going to sew curtains."

"You're going to sew?" Madhu asked.

"Yes," Priya said.

Madhu nodded and turned to leave. He turned

back after taking two steps. "Are you in Energizer Bunny mode?"

"Yes," Priya said, and focused on painting the second wall in the room.

"This means I get lucky tonight?"

Priya looked up from the wall and laughed. "Maybe."

"This whole layoff thing might just be what our sex life needed," Madhu said as he left to change.

"You'd better order some takeout," Priya called after him. "The Energizer Bunny was too busy to cook."

In retrospect, the first week was the hardest.

The boredom was exhausting.

The waiting was debilitating.

She had too much time on her hands, and maybe that was what made her come up with the idea of going to India early. It cemented itself while she was on the phone with Asha. It was ridiculous that they were talking on the phone, struggling to make conversation, when she could just be there, she thought. She could stay with Madhu's parents. She could drive down to Asha, spend time with her, get to know her and her family, and see the belly that was swollen with her child.

Asha had talked about the news crew that would come the following Monday. She sounded less unsure about it than she had the last time they had spoken. She had complained about some backache but had also assured Priya that the masseuse hired by Happy Mothers was helping with that.

She said she was getting tired more easily. But she was enjoying taking the computer classes. With Asha it was always sunshine and rain at the same time. She complained about one thing while she praised another. She seemed almost afraid to bitch and moan about one thing without making a point to appreciate another. And she would always tell Priya that the baby was fine—like three to four times during one conversation.

"I have a backache. But the baby is fine.

"I miss my children. But the baby is fine.

"I'm tired all the time. But the baby is fine."

Maybe it would be better to just be in India and check on Asha directly.

"You'll go out of your mind there," Madhu said.

"No, I won't," Priya said.

Madhu had been traveling for work while she had been fermenting her Indian idea. She hadn't wanted to discuss it over the phone and had offered to pick him up at the airport, bubbling with excitement. She hadn't been able to wait until they were home and out of traffic to start the conversation, and got into it before she had driven them out of the airport onto the freeway.

"My mother will drive you mad with her eat-this-and-eat-that," Madhu said. "And the whole meet-this-person-and-that-person routine. They will try to introduce you to every relative we have in a hundred-mile radius, and that's a lot of relatives, babe."

"Relatives I can handle. Do you think they'll mind if I stayed in their house for two months?" Priya asked.

"Mind? Hell, they'll be delighted. Their daughter-in-law staying with them and then their granddaughter," Madhu said, and then put his hand on her thigh. "You'll find another job, you know. The finance geeks keep saying it's going to get better."

"The finance geeks have not been very good at predicting the world's economic health, so maybe we shouldn't trust them blindly," Priya said.

"Can we think about it for just a little bit before buying a ticket?" Madhu suggested.

And before Priya could respond, he deftly changed the topic. "Wanna hear a good story? I guarantee it'll cheer you up."

"OK," Priya said, changing lanes, her driving slightly more aggressive than usual because she was feeling impatient.

"Something interesting happened to me in Albuquerque. Now, I've been traveling through-out my career. I'm a sales guy; that's what we do. But this was the first time that a woman made a pass at me," Madhu said, sounding very smug.

Priya angled her head, keeping one eye on traffic and one on Madhu, waiting for the punch line.

"So now that women are making passes at me, do you really think it's a good time for you to leave me alone for months on end?" Madhu asked.

"One woman is not *women* making passes at you," Priya said as she took the Guadalupe Parkway exit from 101 to get on 87. "Tell me about this woman."

"Well, of course she was gorgeous."

"Of course."

"She worked for some pharmaceutical company. Also in sales. A Chanel suit type of person," Madhu said.

"And how would you know, Mr. Fashion Forward?" Priya asked sarcastically.

"She told me in reference to taking the Chanel suit off and getting comfortable in her suite. I had a standard room. She had a suite. She was a *top* salesperson," Madhu said, grinning from ear to ear.

"Let's hear the whole story from start to finish, and if it ends with you divesting her of her Chanel suit, you'd better tell me now so I can kick you out of the car," Priya said.

Madhu laughed. "I'm flattered. I was having a drink at the bar alone after dinner. And this woman came and sat next to me. We started to talk, and somehow we were talking about our spouses and how lonely it gets on the road. And then she suggested that we keep each other company."

"And when did she mention her suit was Chanel?" Priya asked, and turned right onto Alma Avenue.

"Right then when she talked about us keeping each other company. She mentioned she'd been wearing her Chanel suit all day and was dying to get out of it and into something more comfortable," Madhu said. "She asked me if I'd like to join her for a nightcap in her room. She actually said 'nightcap.' I told her I was tired and heading to bed. And that was when . . . Are you even jealous? Because if you're not, this is a complete waste of my time."

"Of course I'm jealous. So no nookie in the grand suite?" Priya asked as she drove onto their driveway and buzzed open the garage door.

"Not even a peck on the cheek," Madhu said, and leaned back on the car seat.

"You seem enormously pleased with yourself," Priya said, and laughed. "You liked getting hit on, didn't you?"

"You know, you get married and get settled and you stop looking at women as you used to. And you forget that feeling you get when a woman is interested in you. It felt good," Madhu admitted.

"Stop feeling good," Priya admonished, closing the garage door and shrouding them in the bulb-illuminated darkness of the garage. "You're married with a kid on the way. I don't want to be coming back from India to find panties, bras, and Chanel suits lying around."

"I only like *your* panties," Madhu said as he got out of the car, and then looked at Priya earnestly while she still sat in the driver's seat. "I don't want you to go to India for two months. Not because you'll go out of your mind—because I will."

He might not buy flowers or sexy lingerie, but Madhu knew romance.

Transcript from message board
www.surrogacyforyou.org

Newbie1209: We're going to Anand in Gujarat! My husband has agreed to use a surrogate. And you guys have been such a great help. I even showed him the message board and the other websites you all told me about. He never thought we'd have a baby like this, but now he's all for it. The cost of doing this in India has been most appealing . . . what with the economy and everything. In the States it's crazy expensive. So thank you!

LastHope77: OMG! This is great news. Fabulous. Congrats. When are you going to India?

UnoBaby: This is wonderful news. So, what do you think of the clinic?

Newbie1209: We're going to leave next month. And yes, we have been talking to the clinic. It seems like a very professional place.

NobuNobi: We're leaving this month as well. Our SM is having our baby soon. She crosses the thirty-seven-week mark next week. We can hardly wait to see our baby boy.

Trying1Time: My SM is not due until October, but I just got laid off and I'm thinking of going to India. My husband is Indian and he has family there, so I have someone to stay with. Has anyone done that? How does it work out?

Mommy8774: I did. I couldn't stand it. I'm a stay-at-home mom so it made sense. I went in the seventh month and it was actually difficult. There's the language, of course, and I had a hard time living in India. But I got to see the baby bulge every day and it sort of gave me some peace of mind. But if your husband is Indian and you speak the language, I think you should go for it.

NearlyMother: I would soooooo go if I could. If financially you can afford it, do it. And if you have family there . . . why not?

CantConceive1970: Just do what your heart says. If you want to go, go. Just remember that you're not going to become great friends with your SM. Do you want to? And what about the language barrier, like Mommy8774 mentioned?

Trying1Time: Well, I do speak some Telugu. That's how I have been speaking to her over the phone.

Prietysmommy: Why is it that you want to go? What do you hope to achieve? Don't get me wrong. I fully support your decision, but have you asked yourself why you want to go?

LastHope77: I have been thinking about this, too. Our SM is nearly eight months pregnant but I have a job and I can't just take time off and leave. But even if we could afford for me to go . . . still, I can't think what I'd do there for a whole month before the baby was born. It isn't like I know this woman or have anything to talk to her about.

Trying1Time: I don't know what I'll achieve by going there, but I'm going out of my mind without a job, sitting, worrying about the baby. My husband doesn't want me gone for two months, but I'm very tempted. I'm half Indian but have never lived in India; this could be a way to connect with my heritage and be around my baby.

Prietysmommy: It sounds like you're trying to run away from the fact that you got laid off. I don't make any judgments here, but have you asked the SM if she wants you hanging around her all the time?

Trying1Time: It won't be all the time. Just a little bit every day.

CantConceive1970: Look, you have to do what you feel is the right thing. It sounds like there's more to your going to India than just the baby—you also want to discover your roots. You should go and if you don't like it, it's not like it's for the rest of your life; it's just two months.

Chapter Twelve

There were two white people and three Indians as part of the TV crew that came to Happy Mothers. They brought cameras, big awkward lighting equipment, umbrellas, and shiny round surfaces with them. They talked to one another in English and had taken over the TV room and hall. But no one wanted to watch TV, anyway. The crew talking and yelling at one another was far more interesting than anything on television.

"Light OK?" seemed to be the phrase that was thrown around the most.

Asha wore the nicest sari she had, yellow *pattu* silk with a red border. It had been given to her at her wedding. She had asked Pratap to bring it the previous day. Divya had gotten them jasmine flowers for their hair, and the three women chosen to speak to the news crew were all dressed up as if they were going to a posh wedding.

They all looked like they came from well-off families rather than being poor women who came from slums and were forced to carry the babies of rich people. They looked like women who were indeed doing this out of the goodness of their hearts.

Divya checked on them, asking them if they were OK, if they needed anything, suggesting extra powder on their foreheads, even though the makeup person kept saying that she had been told to do just the minimum, especially since their faces would be covered.

"This is a documentary, not a feature film," the woman said.

Divya introduced Asha, Gangamma, and Vinita to one of the Indian women in the crew. The woman wore brown pants and a loose white shirt. Her name was Farida. A Muslim name. But she didn't wear a burka, as Asha had seen other Muslim women wear. She spoke in Telugu with them, sprinkled with many English words, most of which Asha understood. Hindi and Telugu movies these days were littered with so many English words that even India's most illiterate could pick up some of the language.

"If you're not comfortable with anything, let me know," Farida said to them in Telugu, using the English word *comfortable.*

She introduced them to the others then. Asha didn't pick up the white man's or the white woman's name. The cameraman, as Farida called him, was Indian, and his name was Ashok. He was young, maybe in his twenties, and wore a white T-shirt with the word BENETTON written in English. He spoke no Telugu and tried to communicate with them in a mixture of Hindi and English, which they mostly understood.

"This will be simple," Farida told them. "Sissy here will ask the questions"—she pointed to the white woman, who smiled at them—"and I will translate so you can answer."

Vinita was visibly nervous. This was her first time as a surrogate.

"It will be just like we talked about," Divya said to them. "You don't have to be nervous."

Farida walked around with the cameraman and the white man, moving lights and a large microphone on a stick.

The other women peeked in from the door leading into the television room. There was an air of excitement throughout the house. The daily routine was interrupted. The interviews had replaced the afternoon soap operas for the day.

Keertana had pushed her way ahead and was shushing the women behind her, asking them to quit shoving.

"We would also like to shoot the bedrooms," Farida said to Divya. "Maybe we can interview one of the women there?"

"Sure," Divya said, and looked at the three of them, as if making a decision as to whom to pick. "Gangamma can be in her room when you talk to her."

"OK," Farida said. "Maybe you could wait outside, Divya? We'll start doing some test runs now, and it will be less inhibiting for the women to talk to us without you here."

Farida was speaking in Telugu to Divya, so Asha could understand them.

"But they're nervous, and I think they will feel more comfortable if I'm here," Divya said adamantly.

Vinita and Asha looked at each other. It was obvious that the TV people didn't like it that Divya was here with them. They seemed to want her gone so they could get the "real" story from the women.

"We'll start with you, Asha," Farida said, moving Asha to a comfortable chair in the TV room. They checked the lighting, taking a small device and flashing it next to her and around her, moving the shiny round surface.

"Is this angle good? Am I out of the frame?" Farida asked the cameraman after they had moved the chair and Asha several times. The cameraman gave her a thumbs-up sign.

"We're ready to roll," the cameraman said.

Asha felt her nerves twitch and asked Farida before she could start speaking. "And my face will not show, will it?"

"No," Farida said. "No. We'll hide it. I promise. After the filming you will get a release . . . a contract to sign. And even there it will say that your face cannot be shown. It will be in Telugu. You can read Telugu?"

"Yes," Asha said, but put her sari's *pallu* over her head, covering her face the best she could, just in case.

The white woman started to speak in rapid

English to the cameraman, and then she turned to Asha. She came and sat in a chair opposite Asha.

"How pregnant are you?" she asked, and Farida translated.

"Six months," Asha said, keeping her head down.

Divya was standing by the door, her arms folded as she stared at Asha, willing her to say only what they had practiced.

"How did you decide to become a surrogate?" the white woman asked, and Farida translated almost before the woman was finished speaking.

"Someone in my family had done this also and she said it would be OK," Asha said. "And I wanted to do something to help people who can't have children."

Divya had told them all not to mention money at all unless the interviewer asked, and even then she had coached them on how to answer the question.

"You are getting paid for this. How is this money going to help you?"

Asha licked her lips. "My son is very smart, and the money will help send him to a good school. A school for smart children. Whatever money we have left will go to buy a flat."

The white woman asked about their village and Asha felt a little more relaxed.

"We had a hut, just one room, where we all slept—my husband, my two children, and my mother-in-law when she lived with us," Asha told the woman. "Now we stay with my brother-in-law and his family. They have three rooms. In the village there were no bathrooms, but here we have one with a toilet; it helps a lot for us women."

"How does it help?" Farida asked.

"You know how it is in the village, you have to look for a place somewhere and . . . this is better, more clean," Asha said.

The next question was about the parents. What were they like, and how did Asha feel about them? Asha talked about how they sent presents and talked to her regularly. They seemed like good people, and they were very happy that they were going to have a baby.

"Do you like being a surrogate?" Farida translated the white woman's question.

Asha nodded. "Yes."

"But it's a big thing to do, give birth to a baby," Farida said. "Do you worry about something happening to you during childbirth?"

Asha swallowed; her shoulders were stiff and she was nervous.

"No, I don't worry. Doctor Swati has explained everything to me, and this is a good hospital, better than what I had for my children, and that went well enough," Asha said.

"Do you feel that this baby is being taken care of better than your own babies?" Farida asked, translating the white woman's question.

Divya had not included this question in their practice session.

Asha bit her lower lip, not sure how to answer. She didn't want to look at Divya. She felt frozen. What could she say?

She cleared her throat to buy time and smiled uneasily. "Yes, that is true."

"Do you resent that?"

Asha could feel Divya's nervous energy slam into her.

"No," Asha said simply. "That was then and this is now. I have two healthy and happy children. And I hope that this baby will also be healthy and happy. That's all we can do. The rest"— she looked heavenward—"is up to Lord Venkateshwara Swami."

After that, the questions were simple, just like they had practiced. It took about a half hour at the most, and then it was over.

"You did very well," Divya said, all smiles, taking both of Asha's hands in hers. "So very well."

"Really?" Asha said, glowing under the praise. No matter how old you got, you always wanted to be told that something you did was good.

"I just hope the others are as good," Divya said.

So now Doctor Swati will get my son into the school, yes? Asha almost asked. But she knew this was neither the time nor the place nor the right person to ask. In any case, you didn't say these things out loud. They were done silently, quietly, with nods and smiles and movement of the eyes.

They interviewed Gangamma in her room and then interviewed Chitra in the kitchen while Revati chopped vegetables for *sambhar*. The questions were almost the same for all the women, with small variations. They asked Gangamma if she would do this again. They asked Vinita how she felt about being away from her family for nearly ten months, as she had come to Happy Mothers as soon as she became pregnant.

They were all done and gone before lunch, to everyone's surprise. Divya went with them to the clinic to show them the hospital rooms and interview Doctor Swati and others who worked at Happy Mothers.

The surrogate house was abuzz with TV show talk.

Everyone wanted to talk to Gangamma, Vinita, and Asha. What happened? How did it go? Did Divya really tell them exactly what to say? When would it air? Was there a chance they would be recognized?

Vinita and Gangamma were more amenable to the questions than Asha. She couldn't get the words out. She was stumbling on her thoughts. She hadn't wanted to talk to these people and put her business on display, but Doctor Swati hadn't left her a choice.

Keertana noticed her sullen mood and swooped in for the kill.

"You don't look happy," Keertana said, sitting beside Asha on the coconut charpoy on the verandah.

"I'm fine," Asha said.

"Gangamma and Vinita are so proud that they were chosen to speak with those TV people," Keertana said.

Asha shook her head and felt a weariness engulf her.

"Are you in pain? Are you OK?" Keertana asked.

Asha shook her head again.

"I hate this," Asha said, her anguish making her voice husky. "I hate this."

"Hate what?"

"I can't think like you. I can't think of myself as a coolie," Asha said. "This baby . . . it isn't mine. It's humiliating to do this for money. It's humiliating that Doctor Swati made me talk to those people by saying that she wouldn't help my son get into the good school if I didn't."

"She said that?" Keertana's eyes widened. "That *lanja munda*, the dirty bitch."

Asha sighed. "She's just helping her business. We're just business. We're not people. We're just . . . nothing. I'm a womb . . . a belly. If tomorrow, they could save me or the baby, who would they save, you think?"

"You," Keertana said. "That is in the contract."

"Oh, like they'd tell us the truth. They'll just let me die and let my children grow up without a mother," Asha said.

Keertana put her arm around Asha. "You're not going to die. Women don't die anymore during childbirth."

"I know," Asha said, her shoulders slumping. "But now everyone wants to talk to me and take care of me, but not me, just this person growing inside me. I feel like no one cares about *me*."

Keertana dropped her arm and leaned back on the wall. "Of course they don't care about you. No one cares about us. My own husband doesn't care about me. My kids are only interested in what I can buy them. No one cares, Asha. That's why we have to care for ourselves. A woman in this country is already nobody; now take a poor woman, someone like us . . . we're less than nobody. A dog in the slum has more rights than we do."

"So this is our lot in life?"

"You're changing your life," Keertana said. "You're doing this so that your daughter can study and be a *lanja munda* like Doctor Swati. Strong. Independent."

Pratap fidgeted as he sat on the same coconut charpoy a few hours later. He seemed unsettled. Asha hadn't noticed at first, busy as she was with Manoj and Mohini.

Mohini wanted to show Asha a new dress that Kaveri had bought for her.

"Can you see the butterflies?" she asked her mother, pointing to the blue butterflies scattered around the white frock with a blue bow in the back. "This is my favorite dress now."

Kaveri had even put on a blue headband to keep Mohini's hair off her face.

"The headband is not new," Mohini said when she saw Asha looking at it.

"I want you to have this," Manoj said then, and gave Asha a piece of paper. "It's a poem about . . . you."

Asha unfolded the paper and saw that Manoj had written ten lines neatly in Telugu.

The ten things I love about my mother:
My mother's name is Asha—Asha means
    hope. I like her name.
My mother has long black hair that comes
    down to her back. Her hair is beautiful.
My mother always kisses me good night.
My mother is the best cook. She makes the
    best ladoos in the world.
My mother always kisses me when I get
    hurt. The hurt doesn't get better. But I
    feel better.
My mother has pink lips and pink cheeks.
    She is very pretty.
My mother covers my school books in

brown paper and writes my name
neatly on the labels, Manoj Vardhan.
No one else has books covered as
nicely as mine.

My mother gave me my little sister.
Mohini can be annoying, but I like her.

My mother hugs me when I get scared. I
don't get scared that much, but when I
do, she hugs me. She gives the best
hugs.

My mother has the best laugh. It makes
me laugh when she laughs. I wish she
would laugh all the time.

Asha laughed out loud even as emotion grabbed
her throat. She couldn't help herself.

"You wrote this all by yourself?" Asha asked.

Manoj shrugged.

"Really?" Asha asked, looking at Pratap.

"It's all him," Pratap confirmed.

"Thank you, Manoj," Asha said, and kissed her
son on his forehead. "Thank you so much. This is
precious to me."

"Well," Manoj said, standing up from
charpoy, "I just wanted to give you that. Can we
go inside and see if there is any *chakli* in the
kitchen?"

Asha nodded, and Manoj grabbed Mohini's hand
and she squealed as they ran inside the house.

"I can't believe he writes so well," Asha said.

"Yes," Pratap said, and then scratched his cheek, shifted on the charpoy, and cleared his throat.

"Is everything OK?" Asha asked.

"Yes, yes," he said, and smiled at her. "How was your TV thing?"

"OK," Asha said. "They will hide my face; they promised. Still, I had my *pallu* down to my stomach so no one could see me even if they wanted."

Pratap nodded.

Asha waited for him to say something, and then, reaching the end of her patience, she snapped at him.

"Something is the matter. Say it or leave," she said.

Pratap sat up, clearly surprised to hear his normally sweet-spoken wife so curt with him.

"I was wondering . . . just thinking, you know . . . a flat is up for sale . . . now, don't get angry because I know you think it's your money, but you're my wife and your money is my money, too . . ."

"Really?" Asha demanded, standing up, her rounded belly making her tilt a little. "So you just want to buy a flat and let's not do anything about Manoj's school? I even talked to the TV people for that, and now you don't want to save money for it."

"Sit down," Pratap said. "I didn't say I was going to do it; I said I wanted to talk to you. What is it

250

with you? Whenever you're pregnant you're like *Mahakali*, goddess Durga in warrior incarnation."

"I'm not like *Mahakali*," Asha said, sitting down. "And I'm not like this every time I'm pregnant."

Pratap laughed, which only fueled Asha's temper. He held his hand up. "When you were pregnant with Mohini, you broke the earthen water pot because it was empty and you were thirsty."

"That was an accident," Asha said. Then, seeing the humor in his face, she smiled as well. "So I get a little cranky when I'm pregnant."

He looked at her belly. "And you look beautiful when you're pregnant."

"Don't say things like that," Asha whispered. "This isn't our baby."

Pratap nodded gravely. "But you're still beautiful."

Asha looked at her feet, feeling incredibly shy.

"I can't wait for that baby to be out so I can have my wife back." He put his hand on Asha's. "I want you back, in more ways than one."

It had never happened before, this feeling of . . . desire. But his hand stroking hers suddenly gave her goose bumps and she found herself wanting to kiss him. This was what Kaveri talked about— this wanting to sleep with her husband, this feeling that Asha had never felt.

They always did it furtively, aware that the children were sleeping in the same room and sometimes even Pratap's mother. She had never liked it. Never enjoyed it. Hated his harsh breathing and the sounds he made. She used to turn her head away, closing her eyes to block the sounds and the smell.

But now . . . now she wanted to . . . what?

"The children will be hungry soon," Pratap said. "I should take them home."

Asha watched her family walk away. Pratap carried Mohini in one arm and held Manoj's hand with his free hand.

The baby kicked softly inside her then, and she wondered, not for the first time, what would happen if she just got up and left with them—womb, baby, and all.

Chapter Thirteen

They had spoken to Asha the evening before, and even Madhu admitted she sounded off. They had talked to Doctor Swati as well, who had assured them that everything was just peachy. Pregnant women were just hormonal, and Asha was nearly in her third trimester, so maybe she was tired, nothing to worry about.

She didn't sound tired, Priya thought; she sounded angry.

They went over the conversation as they drove to Nina's house for a dinner party.

"She said that the TV interview thing went fine. Do you think that's what pissed her off?" Priya wondered.

Madhu sighed. "I don't want to start going down this guessing-game path. What has upset her? Why is she angry? I just . . . you know, maybe some of the parents have it right. No contact with the surrogate is best."

"But you agree I'm not imagining things," Priya said.

"I agree that she sounded off. Maybe she was having an off day. Everyone is entitled to an off day," Madhu said.

But what if she hurts the baby because she is having an off day? Priya wanted to ask, but she didn't have the courage to voice the thought. It was a silly thought, anyway. Asha was in a house at the clinic. There were other surrogates there, nurses, a doctor. Nothing could go wrong even if Asha wanted it to go wrong. Right?

"Do you think she's depressed that she's pregnant with a baby that isn't hers?" Priya asked.

Priya thought about all those stories she'd heard about kicking babies keeping mothers awake, and she wondered if Asha stroked her stomach when the baby kicked. All the delights and traumas of being pregnant, she had heard them all—and again she felt the Grand Canyon–size regret inside her that this was the only way for her to have a baby. She would never know what it meant to be pregnant. Never know the flutter of life inside her.

But Asha knew. This was her third time. Genetically, Priya knew, the baby was theirs. But it was Asha's blood that was feeding their baby, helping it grow. It was Asha who was nurturing the baby inside her.

"I think the TV show upset her. We should have said no to Doctor Swati," Priya said thoughtfully. "Maybe it's a bigger deal for them there. We should have refused."

"Do you think it was our call?" Madhu asked. "I think it was up to Asha. And if she had said no, we would've backed her. No one's forcing her to do anything." Madhu paused, seemingly lost in thought as they drove in silence for a few minutes.

"Still, it's a heavy price to pay," he continued. "If you were pregnant and then you had to give that baby away, I'd go berserk. They might be poor, but I imagine they have the same emotions we do."

Priya felt small. While she had spent her time curbing her guilt and emboldening her righteous feeling of using a surrogate, Madhu had obviously given this a lot of thought.

"Do you think she hates carrying our baby?" Priya asked.

"I don't think so. God, I hope not," Madhu said.

"I wish I hadn't said that out loud," Priya said as soon as she tasted her words, the fear behind them.

"Yeah, me, too."

Nina loved throwing dinner parties. It had been her "thing" ever since she had quit her career to be a mom with a capital *M*.

The party was one of those elegant affairs with no kids. Nina's girls were with her mother for the weekend, which left Nina and Jordan without responsibilities for the morning after. This meant that they were both on their second glass of champagne before the guests had even arrived.

Nina was a good hostess but a lousy cook, and they had the sushi catered from Fuki Sushi in Palo Alto. They used to live in Palo Alto, but after Jordan's company had gone public all those years ago during the Internet boom, they had moved to

Los Gatos, into a sprawling house that had been renovated to the nines.

The house looked like something out of Santa Fe on the outside, and inside it was all hardwood floors and beautiful tile. When they first bought it, Nina had loved it. It was a testament to the great careers they had built and all their hard work. Once Nina quit her job, she confessed it sometimes felt like a mausoleum—a trap she couldn't get out of. It irked her even more that they could afford the house without her salary.

It probably didn't help that Jordan had had an affair while Nina was pregnant with their second child, living in the fabulous house she could not afford if she were on her own.

"Sometimes I feel like I didn't divorce him because I was worried about losing the house," Nina had once told Priya, though she followed a few seconds later with, "I'm being stupid. I love Jordan and it worked out, didn't it?"

As Priya walked into Nina and Jordan's home, she wondered if Nina's decisions to quit her job and stay with Jordan despite his adultery had really been worth it. And what did "worth it" really mean?

"I love this wine," Nina said as she took the bottle Priya handed to her. It was a bottle of Barolo—not something Priya would buy while jobless, but they had one lying around, a gift from someone for some dinner party they had thrown.

Since Nina loved Italian wine, she'd brought it along, hoping that Nina had not been the one to give it to them in the first place.

"I hope you'll enjoy it," Priya said, watching Madhu be dragged away by Jordan to meet someone.

"Krysta is going to be late," Nina said as she started to walk toward the kitchen.

It was Priya's least favorite room. It was too heavy, all done in dark wood. It didn't have the cozy feeling a kitchen was supposed to evoke.

Priya and Madhu's kitchen opened onto their dining room and living room—and *was* the heart of their house with the occasional chipped china and cookbooks with dog-eared pages and grease stains. They loved to cook, and when they used to throw dinner parties, their dining table would sag with food and fifteen people eating at a table designed for ten. Once the baby was here and she got a new job, Priya promised herself, she would throw dinner parties again.

"Champagne?" Nina asked, pouring Priya a glass. "You're going to love Anne and Steven. They're a wonderful couple. Anne is French, from Lyon—she's lived in the United States for fifteen years but still has the cutest French accent. And Steven is from New York. Anne's an artist. She sculpts—she's going to be a big deal someday."

Priya sipped her champagne and made the appropriate sounds.

"So, Krysta told me that you lost your job," Nina said as she led Priya into the living room. "Best thing for you. You will have a baby soon, and then you and I can do lunch. What do you say?"

Priya smiled. "I'm going back to work as soon as I can. We've signed up the baby for day care at this place nearby from when she's six months old."

"That's what they all say, honey, but once the baby is here, it's tough to go back to work. I'm a living, breathing example of that," Nina said. "Oh, Karen, you have to meet my friend Priya. She just got laid off and is about to have a baby. I told her it was perfect timing."

Priya learned that Karen, a tall, slender blonde who had an authoritative voice, used to be a VP of marketing for Banana Republic. Once she had kids, she left work and had never felt better.

"The chase and chaos of the morning is gone," Karen said to Priya. "Just knowing that I don't have to scramble to get the kids to school and myself to work is enough to get me out of bed. If I needed to do it all—seriously, I'd slit my wrists."

"You can always get a nanny," Priya suggested.

"Are you thinking of getting one?" Nina asked Priya.

"Did someone say nanny?" asked another woman, another blonde, who looked a little like Reese Witherspoon. "Hi, I'm Sabrina."

Priya and she shook hands.

"Are you having a baby?" Sabrina asked, looking pointedly at Priya's stomach.

"Well . . . we're using a surrogate," Priya said, feeling uncomfortable discussing this with a total stranger.

"Like Sarah Jessica Parker," Sabrina said. "Are you thinking of getting a nanny?"

"No . . . well . . . ," Priya said, and emptied her glass of champagne. "I first need to get my baby, and then I need to find a job, and then I think, yes, we'll definitely think about a nanny."

"Just do it, but don't go back to work," Sabrina said. "I have a nanny and it's the best. I also don't work, which is just fabulous."

Sabrina, Priya found out later from Nina, had not always been a housewife. She used to be an executive, too, at an Internet company. But then she got pregnant, the market went bust, she got laid off, had a baby, and never went back to work. That was ten years ago. (Sabrina's husband was a neurosurgeon who worked all the time, was never home, and clearly made tons of money.)

"Is that cutie your husband?" Sabrina asked, pointing at Madhu.

"Yes," Priya said.

"And he has a job, right? Pays well? Stay home. Enjoy. Have lunch with us," Sabrina said. "Nina, Karen, Anne, and I have lunch every Thursday. We have the best time without the kids. Well,

Anne brings her baby along. Anoushka is just four months old. But she brings her nanny as well so she doesn't have the baby fussing at her all the time."

They all talked a mile a minute, former career women who had given it all up to become housewives—they couldn't recommend it enough.

Priya stole a moment next to Madhu while they ate, standing around the living room and dining area.

"The sushi is *OK*," Madhu said.

"I think it's pretty good," Priya said, and leaned against him. "All these women are stay-at-home moms with nannies. Nina is the only one with no nanny, but that's because her mom lives all but next door."

"And all these guys have seriously expensive cars," Madhu said. "There's a recession out there, and this one guy is talking about buying the brand-new BMW in Germany and having it shipped here. And then this other guy started talking about his new Tesla. You see, he knows Elon Musk very well, so he's getting ahead of the waiting list."

"I'm so out of my league here," Priya said. "These women had real careers, senior positions."

"Most of these guys own their companies like Jordan," Madhu said. "I feel like everyone is more successful than I am. These guys, the *desi* guys from Columbus, everyone."

"You're successful," Priya said, standing up on her tiptoes to kiss him on his lips. "You have a good career. And you have me."

"And even though that does make up for a lot, I think my situation would improve considerably if we could leave this party sooner than later," Madhu said.

"I promised Krysta I'd wait for her."

By the time Krysta arrived, it was nearly two hours into the party, and Priya and Madhu were itching to leave.

"I don't like anyone," Priya told Krysta while they sipped their wine and looked around at the well-dressed crowd.

"You like me," Krysta said.

Priya grinned. "I mean all these people. They're not my type. They're not Madhu's type, either."

"Honestly, I don't think they're Nina's type, either," Krysta said. "These people are acquaintances. Business connections. You and I are the poor friends they rely on at these shindigs to feel normal."

Krysta grabbed some food from the buffet table, and Priya walked with her, keeping her company.

"If you wanna know the truth," Krysta continued, "Nina hates being at home. I mean, look at her. With all that time on her hands, you'd think she'd hit the gym with a personal trainer."

They both looked at Nina. She used to be a

slender woman, but age had caught up with her. She wasn't fat, but no one was calling her fit, either. She was wearing a beautiful rose-colored silk cocktail dress that came to her knees, and though diamonds sparkled on her ears and fingers, her eyes were dull beneath the glitz.

"Oh, she looks fine, and she's too busy with the kids to go to the gym. She told me that you and I were lucky to have the time to go spinning twice a week."

Krysta finished chewing an inside-out crispy shrimp maki before speaking. "She isn't happy. Since Jordan cheated on her, she hasn't been the same. And now he has the big career and all that. It used to be the reverse. He was the struggling entrepreneur, and she was the bacon machine."

As the evening wore on and the food started to thin, the crowd thinned with it. By midnight, almost everyone had gone. Priya and Madhu had stayed at Nina's insistence and were now sitting in the living room, the only guests left besides Krysta.

Jordan brought tumblers of cognac for everyone except Priya, who was driving, and flopped on the couch next to his wife.

They looked like a happy couple, the extramarital affair a distant, almost dreamed-up memory, Priya thought as she watched them hold hands.

"It was good," Nina said.

"It was great," Jordan said. "Nina throws the best parties; don't you think?"

"Absolutely," Krysta said, and Priya and Madhu joined in with their consent.

"As long as we cater," Jordan added. "It's easier on everyone's stomach lining if she doesn't attempt to cook."

"Jordan," Nina said playfully, and threw a pillow at him.

He laughed and put his arm around her and gave her a loud kiss on the mouth.

They were both a bit tipsy.

"Well, it's getting late," Krysta interjected. "Priya, do you think you could give me a ride home? I'll leave my car here, Nina. I'll pick it up tomorrow. I can stop by on my run in the morning."

"Maybe I'll join you for a run," Priya said. "What time do you leave?"

"Around seven," Krysta said.

Nina sighed. "I envy you girls. You have so much time to do what you want. You can go to the gym, run, take cooking classes . . . and here I am stuck at home all the time with the kids."

"You're not stuck," Jordan said. "You enjoy it."

"I don't enjoy it all the time, Jordan," Nina said. "Once in a while I'd like the freedom to have a life, too—like all of you do. I feel trapped."

"You have freedom. The kids go to school and preschool. How busy can you be during the day? We have a cleaning lady who does the cleaning and the laundry. You hardly ever cook. We get our groceries delivered or I go to Whole Foods. What is it you do all day that takes your freedom away?" Jordan demanded, pulling away from Nina.

Not looking so good anymore, Priya thought, looking at Madhu pointedly. It was time to leave.

"You don't go to Whole Foods; I do. Between Rebecca's lactose intolerance and Sasha's allergies, I'm there picking up this and that every fucking day," Nina said. "You're too busy having a career. I'm at home."

"That's your choice," Jordan said. "You want a career, go get it."

"It's not so easy. I've been out of the job market for eight years now, and there's a recession out there if you haven't noticed," Nina said, her voice rising.

"These were your choices. No one put a goddamn gun to your head," Jordan said, and stood up.

Madhu, Priya, and Krysta stood up at the same time as well.

"Well, we should get going," Madhu said.

Jordan and Nina seemed to take deep breaths and looked at their guests.

"Thank you so much for coming," Nina said.

"It was a great party," Priya said. She gave Nina a hug, and then Jordan.

"Christ, that was a fucking disaster," Madhu said when they got home.

"I'm not staying at home," Priya said, and started to take off her jewelry, putting her earrings and only pearl necklace neatly in the silk-lined suede boxes Madhu's mother had given her.

"You can do whatever you want," Madhu said, and kissed her cheek.

Priya slipped out of her black dress and put it back on its hanger, which was lying on their bed. She hung the dress back in the closet.

"Madhu," she said as she watched him undress.

"What?" he asked, sitting down to remove his socks.

"I want to go to India," she said.

Madhu looked at her and sighed.

"No, hear me out. I want to go. I want to see Asha and the baby. I *need* to go," Priya said. "I'll talk to you every day. We'll Skype."

"My parents will drive you up the wall," Madhu said.

"I won't let them," Priya said.

Madhu shook his head and threw his socks in the clothes hamper. He pulled on a pair of gray flannel shorts and a white undershirt.

"Priya, we'll be without each other. Without support," he said. "I don't think I could handle it alone, talking to Asha and hearing her angry or off or whatever. I need you here."

"But that's the point. If I'm there, I'll know exactly what her mood is and why it's like that. I can tell you and you'll have peace of mind,"

Priya said. "We'll still be there for each other, just via Skype."

"For two months?"

"Well, just a month and a half; you'll be there the last two weeks," Priya said.

"And you're sure about this?"

Priya shook her head. "No. But I think I should do it."

"I don't like it . . . but OK," Madhu said as he lay on the bed, his arms stacked behind his head.

"Just don't have an affair with some Chanel-clad woman while I'm gone," Priya said with a smile and lay down beside him in her underwear.

"I'll miss you," Madhu said. "Just the thought of you gone makes me miss you."

"You travel so much. You won't even notice," Priya said. "It'll be the same. You'll just talk to me in India on the phone from Dallas or Phoenix or wherever you are instead of here."

"I do have a lot of travel lined up," Madhu said. "And we do have great phone sex."

"See?" Priya said. "It's going to be just fine. Trust me."

Transcript from message board
www.surrogacyforyou.org

UnoBaby: I'm struggling here. Work has become insane. My company laid off so many people that the workload is just too much. I don't know if I can work like this after the baby. These ten-hour days are fine if it's just DH and me, but once the baby is here I don't know if I'll want to do it. I want to be home, be with my baby. It's been such an uphill battle having this baby—I feel like I'll cheat myself if I work.

Trying1Time: At least you have a job. I got laid off. And I'm honestly scared that I'll never ever work again. I'm not sure I'm the stay-at-home kind, but God knows what I'll become once the baby is here.

Newbie1209: I think you should take a few months off and then make a decision. You'll never know now how it's going to feel to have your baby home.

YummyMummy2008: I don't mean to judge anyone. Everyone makes her choice here. But my advice is to work. If you like your work and it keeps you stimulated, please do work. I am a better mother working than I was not working. But I'm sure it's different for everyone.

Mommy8774: I love being a stay-at-home mom. It's what I always wanted and now I have it. It's perfect. I would not ever work and steal from my time as a mother.

CantConceive1970: FWIW, I never worked. I finished university and got married. I wish I had worked, but now it's too late and in any case I'm so busy schlepping the kids around here and there and taking care of the house, I don't have the time to work. Hats off to the women who do both.

NearlyMother: OMG! Working has kept me sane. After we lost the baby, I was going out of my mind and it was great to go to the office every day and just get my head screwed on right.

LastHope77: I can't quit even though I want to. My husband got laid off and our baby is due in December . . . so I have to work and if my DH doesn't get a job then he will stay home with the baby and I'll continue to work. I wish I could stay home and enjoy my baby. But with this recession, I don't know if I'm going to have that option.

PART IV:
Third Trimester

Chapter Fourteen

Asha wanted to cry as soon as she hung up. She set the mobile phone on the floor beside her bed and buried her face in her hands.

The mother was coming to India. For nearly two months. She was going to visit Happy Mothers and hover around her.

Now Asha wished her parents were like Keertana's parents, who didn't want anything to do with her. It would be better for everyone if she had never met the mother or father.

It had been a difficult few days. Just the day before, Manoj had a big bruise on his elbow.

"How did you get that?" Asha asked.

Manoj shrugged but didn't say anything.

Pratap sighed. "He got into a fight with an older boy."

"The other boy was being stupid," Manoj said. "He said that we have a leap year every four years so he grows older slower than all of us. He's born on the twenty-eighth of February."

"And you got into a fight because of this?" Asha asked.

"It's not true. We need leap years to keep our calendar in alignment with the earth's revolutions around the sun," Manoj said. "Everyone knows this."

Later, when Manoj was playing with Mohini and out of earshot, Pratap told Asha that this was not the first time Manoj had gotten into a fight at school.

"He's bored, his teachers are saying," Pratap said. "He's picking fights, and they're calling him names because they think he shows off his smartness. I was worried, but you know, Asha, all boys go through things like this. I think it'll be fine."

"No, not if we don't do anything. We have to find him a better school with children like him," Asha said.

For days, her mind had been wholly occupied with Manoj's problems, and now the mother wanted to come and bother her. Asha wiped her tears. *If she wants to come, let her come. What's it to me?* Asha told herself. *She can sit here and watch television with us all day if she likes.*

As Asha walked into the TV room and saw all the women with their pregnant bellies sitting and chatting, watching television, she felt claustrophobic. She needed to get away, just for a while. The rules were, they couldn't go out alone. They could go in groups, out to a movie or something like that *once in a while*—but Nursamma had to organize it. Asha would have to talk to someone about it.

Since Asha had come to Happy Mothers, they had gone out as a group only once, to the park in the center of the city. They had packed food and water with them for a picnic. But it was early on, and Asha had spent the entire time missing her children, whom she had come to the park with several times in the past.

Would this time ever evoke one happy memory? she wondered. Or would she forever look back at it as a black mark in her life?

The baby kicked suddenly, and she regretted her thoughts immediately. A baby would come out of this dark time, and if a baby came out of it, how could the time be dark?

"Keertana," Asha said, sitting down next to her on one of the coconut charpoys where the women sat to watch television. "Could you convince Nursamma that we should go for a movie?"

Asha didn't want to ask because the last time at the park had been at her insistence, too.

"That's a good idea. I want to see *Raju Maharaja*," Keertana said. "The songs they showed on *Chitralahari* on TV are so *mast*, fun."

"And Mohan Babu and Ramya Krishnan are in the movie," Gangamma said. "She's still so pretty, even though she's now doing mother roles."

"Mohan Babu, Shmohan Babu. He's an old man," Chitra said. "Let's see *Evaraina Epudaina*. It's with Varun Sandesh."

Keertana shrugged. "I really don't care what

we see as long as we get out of here. I'll talk to Nursamma."

"Wonder how it'll look with all of us pregnant, fifteen pregnant women, all sitting in the same row." Ragini laughed. "I hope I can see the movie before anything happens."

Ragini was due in two weeks, and since this was the third time she was doing this, it could happen at any time. The more babies a woman had, the sooner the babies came. Doctor Swati had given her strict orders to rest and relax.

Asha liked Ragini. She was a strong woman who, like Keertana, didn't think of surrogacy as an emotional experience at all. She just wanted to get enough money to marry off her daughters and be done with it. Her husband was not much use. He spent all the money he made as a construction worker on toddy. In the early years of their marriage, Ragini told Asha, she had tried to change him, but now she didn't even try.

"He can go to hell, that son of a whore," she would say. "Once my daughters are married off, I'll go stay with them. Two months here, three months there—that's going to be my life. I'll play with my grandchildren, stay with my daughters, and let that waste of humanity I married rot alone."

"When you give the baby away, don't you feel something?" Asha once asked her.

Ragini laughed. "Sure I feel something. I feel rich."

They took auto rickshaws to the theater. Five autos for fifteen people—thirteen pregnant women, Revati, and Nursamma. Two of the women had declined to come to the movies because they weren't feeling up to it.

"This was a great idea," Revati said. She was in the same auto as Keertana and Asha. "I've wanted to go see a movie for a long time now, but these days with the TV showing everything, it seems like a waste of money. But a cinema is a cinema."

Revati's life revolved around the Happy Mothers House. She didn't seem to have any family, any life, outside of her responsibilities at the clinic, not like Doctor Swati, who had her own home and family.

"A good, wholesome movie is exactly what I need to cheer me up," Revati said.

Chitra had not won the vote, and they were going to see *Raju Maharaja*, a nice family drama with some well-known but older actors. Young romance was not on anyone's wish list, except maybe Chitra's. In any case, romance movies were for college boys and girls. They were grown, pregnant women; they needed a family setting.

"My husband and I used to see a movie every month," Keertana said. "But now . . ." She put her hand on her belly for a moment and laughed. "But after this baby, we can go right back to it. Don't even have to worry about taking a baby along and having it cry all through the movie."

Revati smiled. "You're all doing such a pious task. You're giving so many people a miracle. I see a lot of parents and surrogate mothers come and go, and I'm always touched by the gift you give and the joy they feel."

Keertana snorted but didn't say anything.

"My baby's mother is coming here," Asha said. "She won't stay here, but she will come and visit every day or something."

Revati didn't exactly make a face, but her discontent was obvious when she spoke. "I don't like those parents who come and try to become friends with the surrogate. It doesn't work. But they don't understand that. I told Doctor Swati to make this a clinic where parents don't talk to the surrogate."

"There are clinics like that?" Asha asked.

"Of course," Revati said, and screeched a little when the auto bumped hard. "Hey, drive carefully, man, I have pregnant women here."

"I'm careful, Amma, but what do you want me to do about holes in the road?" the auto driver said cheerfully. "I have driven lots of pregnant women in this auto, never had any problem."

"Pay attention, for God's sake," Revati screamed as the auto missed a bicycle by a hair.

"You let me drive, Amma," the driver said. "You just relax. So, what movie are you going to see?"

"*Raju Maharaja*," Keertana told him.

"*Mast* movie, Amma," the driver said. "Top movie. Mohan Babu, Ramya Krishnan . . . what a movie."

"Well, if you say it's good, it must be good," Keertana said sarcastically, holding on to the side bar of the auto for dear life as it found another hole in the road.

They stopped outside the theater and Revati paid the auto. Doctor Swati was paying for the autos, but the women had to pay for their own movie tickets.

Rangamma, the maid's son, had gone to the theater in the morning and bought tickets so that the women could skip the long lines at the ticket counter and go straight inside the air-conditioned halls. Even though the women were buying their own tickets, they had splurged and bought balcony seats. The view was much better, and the seats were more comfortable.

Asha always liked the smell of a movie theater. This one, Devaky Cinemas, was a big one. She remembered when Kaveri and Raman first moved to Srirampuram, they had talked excitedly about it, how modern it was and how it could seat fifteen hundred people. Sure enough, today's show was packed.

The balcony seats were lush, comfortable, still velvety to the touch—after all, the theater was just two years old. It even had that unmistakable smell of expensive air-conditioning and fresh samosas.

They had the first row; this meant that they didn't have to move once they sat down, and they had good leg space as well. Asha settled into her seat. When she was young, her favorite thing to see was when the curtains on the screen parted and the movie began. The opening of the curtain was like opening a treasure and seeing what surprise lay within. She sighed contentedly.

Doctor Swati had agreed that even though they couldn't eat anything at the theater because the fried samosas could make them sick, they could have a cold drink each, her treat. As soon as they found their seats, Chitra called out to the cold-drink boy who was walking around the theater with a case of drinks strapped to him.

The women all cried out for what they wanted: Thums Up, Fanta, Limca . . .

"Ah," Chitra said, sighing at the taste of lemony Limca as it coated her throat. "This is so good."

"We should have cold drinks in the house, Revati," Gita said, enjoying her Thums Up.

"These drinks are not good for the babies. Too much sugar," Nursamma said before Revati could respond. "It's OK to drink one here and there, but not every day."

"It's not my baby, so why do I care," Keertana said in a low voice so only Asha could hear.

"Keertana, you're so bad," Asha said, and slowly drank her Fanta, not wanting the bottle to empty too soon.

• • •

The women came back from the movie in high spirits. Such high spirits that Ragini went into labor an hour after they returned. Her parents were in the United States and had been informed. They had tickets to come to India in a week, so they would get the baby then. During that time, the baby would remain at the Happy Mothers clinic and be taken care of by the baby doctor and nurses there.

Ragini's labor was short. Just two hours. She came back the next day, not looking like a woman who had just given birth, but a carefree woman without a worry in the world.

"How did it go?" someone asked.

"How are you feeling?" someone else piped in.

Ragini told them that it went fine. There was hardly any pain, and Doctor Swati had been very good with her.

"Did you see the baby?" Asha asked as she helped Ragini pack her things. Ragini was going home the following day; she couldn't wait to see her daughters again.

"No," Ragini said. "No need to see the baby. It's not mine."

"Did you see any of the babies?" Asha asked. This was Ragini's third time. The last time.

"No," Ragini said. "Neither should you."

Asha nodded. "I know," she said as she folded Ragini's blouses and put them neatly into her black steel trunk.

"You do this a few times and you stop getting attached," Ragini said. "First time, I also thought, how will I give up a baby and all that nonsense. Now I don't even think about it. All I think about is the money in the bank and good matches for my daughters."

Asha sat down on the bed next to the trunk.

"Did you meet your parents?"

"No," Ragini said. "No need to."

"My parents call me once a week. They send me presents. And now the mother is going to come to India . . . early. She will come and visit every other day or something. I don't want her to, but I can't tell her that," Asha said. "I don't like her."

"It's still *her* baby," Ragini said.

"But what if I know that she'll be a bad mother?" Asha demanded. "What if I know? How can I—"

"It's *her* baby and it's none of your business what kind of a mother she is," Ragini said. "Don't do something stupid, Asha. When you do something stupid, it doesn't just mess up your life, it messes up the lives of all the other surrogate mothers. For people like me, this is the only way out. Don't bring this place a bad name."

"I'm not doing anything," Asha said.

"Good," Ragini said, and smiled at her. "It's always hard the first time. When you do it again—"

"I'm never doing this again," Asha said.

Ragini laughed lightly. "That's what I said. But when you need money . . . you'll do what it takes. And this is better than being a whore."

Asha told Doctor Swati about her conversation with the mother during her checkup. While Doctor Swati looked at the baby's picture on the ultrasound machine, Asha voiced her doubts about having the mother in India before the baby was born.

"She just wants to feel close to the baby," Doctor Swati said. Asha wiped her belly with the paper napkin the doctor gave her.

"And we're not the type of clinic that doesn't allow contact between the surrogate and parents. So if she wants to come, then she can. She just has to follow the rules and come here only during visiting hours. She won't disturb your schedule, if you're worried about that."

Asha stood up and started to put her sari in order. The pleats had been pulled out and her petticoat loosened for the ultrasound.

Asha loved watching the baby on the screen. The thump-thump-thump of the heartbeat always brought tears to her eyes, but she held them back. She didn't want Doctor Swati to think she was unduly attached. But it was amazing, a sign of life. She wished she had been able to do this with Manoj and Mohini. She wished Pratap could have heard the heartbeat, seen their baby on the black-and-white screen.

"The baby is inside me," Asha said. "How is the mother going to be close to her?"

"I don't know," Doctor Swati said. "Honestly, I think it's unnecessary, and I have talked to her about her expectations. Once she's here she's going to regret it. There's really nothing for her to do but wait."

"I'm going to be nervous around her."

"Don't be," Doctor Swati said. "And if it bothers you, just tell me and I will talk to her. Do you want me to tell her that she shouldn't come and visit you?"

Asha thought about it for a moment, and it seemed cruel to ask a mother not to feel her baby kicking, even if it was through someone else's belly.

She shook her head. "It's OK."

"By the way, I spoke to the headmaster at the school you want Manoj to be admitted to," Doctor Swati said, and sat down on her chair behind the large wooden table. "He said that Manoj could definitely start there at the beginning of the next school year in September."

"Can't he start this September, now?" Asha asked. She was worried about Manoj; she knew that he needed more of a challenge in his school or his brilliant mind would waste away.

"I'll ask the school, but I doubt it. It's very tight

this year, and it's too late to apply now," Doctor Swati said. "The headmaster said he'll send the admissions materials to me. You can fill them out and pay the admission fees. I think you should wait until after the baby is born and you have the full money to pay the admission fees. They're quite steep. And if you want Manoj to go there year after year . . . you'll need to pay a high amount of money every year, nearly half lakh rupees."

Asha's heart sank. How would they pay for this? How would they manage?

"But that's . . . that's so much money, Doctor Swati."

"We'll find a way. For now, just know that for next year Manoj has admission."

Asha's legs felt heavy as she walked from the clinic to the surrogate house. Five lakh rupees were only enough for six years of school. He would be just eleven years old then.

If she did this again, then they could get another six years, and then what? How would they pay for college? How many more times would she have to do this to ensure Manoj's future?

That evening Pratap came alone. Manoj and Mohini had gone to a birthday party with Kaveri, Raman, and their boys.

"I'm very worried about Manoj," Asha confessed.

"His teachers think that it's going better now

283

that he's two grades up. They think that next year they might push him another grade up and then he will be in the right place," Pratap said.

To deal with Manoj's behavior, the school had moved him up two grades in one week, hoping that the schoolwork would be more challenging.

"So you're saying he doesn't need to go to a special school?" Asha asked. He was going to once again talk about a flat, she just knew it, and she could feel her anger rise.

"No," Pratap said quietly. "I . . . I think that it's OK if he doesn't go to a special school right now. Here he goes to class with much older boys, and that is hard. Just because he's good at math doesn't mean he's good at talking to people or is smart about things that older kids are smart about. But if we can't afford it . . . I'm not going to sacrifice the future of the whole family to put him in a school that may or may not be good for him."

"You just want to buy a flat," Asha spat.

"That's not true," Pratap said, and sighed. "I do want a home. Is that so bad? I've never had a real home. Just huts in a village. No real walls. No bathroom. Is it so bad that I want my family to have a home? Manoj and Mohini love Raman's flat. It's nice. It's big. And I want one, too. Why do you make that sound like a crime?"

"It's not a crime," Asha said. "But Manoj has to be our first priority."

"A proper home will be important for Manoj and Mohini, too," Pratap said confidently. "I'm getting some work . . . business is bad all around the world, but I'm getting work here and there. And I hope to get more. And once business starts to pick up, Raman and I will start our own business. But a home . . . if we have a home, the other dreams can come true, too."

Asha smiled at him. "You're different," she said softly. "Before, you would've just told me how it was going to be. Now you ask me what I want."

Pratap smiled back. "You're different, too, you know. You never would have said what you wanted before. If you had, I would've listened."

"Really?"

"Really," Pratap said. "My mother did what my father wanted. You did what I wanted. The only woman I know who fights with her husband is Kaveri, and I'm glad you're not like her, screaming and yelling all the time. But Raman loves his wife. And I love mine."

He had never said this before. Never used the word *love*. People like them didn't talk about love.

"I love you, too," Asha said shyly, embarrassed, her eyes not meeting his.

"When you come back, we'll go to Tirupati," Pratap said. "Get Lord Venkateshwara Swami's blessing."

"That's a good idea," Asha said.

"It'll be over soon," Pratap said. "And then you'll come home."

"And then I'll come home," Asha said. She grabbed his hand then. The first time she had ever done that, ever initiated touching him. They held hands in silence until it was time for Pratap to leave.

Chapter Fifteen

"I can't believe this is happening," Priya said to Madhu. "And you can stop smiling."

Madhu burst out laughing. "I'm sorry. I know this isn't funny, but in all your fantasies, or your nightmares, I'm not sure which, I'm sure you never saw yourself going to India with your mother."

It had been like all the other times. Priya and Sush had fought, Sush had stopped speaking to her, and then a few weeks later they had sort of made up.

Priya had called to let her father know that she was going to India for two months. Madhu would join her for the last two weeks before they brought their baby home. In those two weeks, they had to get their daughter a passport and get the legal work in place to bring her to the United States.

"Sush has been planning a trip to India as well," her father said. "To Hyderabad for some meetings. You should go together; you can take care of your mother."

"Right, like Sush needs taking care of," Priya said. "And I don't think Mama would be too keen on that."

Priya had been wrong. Sush was quite keen on that.

"Well, we haven't been to India together since you were a little girl. This will be an excellent opportunity," Sush said.

"And you can also meet Asha," Priya suggested, testing the waters.

"I must admit I'm curious to see this clinic and the house where these pregnant women live," Sush said. "It'll be informational."

Sush seemed to have forgotten about her last visit and their fight, and Priya let her. Why fan the flames of a miserable old fire?

So it was decided: Sush would fly into San Francisco, and they would then fly to Singapore together, where they had a three-hour layover before a three-hour flight to Hyderabad.

That was a lot of hours to spend with her mother, Priya thought. They could barely stand each other for a couple of hours; twenty-four hours of nonstop company could cause bodily damage. And once in Hyderabad, it wasn't going to be a picnic, not with Madhu's sister visiting as well.

"My mother, your mother, and Mayuri . . . this isn't happening," Priya said, and leaned her head against Madhu's shoulder.

Mayuri and Sush had met only once and had hated each other. The vendetta started during Priya and Madhu's wedding.

Priya and Madhu got married at a hall near Madhu's parents' home in Hyderabad. The whole wedding had been a blur. The *muhurat*, the "auspicious time," fell at 2:07 a.m. on the twelfth of July. An excruciatingly hot time to begin with, without the added burn of sitting around a fire for the wedding ceremony, wearing a ton of jewelry and a heavy sari.

The whole ceremony had felt alien, and though parts of it had been interesting, by two in the morning, with jet lag hitting hard, Priya had been too tired to enjoy any of it. Madhu had been a rock, his arm around her waist, even as his mother kept asking him to keep his hands to himself.

"It's inappropriate to touch her like this," she said. "She isn't your wife yet, and even if she were, you shouldn't put your arm around her like this in public."

Madhu had turned around and looked his mother in the eye. "Amma, we live together; this is way more appropriate than that."

This wasn't Madhu's usual style with his mother, but with the ceremony dragging on, he was exhausted as well. Prasanna had gaped at him and then shut her mouth as if too disgusted to speak.

At some point in the wedding, the groom's family was supposed to give the bride's mother a sari. Instead of an elaborate silk sari, which was how it was usually done, Prasanna for some odd reason decided to give Sush a rather plain cotton one. Lalita, Sush's cousin, had gone berserk.

289

And once that happened, Sush lost her marbles as well.

Halfway through the wedding ceremony, while Madhu and Priya sat in the wedding *mandap*, a fight broke loose. The main players were Sush, Lalita, Prasanna, and Mayuri, who entered the skirmish when it became obvious that Lalita and Sush were winning the vocal war against Prasanna.

"This is a cheap cotton sari," Lalita said, holding the sari up to Prasanna's face. "Is this the respect you show the bride's family?"

"Respect? You want to talk about respect? We're the groom's side, but we're the ones paying for the wedding. In India, the bride pays for the wedding," Prasanna said.

"My husband has paid for the wedding," Sush piped in.

"No, he hasn't. My Madhu paid for the wedding, and we planned the wedding and did all the work to set it up," Prasanna said.

Madhu had tried to say, "Actually, Amma, Priya's father did send money . . ." but no one was listening to him.

"You don't pay for the wedding, you don't do anything around here, and then you want a good sari? This is the sari we can give you," Prasanna said.

Usually a mild-mannered woman, for some reason Prasanna seemed to fly into full bitch mode.

"We paid for the wedding," Sush said, now

screaming. "And we're letting our daughter marry into a lower social economic class."

"We're Brahmins," Prasanna said. "It's you who are a lower class with your white husband."

Madhu had buried his head in his hands then, and Priya closed her eyes. She was too tired to stand up and fight. She looked at her father pleadingly.

He tried to pull Sush away from the fight, but that just made her angrier.

"They say that your being white is a big problem here," Sush said.

Madhu's father, Sairam, also got into the action, trying to extricate his wife, but like Andrew, he didn't get very far.

"My brother-in-law is a doctor; he's very rich," Lalita said, and Priya groaned at such blatant snobbery. "You have no money, which is obvious, since you gave Sushila a sari like this."

"We're not poor," Mayuri piped in.

"Mayuri," Madhu called out, standing up. The ceremony had now come to a halt. Technically, they were married, but the rest of the ceremony had to be performed for religious purposes.

"What? Her family is yelling at Amma, and you're just sitting there listening," Mayuri said, flashing angry eyes at both Madhu and Priya.

"Stay out of it," Madhu said.

"You stay out of it," Sush said to Madhu.

"Oh for God's sake," Priya said. Standing up

was difficult, with all her wedding finery pulling her down. "It's a fucking sari, Mummy. You don't even wear saris."

"Don't you dare use language like that with me," Sush said, and threw the sari at Prasanna's face. "This is what I think of your lousy gesture."

"How dare you?" Mayuri was ready to go to blows at this point.

Andrew and Sairam came and stood beside Madhu and Priya.

"So sorry, darling," Andrew said.

"This happens in Indian weddings," Sairam said, looking apologetic.

In the meantime, the women were yelling at one another, and the guests were watching them instead of the bride and groom. Even the priest had given up any pretense of being impartial and was supporting Prasanna against the bad Hindu woman who had married a white man.

"There's a car and a driver outside," Sairam said when the discussion went into how long Prasanna thought Madhu and Priya would remain married. She was sure that her son would divorce a daughter raised by a woman like Sush in no time.

"You should go," Andrew said.

"Where?" Priya asked.

"Anywhere," Madhu said, and got details from his father about where the car was parked.

So, in the middle of their wedding ceremony, Priya and Madhu left the wedding hall and drove to

Birla Temple in the middle of the city. It was Madhu's favorite place. He wasn't exactly religious, but it was a beautiful temple with a stunning view of the city, and it was the first place he could think of that would give them some peace.

"I can't believe Mayuri joined that melee," Madhu said.

"Your mother doesn't like me," Priya said.

"She adores you. She just doesn't like your mother, and once she gets angry, she has no clue what she's doing or saying," Madhu said. "You should've seen her with my grandmother. It was mother-in-law versus daughter-in-law, Telugu movie style."

It was nearly five in the morning, and they leaned against each other as they sat outside the gates of the closed temple, the white Honda Civic with their driver in the background. The driver had chatted with them as he had driven them—the news of the catfight in the wedding hall had reached him, and he was amused to drive a bride and groom away from their own wedding half-way through it.

Eventually Sairam called Madhu on his cell phone and convinced him to come back. The women had calmed down, he'd promised.

When they returned to the wedding hall, Sush and Lalita had left, and Andrew had stayed behind. Prasanna and Mayuri apologized to Madhu and Priya for their behavior.

Mayuri later confessed she didn't know what had gotten into her. "I guess I just don't like your mother," she had said.

Priya had nodded. "I understand. It can happen."

Since then, Madhu and Priya had kept his parents away from her parents, and Mayuri away from Sush. They didn't quite know how the chemistry would mix when they met again.

Transcript from message board
www.surrogacyforyou.org

Trying1Time: I'm packed and ready to go to India. I don't know what to expect, but I'm going to go and hope for the best. I'm looking forward to seeing the surrogate house and the SM. And I really want to feel the baby kick. And in two months I'll get to hold her.

NobuNobi: OMG, you're really doing it! We just got back with the baby and it's fabulous, just wonderful. Little Cooper is amazing and I have never been this much in love before. DH and I just sit and stare at him for hours. And my in-laws who were so against us using a surrogate are thrilled to be around him. I couldn't be happier.

Newbie1209: I'm so happy for you. We'll be going in a few months, too, to get our baby and I can hardly wait. But Trying1Time, won't it drive you crazy to be in India for two full months? I mean, you did say that you had family there, but still? Do you intend to stay at the surrogate house with the mother?

Trying1Time: I don't think they allow that! And I don't think I'd want to stay in the surrogate house. There's the language issue. I speak some Telugu but not a whole lot. My mother is coming along with me to India and my sister-in-law will be at my in-laws' place as well. So I'll have plenty of company. I think it'll be fine . . . who knows, maybe even fun.

LastHope77: Just do what your heart says. If you're miserable, you can always come back and then go again. But if you feel it's important to see the SM and touch your baby while it's in the SM's womb, then do it.

YummyMummy2008: I was there a week before the baby and two days before the due date and it drove me up the wall. All that waiting. Is it now? Is it now? We waited for the phone to ring constantly and we were worried that the baby wouldn't be born on the due date—I mean tickets to India and the hotel stay were expensive. But they said they'd just induce if a week passed by. Thankfully the SM went into labor. It's nerve-racking enough when you're pregnant and you don't know when you'll go into labor—but this was pure torture.

UnoBaby: I told my friends that I might do what you're doing, Trying1Time, and they said that it would be torture—but it's torture being this far away, isn't it? No matter how you do it, this process is painful. I'm tired of feeling this helpless. And I'm angry that this was the only way we could have our own baby. They put a man on the moon—you'd think they'd have found a way to deal with an inverted uterus.

CantConceive1970: Or get men pregnant?

Mommy8774: LOL. I wish both the man and woman could get pregnant—then at least one of us could conceive. But I agree—using a surrogate is so hard and so painful. It puts you through the emotional wringer.

Chapter Sixteen

The backache began in the middle of the night.

Asha woke up moaning. She tried to find the best position to sleep in, but the pain was incessant. In the end, she gave up trying to lie down and sat up. She would have liked to turn the light on and read the Telugu book she had borrowed from one of the other mothers, but that would wake up Gangamma, so Asha found her book in the darkness and left the room.

In the dim moonlight the house looked beautiful. You couldn't see the chipped walls or the uneven cement floors, and even the charpoys that were the furniture of choice in the TV room and hall looked elegant. She was startled to note that the light was not coming from the moon but from the television.

"Who is there?" she heard Revati's tentative voice call out.

"Asha," she responded, and found the housemother sitting on one of the charpoys. Now that her eyes had gotten used to the dark, she could see better.

"What's wrong?"

"My back is hurting," Asha said as she waddled up to the charpoy next to the one Revati was half lying on with the remote control in hand.

"Come sit." Revati sat up and gestured to the charpoy Asha was walking toward. "I can't sleep anymore. It's the age. I need to sleep because I'm tired all the time, but I can't, and then I'm even more tired. It's a curse. Old age is a curse."

"You're not that old," Asha said with a smile. Sure, Revati had gray hair, but her body was still sturdy, her eyes didn't need glasses to see, and everyone in the house had noted how white and strong her teeth were.

"Old enough that sleep has abandoned me," Revati said. "Do you want a back rub? Something to eat or drink?"

"I'm fine," Asha said, and sat tentatively on the charpoy, holding on to the load in front of her as she sank. "It starts now for me, the backache, and it doesn't stop until the baby comes out."

"You'll be done in . . . what . . . two months now?" Revati asked.

"Almost," Asha said. "Doctor Swati said nine more weeks. I can hardly wait."

"Was it easy, the labor and delivery with your own children?" Revati asked.

Asha shrugged. "As easy as it can be. You can't avoid the pain. There is nothing to do about that. It's just the way it is."

"God gave this chore to us because he knew that man could not bear such pain," Revati said. "Our bodies are designed for this. In the old days, women had eight to ten children; now we have one or two."

"This is my third," Asha said, and then bit her lip. "Well, this one is not mine."

Revati nodded.

"What are you watching?" Asha asked.

"Telugu movie songs," Revati said. "They show old ones at night and I like to watch them. Women used to keep their clothes on then. Now they're half-naked and shaking their breasts about. It's not decent."

"Times have changed."

Revati shook her head. "Times have changed for those who have money, not for you and me. What has changed for you? Has your life changed a lot because of all that IT business they say India has? Our lot in life remains the same. The rich get richer and the poor stay poor."

"My sister-in-law lives in a flat now. My children and husband are there with them. They have never lived in anything but a hut in our village. That's change," Asha said.

"And what, it came free to her? No, Kaveri sat right where you are and got pregnant with some white people's baby," Revati said. "We still have to do work and struggle to get anywhere. The rich, they just sit on their asses and things happen for them."

Asha had spent time with Revati before and enjoyed her straightforwardness. She was a good woman who fiercely watched over the surrogate mothers and took good care of them. She was polite and gentle but also firm. She was a mother to the core, Asha thought, a strict mother with a big heart.

"You don't think what we're doing is a good thing?" Asha asked.

"Good thing for whom? The white people and the rich people? Sure. Is it good for you? I don't know," Revati said. "You have to sell your body and have a baby. I understand it's a gift you give to a barren couple, don't get me wrong. And I understand that it helps you live a better life, but . . . they get a baby; what do you get? Hemorrhoids and a sagging stomach."

Asha laughed.

"Oh, you get the money," Revati continued. "But it's not going to change your life, is it? That's why women keep coming back here. They have one, two, three children like this to make more money while their no-good husbands sit at home, doing nothing."

Asha had never realized that Revati didn't approve of surrogacy. It was a strange role she played as housemother when she disapproved of the process, and Asha told her so.

"No, no," Revati said, waving her hands. "I don't disapprove. You misunderstand. I think it's wonderful. I just think . . . well, I think the mothers should get more money."

"We get what we get, and it's more than we ever had," Asha said. But the women did talk about it. How they got just five lakh rupees while Doctor Swati kept ten or more; no one was sure of the exact figure.

"But it's such a big sacrifice."

"Not really," Asha said, not wanting to believe that this was bigger than it was. It was important, she told herself, not to use words like *sacrifice*. "We're like coolies, carrying someone else's load for a while," she said, borrowing Keertana's words. "Once we're done, we hand over the baggage and it's over."

"You really think it's that easy?" Revati asked.

"I hope it's that easy," Asha said.

"Well, then, I'll pray for your sake that it is that easy," Revati said.

They watched television for a while after that, and Asha fell asleep on the charpoy, waking up feeling sore and very tired.

A few days before the mother was supposed to come, Asha read a story in the newspaper on the computer about a Japanese couple who had used a surrogate in Gujarat. Apparently the couple had gotten divorced, and now the mother didn't want the baby but the father did. However, in India, a single father cannot adopt a baby, and since he needed the permission of the Indian authorities to take the baby out of the country, there was a problem.

The surrogate who had given birth to the baby didn't want the baby, either, so the baby's Japanese grandmother was taking care of it, hoping to get all the legal things taken care of so she could take the baby back to Japan.

Asha couldn't help but wonder if she would get the chance to keep the baby if her mother and father got divorced in the next couple of months. Was that why the mother was coming early? Because things weren't working out between them? Maybe if they got divorced she wouldn't want the baby anymore and then Asha would get to keep it. That could happen. Everyone knew that these foreigners didn't have good family values. They got married many times, divorced many times; it happened all the time.

It was a regular checkup. Doctor Swati checked her blood pressure and her temperature, and they took her urine in a cup.

Asha wondered if she would have to lie down today on the bed Doctor Swati had in her checkup room and wait for the cold jellylike thing to be put on her stomach before Doctor Swati used the plastic thing that helped them see inside her womb.

Asha loved this part. She would see the baby and feel anew the surge of love she felt for this life growing inside her.

"Should I lie down?" Asha asked expectantly.

Doctor Swati shook her head. "No, no, not today. We'll do it next week when Priya and her mother are here. You don't mind, do you?"

She did mind, but what could she say?

"When are they coming?" Asha asked, trying to keep the irritation she felt out of her voice.

"This Monday. Around noon or so, after lunch," Doctor Swati said. "I couldn't ask them to stick to the visiting hours, you know. They're driving all the way from Hyderabad. And she's come all the way from America. We have to give them some concession. And since your family comes during visiting hours, it seemed like the right thing to have them come earlier."

Suddenly everything felt like too much. Asha wanted to scream.

"Are you OK?" Doctor Swati asked.

"I have a headache," Asha said, her voice snappy. "Are we done?"

Doctor Swati put her hand on Asha's shoulder. "Something's wrong," she persisted.

"I . . . I just get a little moody when I'm pregnant," Asha said, almost mumbling the words. The doctor's concern was making her feel guilty for her behavior. She was acting like an idiot, like a child—she should behave herself and not throw tantrums like Mohini did when she didn't get what she wanted.

Doctor Swati smiled. "Most pregnant women get irritable at some point or other. No surprise there. I just . . . you always seem so calm that I never expected it of you."

Now she felt even more foolish. "It just happens. My husband also said I was a little . . . well, moody."

"Of course," Doctor Swati said. "And how are Pratap and your children?"

"Good," Asha said. "We're just so worried about Manoj's future. The school sounds good, but . . . so expensive. I don't know how we will be able to send him there."

She thought Doctor Swati was the one who was a little irritable now. "You should not burden yourself with these worries. I told you we'll figure it out. Just find peace and get through your pregnancy. If you're worried, it's not good for the baby."

"But how can I not be worried?" Asha asked, feeling a prick of anger. "He's my son and I'm doing this for him."

"I know," Doctor Swati said, and looked at her wristwatch impatiently. "Look, we'll talk about this later, OK? I have a few more patients to see, and I have some new parents visiting soon as well; just go on over to the house and try to rest. Worry isn't good for a pregnant woman."

Easy enough for you to say, Asha thought. Why, she could probably send her child to America or London or someplace like that where they had even better schools.

. . .

Asha remained angry when Pratap came to visit with the children. She didn't talk to him much, but spent the entire time talking to her children and holding them close to her.

"What did you learn in school today?" Asha asked Manoj, who was playing with a cube with blocks of color on it.

"I learned about magnets," Manoj said. "Do you know what the biggest magnet in the world is?"

Asha shook her head.

"The world," Manoj said. "The planet Earth is the biggest magnet."

Asha didn't understand and just nodded vaguely.

"What is this you're playing with?" she asked as she held Mohini close, kissing her hair as she waited for Manoj to answer.

"It's called a Rubik's cube," he said. "I have to find a way to make all the sides have one color only. Look, now there is red, yellow, blue, and green on this side; I have to make it all one color."

"Can you do it, you think?"

"He's already done it several times," Pratap said, and was met with a chilly glance from Asha. "What? I'm not supposed to say anything?" he asked calmly.

Asha sighed. This was just not like her, but there didn't seem to be much she could do about it. She was trying to be nice and normal, but her mind was spinning out of control.

Mohini felt the baby kick at her back and giggled.

Asha smiled at her. "That's the baby kicking," she said, and turned Mohini to face her. She took Mohini's little hand and placed it on her round belly. The baby kicked again and Mohini's eyes widened.

But before Mohini could feel it again, Pratap lifted her from Asha's lap and pointed to a butterfly that was sitting on a flower growing next to the terrace. "Look," he said. "Isn't that pretty?"

Mohini went to explore it, and he turned to Asha. "Don't talk about the baby like that to them," he said softly, his voice a bare whisper.

"Why not?" Asha demanded, not whispering.

"Because," Pratap said, his voice still low. "Because . . . you know why, Asha."

She did know why.

And in an instant, all her anger and resentment were washed away by an immense sadness.

"I didn't think," Asha said numbly, and was saved from saying more because Manoj leaped up from the ground where he was sitting with the cube in hand.

"Look, I did it again," he said triumphantly.

"So you did," Asha said, taking the cube from him and examining its sides, now each in one color. "You're such a smart boy," she said, and pulled him into her arms.

"I did it before, too," Manoj said. "But it's so

much fun each time. *Nana*, can you mix them up again?" He took the cube from Asha's hand and gave it to his father. "Nana mixes the colors again so I can put them back together."

As Pratap moved the various sides of the cube, Asha watched his large hands and realized for the first time that Pratap was different from other fathers in so many ways. Her husband actually took care of Manoj and Mohini, all on his own. Sure, Kaveri was there to help, but he brought them here alone and then took them back alone. He obviously played this cube game with Manoj and sat with him while he did his homework even though he couldn't help him. The other surrogate mothers complained about their lazy husbands and how they beat the children, but not Asha. Pratap never beat the children. Kaveri and Raman hit their kids all the time, but Pratap had told her when Manoj was little that no one would beat his children.

"I hated it when my father and mother beat me. I used to feel small and helpless, scared," he had told Asha. "I don't want my children to feel that way."

Pratap was a good man. A very good man.

And Pratap wasn't lazy. He worked and struggled to bring home money. He took care of them, but even he couldn't make enough money to help Manoj. As a painter, he would never make that much money; it would never happen.

He brought money home without complaining about it, but this one time it was her turn to bring money home, and she was doing nothing but complain, complain, complain. She felt small. She should appreciate him more, Asha thought.

"Thank you," Asha said suddenly to Pratap.

He raised his eyebrows in inquiry.

"For never hitting me," Asha said, making sure that Mohini and Manoj were out of earshot.

He looked bewildered.

"I know some men hit their wives and their children, but you never have. You won't even let me hit the children. Raman hits his children. My father used to beat my brother all the time, and my mother beat me, too. But you don't."

"Why would I?" Pratap asked. "I have the best wife and the best children in the world." He winked at her then, his eyes bright with laughter, and she smiled back at him, suddenly deliriously happy, sharing this moment with him.

Chapter Seventeen

General Parikshit's son, Colonel Vikas Parikshit, came to pick up Priya and Sush in an olive-green army jeep. Priya had never met Vikas before but had heard countless stories about him from her mother since they'd met at some poverty conference many years ago. The Parikshits had kept in touch since then and become family friends.

General Parikshit had two sons, both over-achievers. Vikas was in the army, quickly rising through the ranks, while his brother was a neurosurgeon in New York, minting money when he wasn't volunteering in Africa with Doctors without Borders. Priya knew Sush would have liked her to be like them, successful and impressive, an amazing child who would make Sush look good in front of her friends. "Graphic designer" just didn't cut it.

Priya and Vikas shook hands while the driver of the jeep helped put their luggage in the trunk.

"How was your flight, Auntie?" Vikas asked.

In India everyone was auntie and uncle, though Priya had decided to stand her ground and call General Parikshit "General Parikshit." He wasn't her uncle, and she wasn't about to start calling him that.

"It was long, and then we had that stop in Singapore," Sush said with a smile. "It's so nice of you to come and pick us up."

She was a true chameleon, Priya thought. As soon as there was someone around who was nonfamily, she changed colors. She'd become sociable, polite, gentle even. Sush didn't even complain to Vikas about the stupid woman at passport control. She talked about how wonderful the service was everywhere. Priya angled her head, watching on in amazement; she had to hand it to her mother.

"So, you're here to spend time with your husband's family?" Vikas asked Priya from the passenger seat, turning around to face them.

Before Priya could answer, Sush interrupted.

"Madhu's mother isn't feeling well, and Priya got laid off—you know, the recession—so she's here to spend some time with her, take care of her," Sush said.

Priya stared at her mother, aghast. She was keeping Asha and their baby a secret.

"That's very nice of you," Vikas said. "Your husband must be so grateful that you can take time to come here and help his mother."

Priya was about to speak again when Sush put her hand on Priya's and squeezed.

"Madhu is a wonderful husband," Sush said. "Just like you. I absolutely adore him."

No, you don't, Priya wanted to scream. *You're*

hardly ever nice to him. Who was this woman?

General Parikshit's house was far removed from the slums and dingy housing that they had driven past. As soon as the electric gates opened, letting the jeep through, they found a beautiful garden with a gardener busily digging up something. It was perfectly manicured. The mansion was typically Indian, with a wide veranda surrounding part of the house. The entrance was a large wooden door with an ornate brass knocker shaped like a bell.

"Vikas lives with his parents," Sush told Priya with some pride as Vikas led them into the house. The driver and a servant who had come running out of the house when they arrived were bringing in their luggage.

"Really," Priya said, not sure how this was a matter of great pride. Only losers lived with their parents.

"I believe in a joint family," Vikas said, pushing the door open. "My brother, Vishal, is a doctor in New York, but when he moves back to India, he's going to live right here with his family, too. We have the room."

"How nice," Priya said politely, feeling out of place. This was a different side of India, more like what you saw in Bollywood films than real life.

Madhu's parents didn't live like this. They had a maid to help clean and do errands, but this was a houseful of servants, just like in one of Sooraj

311

Barjatya's movies, where all the characters led luxurious lives, beset only by problems of unrequited love.

"Sush, darling!" a woman called as she came into the front room.

She was dressed in a purple silk caftan, her hair to her shoulders falling in salon curls. Gold and diamonds twinkled on her ears, neck, and wrists. She matched the front room, which was chock-full of gaudy Indian arts and crafts and over-loaded with heavy ornate rosewood chairs and a coffee table. The legs of both the chairs and the coffee table were carved like ropes, while the chair's cushion was covered in thick red-and-gold fabric. The coffee table had a glass cover, and underneath the glass were more carvings. A large, ornate mirror covered one wall while another had alarge painting of Sri Krishna imparting the Bhagvada Gita to Arjun during the battle of Mahabharata. The painting was signed. It was an original.

The woman and Sush hugged and kissed, European-style, a kiss on each cheek.

"Oh, you must be Priya," the woman said, and hugged her. Priya responded the best she could and smiled. She felt like she was five years old again, doing what her mother prepped her to do for guests.

"This is my mother," Vikas said, putting his arm around his mother.

"And my good friend Romila," Sush said.

It felt like they were actors in a play, each with their set lines. Priya didn't know what hers were.

"Well, I'd better go and get changed," Vikas said. "I have to go to work. I look forward to speaking more with both of you at dinner."

"Come in, come in." Romila held Priya's hand and took her inside the house.

Another ornate room, the sitting room this time, welcomed them. There was no television here, and it had an unused look to it—or maybe the servants constantly kept it tidy.

The centerpiece of the room was a very large elephant made in dark metal. It filled an entire corner of the large room. There were enough couches to seat about ten people with ease and two coffee tables topped off with heavy books, Ansel Adams and a book called *Monumental India* with the Taj Mahal on the cover.

The floors were white tile with green flecks, some kind of marble, Priya guessed. The carpets, handwoven and silk, were plentiful and should have been unnecessary, since India was plenty hot, but the house was cool, and obviously air-conditioned.

"The elephant is beautiful, Romila," Sush said.

"The Charcoal Project, everyone swears by it these days," Romila said. "You know Hrithik Roshan? The actor?"

When both Priya and Sush gave her a blank

look, Romila continued. "You don't watch enough Hindi movies to know, but he's a big deal, and his wife is a talented designer. She has a home décor chain of stores called the Charcoal Project, and when we were there last month in Mumbai, I just had to pick up a few pieces."

Romila led them outside through large French doors to the courtyard. The house was spectacularly designed, Priya thought, and couldn't wait to call Madhu and tell him about it. The courtyard was a large open space in the middle of the house with two mango and three coconut trees and several rosebushes. Metal outdoor furniture painted white stood majestically under a mango tree on some kind of brown tiled floor, the white parasol closed and probably never used, as the mango tree gave enough shade.

"It's too hot to sit outside, but the evenings are almost bearable these days," Romila told them as she took them across the courtyard into another living room.

This one had a lived-in look and was much less ornate than the other rooms. Casual and colorful carpets covered the tiled floor, and the furniture was light and very Western; there was not an Indian floral curve in sight.

They sat on comfortable sofa chairs, and almost as soon as they sat down, a woman arrived with a tray of food and tea.

"Would you like some tea, dear Priya, or do you

want something cold?" Romila asked her. "I'm sorry, I didn't even ask. Sush drinks tea and I was only thinking of that. And I had the cook make your favorite."

"Oh, *kachoris*, it's been years since I had an authentic one," Sush said, placing one of the flat, round pastries on a plate and handing it to Priya. "Priya loves samosas, but she won't say no to a *kachori*."

Priya took the plate and realized that her opportunity to ask for a cup of coffee had come and gone with the *kachori* tray. She bit into one carefully, not wanting to spill the fried lentil stuffing onto her clothes or, God forbid, the spotless sofa. She desperately needed a shower and a nap and in that order, but she felt it would be rude to get up and go.

"So, how are things, Sush? And how is Andrew? We wish he were here as well," Romila said.

"Andrew and Edward have a whole week of fly-fishing planned," Sush said. "They're driving down to Oregon."

Edward was Priya's father's best friend, a professor at NYU.

"We just love Edward," Romila said, and seeing the puzzled look on Priya's face, added, "We met last year in New York. We were visiting our son Vishal, and he was there with Andrew and Sush. Such a brilliant family."

They chitchatted some more about how

315

wonderful Sush's family was and how wonderful Romila's family was. It was your average scratch-each-other's-back kind of exchange, Sush glossing over the facts a bit to tell Romila how wildly successful Madhu was, and how his family was just "so intelligent." Even Mayuri was praised for her "fabulous" career as a fashion designer in London. She was swelling so enormously with made-up pride that Priya didn't have the heart to burst her bubble by telling her that Mayuri had been laid off, too.

Priya was about to keel over and had decided to politely excuse herself when a little woman in tight jeans and a white blouse came running into the room.

"Sush Auntie," the petite woman cried out, and launched herself at Sush, hugging her.

Wow, Priya thought. If she hadn't seen it, she wouldn't have believed that her mother could evoke such affection in another person. It was almost a revelation to watch her with her friends. If Sush were only this pleasant with her, they would get along just fine.

"Mona, my darling," Sush said.

"Oh, it's so good to see you," Mona darling said.

Priya popped another *kachori* in her mouth and chewed on it thoughtfully. This was better than watching television.

"Priya, *beta*, this is Mona, Vikas's wife," Sush said.

"Hi," Priya said, blinking away the surprise at being called *beta*, daughter, by her mother. Mona was gorgeous, no way around it. And she was young, midtwenties at most.

"Mona and Vikas got married two years ago," Romila said. "A love match made in heaven. We absolutely adore our Mona."

These people seemed to *absolutely* love and adore everyone, Priya thought. This was far, far away from her world.

"You just have to hear how they met," Romila said. "It's the loveliest story."

Mona's eyes glittered. "And I'll tell you during dinner. You look tired, Priya. Why don't I show you to your room? How about you, Sush Auntie?"

"We've put you in your regular room," Romila said to Sush with a smile.

Sush Auntie has a regular room here, Priya thought. Her mother had this whole life that she knew nothing about. It was good to get to see this side of her; it made her . . . well, less annoying.

"I'll just catch up with Romila for a bit first," Sush said. "You go on, Priya. Get a little sleep. I'm going to tough it out and go to bed after dinner. I want to get done with jet lag as soon as possible."

Mona took her through a corridor lined with

bedrooms and walked her into one with a view of the courtyard.

"I hope you'll be comfortable here," Mona said as she drew thin white curtains on French windows facing the courtyard.

"This is lovely," Priya said.

Better than a hotel for sure. The bed had four posters with a wooden bedside table, and there was an en suite bathroom with a glassed shower cabin and shell scoop sink.

"Vikas's parents built this house, and they spared no expense," Mona said, and flopped on one of two chairs flanking a small table by the French windows.

Priya sat down on the bed. She really wanted to lie down but felt guilty, considering how grimy she was.

"Oh, Nandita unpacked your things and put them in the closet," Mona said. "I hope that's OK."

Priya had to bite her tongue from protesting. She had all those baby clothes; where did they go? She walked up to the closet and opened it.

Her clothes were either hanging or neatly arranged on shelves. All the baby things were placed on shelves as well.

Mona could see the contents of the closet. "Are you visiting a friend who had a baby?"

Priya turned to look at her. She didn't want to rain on Sush's parade, but she also didn't want to lie. She wasn't ashamed of how she was having a child. She was proud, happy to have it any way she could. It was important that she remember this.

"Actually, *I'm* having a baby . . . that is, my husband and I are having a baby," Priya said. "But I'm unable to carry to term, so we've hired a surrogate to do it for us. She's due in October, and I brought the clothes along for then."

"You're going to stay here until October?" Mona asked. "Oh, I mean, you're welcome of course, very welcome to stay here. I'm just surprised that you'll be away from your husband for that long."

Priya smiled. "That will be the hard part. But I want to spend some time with Madhu's—that's my husband—his parents and the surrogate mother. I'm going to go and stay with Madhu's parents once I leave here next week."

"You *really* are welcome to stay here," Mona said.

"I know, but Madhu's parents are expecting me," Priya said. "And his sister is going to be back from London this weekend as well. I haven't seen her in months."

"Isn't family wonderful?" Mona said.

It certainly was, Priya thought. And she was going to have one of her own soon. But she knew what Mona meant. Parents, sisters, parent-in-laws . . . all these people who were part of your life and were there for you when you needed them. Madhu's parents had been ecstatic to have Priya stay with them. Sush, well, *this* Sush—the new one—hadn't said one vile thing about surrogacy throughout the flight and had brought her here, was going to come with her to see Asha.

When Priya didn't respond and had a faraway look, Mona came up to her and put her hand on Priya's. "Congratulations on your baby."

"Thank you," Priya said.

"Will you be visiting your surrogate?" Mona asked.

"That's the plan," Priya said. "Vikas has been nice to give us a car and driver for tomorrow."

"Of course," Mona said. "May I come along? Or would that be too weird?"

That would be too weird, Priya thought.

"Maybe the next time we go," Priya suggested. "It's just that this is my first time visiting her like this, and my mother is coming along. I don't want to upset her by bringing too many people over."

"Oh yes, yes," Mona said. "I understand."

But she sounded disappointed.

"I intend to go again before I leave here. You can come along then," Priya said. "It's a two-hour drive, but if you're up for it, I'd love the company."

"I'd love to," Mona said, and left.

Priya didn't know what to make of Mona. She wasn't like Romila; she didn't seem fake, but

320

was genuinely interested. When she said she wanted to see Asha, she wasn't being polite but sincere, without vulgar curiosity.

She knew Indians demanded immediate intimacy. Like Madhu's friends' wives—they expected Priya to open up to them because their husbands were friends. Madhu's parents who wanted her to immediately become close to them. Priya had found it unsettling but had learned to create boundaries. Madhu's parents, no problems. The wives of friends, well, within limits.

Mona seemed different, and Priya was curious to find out why. Yes, she would take Mona with her. She'd like to get to know her better.

Chapter Eighteen

They came after lunch in a big black car with a driver dressed in white clothes.

The mother wore blue pants with a white shirt. The mother's mother wore a yellow *salwar kameez*. They looked even wealthier than she remembered.

Asha couldn't help but envy the mother's mother's shoes. They were white, strappy *chappals* with silver designs on them. The mother's mother's toes were painted red, and her feet looked smooth and soft, unlike Asha's, which were always dry and hard, cracked at the heels.

Asha couldn't see the mother's feet. She was wearing brown shoes that covered her feet completely. They were pretty shoes, too. She'd never seen shoes like that. She had only slippers, two pairs, one for inside the house and one for outside, no more. Pratap had bought the outside slippers for her two years ago when he'd gotten a bonus from a contractor for finishing a painting job quickly. Asha wondered how many slippers and shoes these women had, probably a pair for each dress they wore. The things some people could spend their money on.

Asha watched them from the window in the TV

room, the one that had two panes covered in thick plastic. The windowpanes had broken when the TV people had come and were moving their equipment around. Revati had put the plastic sheets up in their place. No one was going to replace those windows, according to her, and this was the best they could expect. It wasn't that the house was falling apart—it wasn't. It was one of the nicest houses Asha had ever lived in, but as the mother and her mother arrived, Asha looked around and saw that it was actually quite shabby. Thin cotton sheets, faded and even torn in some places, were draped over the charpoys in the TV room. There were straw mats spread around the floor, which was where the women got together to play cards. Pillows covered in lightly stained pillowcases were spread over the mats.

The ceiling fan buzzed away while a floor fan swiveled around, its blades moving at dizzying speed. The floor fan had become a necessity as the summer months had progressed. It was always hot in July, but this had been the hottest of them all. Almost all the women had received miniature portable fans that they could put near their faces and necks when the heat was at its worst and they cut out the electricity. The clinic had a generator that came on during power cuts, but the surrogate house didn't have such luxuries. When the current went out, everyone came out of their rooms like ants scurrying out of the walls, into the TV room or onto the veranda, which were cooler.

"Are they here?" Keertana asked. She, Gangamma, Gita, and Urmila were playing cards. The television was turned on, and a few women sat on charpoys, half lying down with their hands on their swollen bellies. Before long they would start snoring softly, sleeping.

That's all the women really did in the house, Asha thought bitterly. They ate, they stretched a little, and then they slept. When Asha first came to the house, she thought how nice it was that they could learn how to use the computer and learn English and get some job training. But as the days had passed, she realized that the English classes were canceled most of the time, and they really didn't learn anything about computers except how to read the tabloids and listen to songs. Even the exercises they were made to do didn't take place every day. If Divya wasn't feeling well or had other appointments, she wouldn't lead the daily yoga. Nor would she teach the English class or open the computer room.

The only guarantee the women really had was that if they had a backache, Revati would give them a good and thorough massage. Even Asha had had a massage when her back was especially bad, and she had to admit she felt much better after it.

She saw the mother and her mother open the gate to the house, and she turned to face the women in the TV room. "They're here," Asha said.

Divya received them on the veranda, where she usually sat with her mobile phone stuck to her ear, talking in a mixture of English and Telugu to her friends. The women at the house suspected that Divya had a boyfriend, and that's what the giggling on the phone was all about.

Asha heard Divya chat animatedly with the mother and her mother while her heart thumped. What was she supposed to do now? What on earth were they expecting from her?

"It's after lunch so they're all lazing around," Divya said as she led the women in. "And soon enough they will cut the current so there will be no TV to watch. And when the fans stop working, it's ridiculously hot—nothing more to do than take a nap."

"Asha," the mother called out when she saw Asha, and moved toward her, sidestepping the unoccupied mats on the floor. She took a step forward and hugged her. Asha stood stiff for a moment, then softened.

"How wonderful to see you," the mother said, and looked at her belly, bulging out of her blue-and-white cotton sari. "Oh, your belly has grown so."

There were tears in the mother's eyes, and that

irritated Asha. What was there to be so emotional about? Why all the drama?

"How are you feeling?" the mother asked.

"Fine," Asha said.

"*Namaskaram*," the mother's mother said, folding her hands and prompting Asha to do the same. "I'm Sushila; I'm Priya's mother." She spoke in Telugu. No accent.

"*Namaskaram*," Asha said, now very uncomfortable. All the other mothers were looking at them.

"Why don't you sit on the veranda," Divya suggested. "It's always cooler there because of the trees."

Asha walked with the mother and Sushila to the veranda, and they all sat down. This was where Asha spent every evening with her children and Pratap. She and Pratap would watch Mohini and Manoj run around the tulasi plant in the center of the yard or the small bushes. Sometimes they would go around the side of the house and look wistfully up at the tall mango trees that surrounded the house, which they couldn't yet climb. Visiting hours were the best time of Asha's day, and every time she looked at the veranda, it was with joy, a feeling of remembered pleasure. But now she was here with these women and she felt no pleasure whatsoever, just a heavy sense of burden.

The mother opened her bag quickly and brought

out a small box. "This is for you," she said. "I didn't know what else to get you, but . . . I thought . . . maybe you'll like it."

Asha saw the small blue box and frowned. She opened it and gasped; there were little pearl earrings inside: a big pearl, and from there hung three smaller ones.

"Do you like them?" the mother asked.

"I can't take this," Asha said in shock. These were real pearls; even she could see that. These things cost money.

"You don't like them?" the mother asked.

"No, they're beautiful," Asha said. "But so expensive and—"

"Please, they're nothing," the mother said, as if buying jewelry was like buying mangoes at the fruit stall. "You must take them."

Asha reluctantly accepted the gift, a part of her admittedly giddy to own something so beautiful.

"How are you feeling?" Sushila asked.

"I'm fine," Asha said. "Doctor Swati takes good care of me." She felt like a puppet, still speaking to the TV people.

"We saw the clinic," Sushila said. "It's nice."

"Swati Atha has worked so hard to make all this happen," Divya said.

Asha had expected Divya to leave them alone, but she sat with them, keeping watch just as she had done when they'd made the TV show, as if making sure Asha didn't say anything untoward.

"Maybe in a bit you can give us a tour of the house, Asha," Sushila said, as if ignoring Divya, and Asha liked her for that.

"And we were hoping we would have a chance to meet your family," the mother said.

"Why?" Asha asked before she could stop herself.

The mother looked flustered.

But Sushila just smiled. "We have some presents for your children and husband, and we just wanted to see them and say hello. Will that be OK?"

She seemed so nice, Asha thought, the mother's mother. Compared to the mother, Sushila was definitely more Indian and spoke Telugu so well.

"If it's OK with you, that is," the mother tacked on, as if suddenly realizing that Asha might take issue with their meeting her family.

That was it, Asha understood; the mother was completely fake, and this was why she had never liked her. Sushila, on the other hand, seemed genuine.

"No, no," Asha said. "They will come at four. That's when they can visit. You can visit anytime, but they can only come at four, and for just one hour. That's the visiting time."

She didn't want it to sound like an accusation, like they were getting preferential treatment, but that's how it came out.

"Well, it's nearly three," Sushila said, looking at

her wristwatch. "We can wait. Do you want to try on the earrings and see how they look?"

Asha was the one who felt flustered now, but she removed her small gold studs, the ones that her parents have given her when she got married. They were quite small and had more copper than gold, but they were her only pieces of jewelry, besides her two gold bangles and *mangalsutra*, the necklace that a husband ties around a woman's neck to make her his wife, and she treasured them.

She put her gold studs inside the box with the pearl earrings and put the other earrings on, slowly, savoring the smooth, cool feel of the pearls as she closed the gold clasp.

"They look lovely," Divya said with a loud clap.

"Here," Sushila said, and pulled out a small mirror from her purse.

Asha saw that her face was slightly pinched, as it was when she was irritated, but the pearl earrings brightened her appearance nonetheless.

"They're beautiful," Asha said, breathless at the sight of such lovely jewelry on her ears. "Thank you."

"You're welcome," the mother said, sounding very pleased with herself. Her voice grated on Asha's nerves.

"You should keep them on," Sushila said. "They look good on you."

Asha closed the box with her studs, holding it close to her swollen belly.

"Maybe you can show us where you sleep," the mother suggested. "And then you can put your earrings away as well."

They all walked through the TV room to the hallway that took them to the seven small rooms that lined up one after the other. Six of the rooms were on either side of the hallway, and the seventh room, which was big enough for four women, was at the end of the hallway.

"We saw other surrogate houses before we built this," Divya told Sushila and the mother. "And there, all the women stay in one big room, which is just full of beds and nothing else. We didn't want that. We wanted to keep the women comfortable. We think privacy is very important; these women are away from their home and families, and they need some space for themselves."

"When was this house built?" Sushila asked when they came to Asha's room.

Asha wished she could open the small, rickety window because the room smelled. She put the box with her studs inside the trunk that was under her bed and then stood uncomfortably, her hands twisting her *pallu* nervously. What did they want from her? she thought in near desperation.

"Seven years ago," Divya said.

Sushila looked around the room. "Just seven years? It looks much older."

"Oh, we haven't had time to . . . you know . . .

330

spruce it up. We have so many women here all the time that we just haven't had time," Divya said while she worried her lower lip.

Divya was embarrassed, Asha thought with a little glee.

"Still," Sushila said. "It doesn't have to look like a refugee camp, you know. Maybe we'll get a chance to talk to your aunt about it."

The mother said something to her mother in English. She called her Mummy, Asha noticed.

"No, no, it's OK," Divya said in English as well.

Asha felt left out and relieved. Maybe they'd just talk to one another in English the rest of the day and keep her out of it.

"We have a computer room next to the kitchen," Divya said, as if to make up for the dirty walls and ill-kempt house, and took them for a tour of the computer room. But the mother was not impressed, it seemed.

"This is nice, but just two computers?" she asked.

"Well, we don't need more than that," Divya said defensively.

"Can we sit outside again?" Sush said in Telugu, her displeasure evident.

They all walked out again, going through the television room, with all the pregnant women in the room looking at them.

"Does the baby kick a lot?" the mother asked when they settled back in the chairs and charpoys on the veranda.

"Yes," Asha said. She paused for a moment, and then said, "Would you like to feel?"

The mother nodded.

"OK, next time she kicks, I'll let you know," Asha said. She hadn't wanted to offer this, but the mother seemed so pathetic that she couldn't help but feel some pity for the woman.

She might have money and she could buy Asha earrings, but she could never have a baby. She would never know how this felt, never feel that closeness to a baby when you gave birth to it, never hold it as soon as it was born. It made Asha feel a little sympathy for the mother, even as it made her feel like a better woman for knowing what it meant to be a *real* mother.

"Well, Swati Atha wants us at the clinic in fifteen minutes or so," Divya said, looking at her watch. "She has arranged for an ultrasound."

The mother's face lit up. And though she'd felt compassion for her a moment ago, Asha wished she could find a way to knock that happiness right off the mother's face. Maybe she could come up with an excuse not to go to the clinic, and then the mother wouldn't be able to see the baby on the machine.

Asha was shocked at her own malicious thoughts. She was not a mean person, but something was happening to her; this baby was doing something to her, making her resentful and angry.

• • •

The ultrasound made the mother cry some more. This time Asha didn't look at the picture on the screen; she felt it wasn't her right.

"Oh, look at her tiny feet!" Sushila exclaimed.

The mother put her arm around Sushila and put her head on her shoulder. She said something in English.

Asha felt unnerved looking at the two women. This baby was theirs, she realized as panic fluttered inside her. Her baby was theirs.

The mother moved away from Sushila and put her hand on Asha's shoulder. "Thank you," she whispered, her voice thick with emotion.

Asha didn't answer, just blindly looked away from the monitor. This was their baby. She had known it all along, but she supposed that there had been a tiny part of her that fantasized that the baby somehow, some way, could be hers. Now with the mother standing there, staking her claim, her fantasies dissipated and she felt beyond foolish.

"You don't have to stay and meet the children," she said in Telugu, as politely as she could. "I mean . . . if you have to leave, that's OK."

"We're in no rush," Sushila said. "We have the car for the day, the week if we want it."

The mother seemed to understand her better and asked in her strange and accented Telugu, "Do you not want us to meet your children?"

"No, no," Asha said quickly. "You're welcome to meet them. I just didn't . . . I mean, why would I not want you to meet the children? Meet the children. They're wonderful children."

She felt silly talking like this. Why couldn't she just tell them that she didn't want them here, didn't want them intruding in her life? Wasn't her shame already complete with these people looking inside her? Now they wanted to see inside her family? What, did they want to take them to America as well?

"You said your son was very smart," the mother said.

What, poor people couldn't have smart children? Asha thought snappishly.

"Yes, he is," she said with pride. "He's only five, but they have put him in the third class because he's far ahead of children his own age."

"Asha's son is a cutie," Divya said. "They come and visit every day. Asha is the only mother we have who has family visiting her regularly. The others come from places too far."

"Is he going to a special school for gifted children?" Sushila asked.

Asha felt uncomfortable.

"We didn't have the money . . ." She paused; she felt poorer than she ever had before. "But now with this"—she looked at her belly—"we hope to send him to a special school. We have one outside of Srirampuram. Doctor Swati said she'll

334

help us with a recommendation and everything, and then maybe next year he can start there."

"These schools are very expensive," Sushila said. "How much money are you getting? How much, Priya?"

"Mummy," the mother protested.

"Please, this is not appropriate conversation," Divya added, looking sternly at Asha.

"Oh come on, the boy needs an education," Sushila said. "How much?"

Divya raised her hand and came in front of Sushila. "Please, you're upsetting her."

Asha was glad for Divya's intervention. This was humiliating, she thought, talking about money like this. Maybe she had been too quick in liking Sushila after all.

"We'll manage," Asha said, her head high, before Divya could speak. "We'll make sure our son has a future."

"Of course you will," Sushila said. "I mean, look at the sacrifice you're already making to make it happen. You're an amazing mother for doing this."

Asha almost said something then; something like she was also doing this to help Sushila's daughter and son-in-law, but the gate opened then, and Asha saw Pratap. He was carrying Mohini, and Manoj was behind them, holding his father's shirt with one hand and a notebook with the other.

He saw Asha and left his father to run to her.

"Look, Amma, look at what I got!" He thrust the notebook at her and Asha flipped through it.

"I got a hundred in maths," he said. "No one got a hundred. Only me."

Asha's chest swelled and she hugged him. "You're such a smart boy."

He stopped then and noticed the others on the veranda and smiled at them. "I'm Manoj," he said in Telugu.

"I'm Sushila," Sushila said.

"I'm Priya," the mother said, and held her hand out for Manoj to shake it.

Pratap put Mohini down, folded his hands, and said "*Namaskaram*" to the women. Asha had told him that they were coming but had assured him that they would be gone by the time he came with the kids.

Divya left them alone now, and they all sat down, uncomfortable with one another. Only Mohini and Manoj were oblivious to the tension.

The mother had brought presents for the children and Pratap. Mohini got a beautiful princess dress in pink and white with a crown. She immediately insisted on wearing it and pranced around, asking if she looked pretty.

"I asked the people at the toy store what would be good for a gifted child like Manoj, and they gave me this," the mother said, and held up a big box wrapped in pretty colors. Manoj took the box. "I also got him some books." She held out another wrapped box that she gave to Pratap.

Manoj said thank you in English and attacked the wrapping paper.

"It's a construction set," the mother said. "It's supposed to be good for smart kids like Manoj. It helps them build things; they can build anything with it."

Manoj looked at the box and read easily, "Capsela, ninety-one pieces, forty-seven models, fifteen principles," he said.

"Excellent," Sushila said. "You *are* a very smart boy, aren't you?"

"I got a hundred in maths," he said in response.

As he opened the box, the mother gave another box to Pratap.

"No, no," he said, putting his hands up. "You already gave me a watch; I can't take any more."

"Please," the mother said. "It's a small present. I think . . . I think you'll like it."

Pratap looked at Asha and she nodded. She would have to ask Pratap to bring something for the mother—but what present could they possibly give?

Pratap gasped when he removed the wrapping paper. Underneath was a box with a picture of a camera.

"It doesn't use film. It has a chip, and if you take it to any photo shop, I checked, they will print the pictures for you," the mother said hurriedly.

Pratap turned the box around in his big hands and opened it. He pulled the black camera out, wrapped in translucent paper for protection.

"I've never had a camera before," Pratap said in awe. "And I always wanted one. Especially to take pictures of the children."

The mother smiled widely. "I'm so glad you like it. I can show you how to use it."

"Oh my God," Divya said, coming onto the veranda. It was obvious that, even though she had left, she was watching from inside. "It certainly is an expensive present."

"*Challa* thanks," Pratap said, flushed with excitement. "This must be so expensive. You really don't have to bring us presents . . ."

"It's *not* expensive," Sushila said. "You shouldn't think about it. Just enjoy the camera. Take pictures of your children and your family, something you can look back at when your children are older."

The evening became easy after that. The mother taught Pratap to use the camera, and he took pictures of everything, showing each picture he took to Asha and the children after snapping it. It helped when Divya sat a little away from them, seemingly busy with her phone with the wide screen, finally no longer keeping a watchful eye on them.

Asha hated to admit it, but the presents had made her soften toward the mother. She showed Pratap her new earrings, and he agreed that they made her glow.

"Has Manoj been tested?" the mother asked as they talked about the children.

"Tested?" Asha asked.

"Yes, to see how smart he is," the mother said.

Asha frowned. "He is smart. You have doubts?"

"That's not what she's saying," Sushila said. "It's just a way to find out what level he's at so he can be taught better."

Asha looked at Pratap and they shrugged. They didn't know anything about testing.

Sushila nodded. "You said Doctor Swati was helping you with the school?"

"Yes, there's a special school . . . outside Srirampuram," Pratap said. "Doctor Swati will get Manoj into that school."

"But he hasn't been tested at the school?" the mother asked.

"No," Pratap said. "She said it was too late to apply this year, but we could for next year. He will start there next year."

The mother and Sushila looked at each other and then smiled at Pratap and Asha.

"What?" Asha asked.

"Well," Sushila began, and then sighed. "It's strange that he hasn't been tested. Any school will want to test him before they even consider taking him in."

"Doctor Swati said that they will send us admissions material soon," Asha said. "Are you saying he can't get in?"

"I'm sure he can," the mother said. "Can you tell me the name of the school? Maybe we can look it up as well and see how good it is."

"It's a good school. We know it's a good school," Asha said, but she wasn't so sure anymore. Doctor Swati had said it was and she believed her, but now these people were talking about testing and whatnot. And now that she thought about it, it did raise her suspicions that the school had just believed them that their son was smart; how did they know he was?

"I'm sure it's a good school," the mother said. "We just . . . you know, I'm sure you know what you're doing."

Asha gave them the name of the school then. "It's one of the best schools here," she said defensively.

"Thanks," the mother said, and looked at her watch.

"How about you take a picture of all of us, Pratap?" Sushila said as she stood up.

"Stand together," he said to the women.

The mother and Sushila flanked Asha, who self-consciously put her hands around her belly. Pratap snapped the picture and Asha wished he hadn't. He had for posterity locked this time, this time when she was pregnant, standing with these women who would never have known her but for the fact that the mother couldn't have children.

Chapter Nineteen

"OK, you gave me hell for getting a surrogate, but you're like a mother hen with Asha," Priya said to Sushila as they drove back to Hyderabad.

"It isn't her fault that you're exploiting her," Sush said, and then shrugged, shaking her head. "I have been tough on you. I know. Andrew made me see how it may have sounded to you."

Priya waited. Was an apology on its way? This had never happened before.

Sush took a deep breath. "So I'm making amends. I know I've been hard on you, and I could have done better. Andrew also said that if I piss you off too much you won't let us see our grandchild. And . . . as I would like to know my grandbaby . . ."

"Ah," Priya said, and couldn't stop from smiling.

"And we will not speak of this anymore," Sush said, smiling as well.

"Yes, Mummy," Priya said, and felt a weight lift off her.

"Doesn't something smell fishy with that school business?" Priya said. "How can they get admission to a school for special children without an interview?"

"I didn't like that doctor," Sushila said.

"Doctor Swati is lovely," Priya said. "You just think she's exploiting these women. But this money is making it possible to give Manoj an education."

"You know that five lakh rupees won't go a long way, don't you?" Sushila said. "It used to be a lot of money a long time ago, but now it's not enough to build a life on."

"The kid first needs to be tested," Priya said. "And let's check out this school. And then . . . how can we help with his schooling? I mean . . . if I had a job, I'd tell Madhu that we should just fund it, but I don't have a job and I don't know when I'll have one."

Sushila nodded. "No, it's a big burden for a private person, but maybe we can find him a scholarship."

"That's a great idea," Priya said. "Do you know anyone through UNICEF who can help?"

Sushila seemed thoughtful. "I'll think about it. I'm sure we can come up with something. We could talk to the Parikshits as well. They are very much into helping schools and students. It could be an option."

"That would be great," Priya said. "Or I could do an e-mail drive to raise money; what do you think?"

Sush nodded again, but she wasn't really listening. "It's like a baby factory there," she said. "And that house? My God, it was peeling off the edges. I know, I know, it's better than the slums.

That's India, everything could be better, but then again, it could be much worse."

When they got back, Priya called Madhu, waking him up. He wanted to be woken up, he had told her the night before; he wanted to hear about the baby and how Asha was doing.

"She has ten toes and ten fingers," Priya told Madhu about the ultrasound, and he laughed.

"And she's beautiful, right?"

"She looks like a weather map, but the most beautiful weather map I have ever seen," Priya said. "Asha loved the earrings. She thought so much of them, and to think they were on sale, seventy percent off at Macy's. I paid next to nothing for them."

"And did he like the camera?"

"Absolutely," Priya said. "But I don't know . . . I felt that our gifts made them feel less, as if they were poor."

"They are poor, Priya," Madhu said. "If they had money, they wouldn't need to do this."

Then Priya told him about Manoj and his schooling issues. She was suspicious that Doctor Swati had done no research whatsoever into special schools and had just said so to reassure Asha, and maybe to motivate her to sign up again sometime down the line.

"Maybe you should talk to Doctor Swati," Madhu suggested.

"And say what? I don't want to create any problems, not now, not with the baby due in eight weeks," Priya said. "But I'll do some research. Mummy said she would look into a scholarship."

"Did you just say Mummy? Usually it's Sush or just 'she,'" Madhu said.

"She's being supportive. She's making amends; she actually used the term *making amends* because she's worried I won't let her see her granddaughter. She admitted she was being too hard on me," Priya told him.

"And hell hasn't even frozen over," Madhu said. "So she thinks she can find a way to help this kid?"

"She said she'll look into scholarships," Priya said.

"You know if it's just money, we can just . . . I don't know, send an e-mail out to everyone we know and collect as much as we can. Even if everyone we know gives fifty dollars or so, we can raise a good chunk of money," Madhu said.

"I thought about that, too, but will that sustain years of schooling? I think a scholarship would be better. If that doesn't work out, then we can raise money or, you know, send money, whatever we can," Priya said.

"We're not the Rockefellers, honey," Madhu said. "No one said we have to save the world. But we can try to help this boy. Will you get him tested?"

"Mummy said she'll find out how we can do that," Priya said. "We can bring him to Hyderabad for it. The Parikshits have been great, by the way. They just handed me a car and a driver."

"My parents' house is going to be poor digs compared to this," Madhu said, but Priya could hear he was joking.

"Maybe I should just stay here. They've offered me the place for the whole two months if I want," Priya said.

"You just want to avoid a scene between my parents and Sush," Madhu said.

"I don't know, Madhu. She's a different person here. She's not critical, not judgmental. These people genuinely adore her," Priya said. "And on the trip to see Asha, she was a rock. She's really trying. I swear, we have never had this kind of intimacy before."

"Never too late," Madhu said.

They talked some more and Priya hung up laughing because Madhu charmingly but unsuccessfully tried to have phone sex with her.

The whole family was present at dinner, as they almost always were. Vikas made it a point to be home for at least one meal every day, he had told Priya.

Priya could see the easy relationship Mona had with her in-laws and hoped that her time at Prasanna and Sairam's would be similar.

Sush had updated the Parikshits on the surrogate house and told them about Manoj. Once Priya had told Mona about Asha, Sush had stopped hiding it like it was some dirty secret.

"We give out a scholarship once a year," General Parikshit said. "Well, by we, I mean our foundation does. We set it up several years ago at Vishal's, my older son's, insistence. We have helped several young people with funding to go to the States to do their master's, and we have offered support for students to go abroad for various courses. We usually don't offer support for such young children, but if this boy is as intelligent as you say, maybe we can swing something."

"You mean that?" Priya said, unable to believe that this might actually be easy.

"Absolutely," the general said. "In India, Priya, it's all about who you know."

"Of course, we need to have him tested first," Vikas said. "There are several applicants every year for this scholarship. We only offer one, and we try to give it to the best applicant possible."

"Your recommendation will definitely put him at the top of our list," Mona said. "I manage the foundation, more or less, because Papa and Vikas are so busy with everything."

Priya looked at Mona curiously.

"What do you do . . . I mean, for the foundation?" Priya asked as she refused another helping of butter chicken. There was only one server tonight, as it was just the family and them. She could get used to this. Good food, cooked for you, served to you—this wasn't a bad way to live.

"Everything," Romila said fondly. "She manages the finances. Of course, we have an accountant, but she works with him. Mona has a bachelor's degree in finance, and she's even a certified chartered accountant. Those exams are very difficult to pass, but our Mona, she cleared them in one go."

Mona flushed. "It wasn't a big deal."

"Of course it was," Vikas said. "Mona also does all the fund-raising and dispensing of the funds. Besides the scholarship, we also have a program to help single mothers, especially in villages. They're socially ostracized once their husbands die, and financially strapped. Mona travels to these villages and works with some NGOs that specialize in such matters. And we bought a farm last year; it's an hour outside of Hyderabad. When someone contracts AIDS in a village, they're thrown out, but on this farm they all live together and they also work. A lot of the food on this table comes from produce grown at the farm, and that is Mona's baby. She bought the land, got the farm going, found the right NGOs to help run the place, everything."

Priya had not expected Mona to have much to offer beneath the surface. She looked like someone whose idea of exerting herself was getting to her facials, pedicures, manicures, and haircuts on time. Apparently there was merit to the statement "Don't judge a book by its cover." Priya was impressed.

"They think it is *so much work,* which it's not," Mona said.

"It's very commendable what you do," Sush said. "I'm proud of all your accomplishments."

Mona promised to help with setting up an IQ test for Manoj in the next few weeks, and then work with them on finding the right school for him. She warned that most of these schools were in big cities, and she doubted that Manoj would be able to live at home. A boarding school would likely be the only viable option.

Mona came with Priya the next time she went to Srirampuram. This time Priya felt surer about her visit. She had something to convey to Asha. Mona had set up an IQ test with MENSA. They had to talk to Asha and see if they could take Manoj to Hyderabad and let him take the test there. Then they would bring him back. But Srirampuram was two hours away, which meant that there would be an overnight stay involved, and Priya wasn't sure how Asha would feel about Manoj staying with strangers for the night.

"Maybe we can bring Asha along as well," Mona suggested on their drive to Srirampuram.

"I don't think the clinic will allow that," Priya

said. "And honestly, I wouldn't want it, either. She's nearly eight months pregnant, and I don't want to risk it."

"And in any case, she needs to learn to be away from the boy," Mona said. "I found two schools in Hyderabad and one in Visakhapatnam that someone at MENSA told me would be the right school for this boy . . . that is, if his IQ is over one forty."

"He's five and he can read and write fluently," Priya said. "And he's been doing it for a while both in English and Telugu. His math skills are pretty high as well. The test he showed me he got a one hundred in had division and multiplication, beyond his years."

"Well, he needs to be tested so we can be sure," Mona said. "And the schools will want to test as well. Might as well do it now with MENSA and avoid any hassle later."

It had been good for Priya to work with Mona on this, because it took her mind away from the baby and worrying about all the legalities and official nonsense they had to get through before they could take her home. She had been seriously thinking about extending her stay with the Parikshits until this was resolved, but even as she had broached the subject on the phone with Madhu's parents, she could hear Prasanna's disappointment, so she scrapped the idea. She had spoken to Mayuri, who had all but pleaded with Priya to come as soon as possible—her parents were driving her mad.

"Now that I don't live in London, don't have a work visa or a job, they think the best thing for me is to get married," Mayuri said. "They put my profile into the database of a local matchmaking agency. They're determined to find a 'nice boy' for me."

"What's wrong with that? You're what, thirty? You're not getting any younger, and since you don't have any long-term relationships in your past, maybe arranged marriage is the best thing for you," Priya teased.

"Oh, fuck you," Mayuri said.

They sat on the veranda again. Divya sat with them, and Priya wondered why the woman had to be with them all the time. It was obvious Divya was spying on them—making sure that Asha didn't say anything untoward about Happy Mothers. The thought sent a chill down Priya's spine. What were they doing here that they were so worried about? Had all their phone calls with Asha also been monitored?

"So what do you think?" Priya asked Asha as Mona and she laid down their plan for Manoj.

"He'll be alone with you?" Asha asked.

"Well . . . my mother will be there, and so will Mona's in-laws," Priya said. "Maybe your husband can come along?"

350

"He has to work," Asha said numbly.

"Of course," Mona said. "But we will take good care of your son. We promise. He can stay at our house. My in-laws love children."

Asha seemed skeptical, so Priya asked her to talk it over with Pratap and get back to them. She would be back again next week, and they could talk more then, firm their plans.

Asha was even more reluctant to send Manoj with them when Mona said that most of the schools for special children were in the city, which meant that the only option for the boy would be a boarding school.

"Unless you move to Hyderabad," Mona said. "Would you be able to do that?"

"I don't know," Asha said. "I don't know how easy it would be for Pratap to find work there, and it's also so expensive. Here we can afford to buy a flat. There we won't be able to do that, will we?"

And then she sighed and leaned back on her chair, stroking her belly. She looked at Priya and smiled. "She's kicking; you want to feel?"

Priya walked up to her tentatively and put a hand on her belly. She felt the tiny touch of her child through Asha's flesh and felt an answering tug inside her. She put both her hands on Asha's belly, naked under her blouse, her cotton sari's *pallu* caressing Priya's hands.

"Oh my God," Priya gasped. "Oh my God. Hello, baby. Hello, my darling."

Her eyes filled up as the baby kicked again as if responding to her touch. *Oh how I wish you were inside me,* she thought. Nothing, just about nothing compared to the feel of touching her child like this, and Priya knew then that holding her baby in her arms would be the single most important thing in her life, a defining moment, an all-encompassing emotion.

The baby stopped kicking, and Priya reluctantly removed her hands.

"Thank you," she said.

"It's your baby," Asha said softly.

They went back to talking about schools for Manoj, Mona telling her how many schools there were in the state of Andhra Pradesh and their caliber.

"A boarding school—but then he won't be with us," Asha said. "And what about the money—won't it be more expensive?"

"It won't cost you anything," Mona said. "We'll find a scholarship for him."

Asha shook her head, as if trying to sort through what they were *really* saying. "Sometimes I wish Manoj were a normal boy. Now he has to go to a boarding school, and how will I stand it, not seeing him every day?"

"That's why Swati Atha suggested the school close to Srirampuram. They even have a school bus," Divya said.

"But it's not a school for gifted children," Priya said.

She had done her research. It was a private school. What was more, she had learned, Doctor Swati's husband, Doctor Ravi Gudla, was a board member. She couldn't understand why Doctor Swati had made a big deal about the weight of her recommendation while also saying that he couldn't get in this year. This was a new school, looking for new students. In fact, Priya wondered why Doctor Swati didn't waive tuition altogether for Manoj. After all, having a child of a high IQ in their school would only raise the school's image.

"But it's a good school," Divya said. "We have a lot of connections there. We can get Asha's son in."

"But it's a regular school," Priya repeated. And if Manoj has to go to a regular school, he might as well go to the one he's going to now."

"That's *not* a good school," Divya said peevishly. "I know the schools in this area, and that is a third-rate school."

Priya saw Asha's face fall.

"It's a good school," Asha said. "We pay five hundred rupees a month for it."

Divya shrugged. "Look, it's up to you. Swati Atha pulled a lot of strings for your son—but if you want to send him to another school, that's up to you."

"If Manoj has a high IQ, this school will not be able to handle his education," Priya said, wanting to shut Divya up. She gave her the creeps, sitting here all the time, interfering in their conversation and manipulating Asha.

Divya just shrugged again and went back to the magazine she was reading.

Priya wasn't sure she liked the doctor or her niece. Were they trying to push Asha into sending her son to this school, where she would have to pay an exorbitant amount of money for an ordinary education? Would Doctor Swati's husband profit from this as a member of the board? And how would poor people like Asha and Pratap continue to pay tuition? Probably— |she hated to think of it—by coming back to Happy Mothers to be a surrogate, where Doctor Swati was sure to gain a profit again.

Priya wondered if Doctor Swati would mention the school when they talked later, but she didn't. Instead, she said something about being careful with bringing too many presents for Asha.

"I understand your need to give her gifts, but don't bring something every time you come here," Doctor Swati said. "There are other women in the house, and we don't need jealousy brewing among them, do we?"

Priya had always liked Doctor Swati. But now, face-to-face, she didn't seem quite as noble and sincere as she did over Skype.

Once Priya apologized, promising to be more circumspect in the future, Doctor Swati talked about the labor and delivery and how they should proceed after that.

"We will call you when she goes into labor," Doctor Swati said. "Since you're here, I'm assuming you will come to the hospital."

"Yes, absolutely," Priya said. "Madhu might be here then as well, depending on when it happens."

"I don't know if you can be in the delivery room. It depends upon Asha, and usually the women like to just have someone from their family there," Doctor Swati said. "But then all our parents usually get here right after the baby is born. You are an unusual case."

"So no one comes here before the baby?"

"Oh, they do, but a week or two before at the most . . . but you can't plan delivery, so sometimes the baby comes early and they are here right after," Doctor Swati said. "I can ask Asha, if you want to be in the delivery room."

Priya thought about it and said, "No, please don't. I don't want to pressure her. This is such a private thing, and I don't want to impose any more than we already have."

"OK, I'll respect your wishes," Doctor Swati said. "To be frank, I'm relieved, because that would complicate things for us as well."

"How come?" Mona asked. She had been quiet the entire time, but she spoke now.

"It's never easy to have the biological mother

and surrogate in the same room when the baby is coming—we want to focus on the baby, and I could tell you stories of full-blown hysteria in the labor room, and not from the woman giving birth," Doctor Swati said.

Mona nodded in response and gave Doctor Swati a small smile for her attempt at humor. She hadn't said anything to Priya, but Priya had felt Mona's displeasure at seeing all those pregnant women squeezed into the surrogate house.

Priya was affected as well. She had been here before; still, it surprised her, the dilapidation around her. She didn't quite remember it like this. Then, she had been wearing rose-colored glasses. She didn't know Asha. The house had seemed cozy. Now it seemed dingy, beaten down, worn out and ill maintained.

"Maybe we should give her more money," Priya said to Mona as they drove back to Hyderabad.

Mona shook her head. "No, no more money. People think giving money is the solution. It's not. Giving tools is the solution. Giving a scholarship to her son is the right thing. You think she will allow him to be tested?"

"I do. I mean, she cares about his future so much. It's so important to her. She's pregnant with our baby for it," Priya said. "But oh, it would break a mother's heart to send her child far away. And he's so young. Wouldn't it mess him up?"

"It'll mess him up more not to be challenged,"

Mona said. "Gifted children tend to be very impatient and need constant stimulation, otherwise they become aggressive. Vishal, my brother-in-law, his son is a member of MENSA. He's sixteen and has a one fifty IQ. Very smart kid, and when he was young they didn't want him to go to a special school. They wanted Kabir to go to school with his sister, Mira. But then Kabir, who is three years younger than Mira, would be in her class. And then he started getting into trouble because he was so bored. They had no choice but to move him. It was for the best. He's already in university, will have a PhD by the time he's twenty-one."

Priya thought about that for a moment and said, "But Asha and Pratap don't have the possibilities your brother has. He's a doctor in New York. Pratap is a painter in Srirampuram supplementing his family's income through surrogacy. I wonder if Manoj can really have the future a child like him deserves."

"If he's got the smarts and we make sure he gets the right guidance, why not?" Mona said. "I know it looks hopeless. You look at the poverty in India and you think it's so massive, so huge, there's nothing we can do. But I believe that we can make a difference, one child at a time, one single mother at a time."

"You're very passionate about helping people," Priya said with a smile. She had not expected

Mona to be passionate about anything but Prada boots and her family, in that order.

Mona grinned. "I know, I know. People look at me, see a twenty-three-year-old girl who married into a wealthy family and decide I must be a trophy wife. But the fact is that I come from money. I would've always married into a wealthy family unless I fell in love with a bus driver, which only happens in the movies. Because, really, when would someone like me take the bus?"

She wasn't being snobbish, just honest and genuine. She grew up with money and married into money, and she didn't see what the fuss was all about.

"I choose to have this life," Mona said. "I don't feel guilty about having money. I like money; it buys us things and makes our lives very comfortable. But I can also use it to do good. And not just our money; I throw all these fund-raisers to get Papa's friends involved in our foundation, too."

"Excellent philosophy to live by," Priya said. "And if you can help Asha and her son, I'll be indebted to you for life."

Mona laughed. "And I *will* call on that debt," she said. "So be forewarned."

Chapter Twenty

One sixty.

They kept saying that number, kept repeating how high it was. Asha didn't understand what it meant. Priya was very excited. She said that the other woman, Mona, who had come with her the previous week, was looking into arranging a scholarship for Manoj.

"It was so much fun, Amma," Manoj said. "Mona's parents have such a big house. And I got to sleep in Priya's room, with Priya."

Priya smiled at him and touched his face gently.

Not your baby. This one is mine, Asha wanted to say, but Manoj was oblivious to her jealousy.

"They have so many servants, but the best was Mona's father-in-law. He used to be a general in the army, and he was so funny. We played cricket together in the garden. I threw the ball sideways and broke a window . . ."

"Oh my God, were they angry with you?" Asha asked.

Manoj shook his head as if that were a strange question. "No. But he said that we would pretend when Romila, that's his wife, asked, that we didn't know what happened." Manoj laughed then. "But she knew and she gave me a chocolate anyway."

Priya sat on a charpoy by the swing where

Manoj sat with his mother, his excitement spilling out of him in waves of conversation.

"He was a perfect angel and everyone is in love with him," Priya told her. "He could've had a room of his own, but I thought five might be too young."

"And it was such a great room," Manoj said. "And I played on Priya's iPad. It's like a computer, but the size of a magazine. Priya downloaded three games for me, and I won them all."

Asha just wanted to hug him and ask him to stop talking. He was speaking too fast, about things she didn't know.

"He had a good time," Priya said, smiling. "He's a great kid."

"And the test, was the test difficult?" Asha asked Manoj.

Manoj made a face. "Of course not. It was very easy. I have an IQ of one sixty, Amma. They told me. That's a high IQ."

He was already not her Manoj, Asha thought. One night, just one night he was gone, and there was a different swagger to him. He spoke differently. He seemed to have already changed.

"Oh, and the school was . . . fantastic." Manoj said the sentence in Telugu but said *fantastic* in English like they did in the movies.

Asha hated the idea of a boarding school. He would not be able to live with them and would see them only once every three to four months unless they moved to Hyderabad, and even then they could see him only every Saturday and Sunday. Priya had said that was the only way. It broke Asha's heart to think about not hugging her son every day. But was there a choice for her?

"Are we supposed to move to Hyderabad?" Pratap wondered later.

When Asha had asked him about them taking Manoj to Hyderabad for the night, he thought it would be OK; why not, he'd said; his son would enjoy driving in a big air-conditioned car, staying in a fancy house, showing these rich people how smart he was. But now it was turning into a reality—this whole dream of sending him to a school for smart children—and Asha could see that Pratap was wavering. "I don't know about Manoj going to a boarding school," Pratap said.

"This is for his own good, for his future. I hate it, too, but . . . we have to do this," Asha said. "Maybe I should ask Priya to talk to you."

"How can you even think about sending him away?" Pratap asked. "You couldn't even imagine not seeing him every day while you're here."

"I know," Asha said sadly. "But we have Mohini to think about as well. We can't just move to Hyderabad and ruin Mohini's chances for astable life. She'll have a home with us here, a permanent home, a flat. And . . . Hyderabad is just three hours by bus. We can go see Manoj all the time."

"So you want to buy a flat now?" Pratap asked.

"If Manoj gets a scholarship, we should, don't you think?"

"Yes," Pratap said.

"He's really smart, they say," Asha said, and smiled. "And Manoj can't stop talking about the house he stayed in. It was full of servants, and he got to eat chicken curry with *rotis*, not rice."

"And he got chocolate ice cream," Pratap said. "He's been talking nonstop about it at home, too. Priya's much nicer than I thought she would be."

"She is," Asha said. "She's so determined to make sure Manoj's future is secure. I didn't think she would care. I mean . . . all I thought she cared about was the baby."

Asha hadn't wanted to like Priya. But she was impressed with her dedication toward Manoj. She was impressed with how she had gathered her rich friends to help her child. How could she dislike someone who was trying to save her child?

They watched Manoj help Mohini shake the dirt from her hands outside before coming to sit by their parents.

"Did you like the people you stayed with?" Asha asked Manoj again. She wanted to make certain; he would go again next week with Priya to be interviewed at the school for children like him who scored high on the tests.

"They were so nice, Amma," Manoj said. "And the woman there, Mona, she and Priya took me to see the school. I could go to that school. It was so great, Amma. They had computers everywhere and flowers and gardens. They had horses in the school, horses to ride on. All students can learn how to ride, and there was a big swimming pool to learn swimming. They also had rooms for students to live in. I'll live there if I get in. For boys my age, there are four boys to a room, but the rooms are big, bigger than Kaveri Atha's whole flat."

"So you would like to live there?" Asha asked, her voice constricted.

"I'll miss you and Nana and Mohini and Kaveri Atha and Sairam Mava and Sirish and Girish *Anna*. Will you be very angry if I say that I would like to stay there?" Manoj asked.

"No, I won't be angry," Asha said. Priya was taking this baby inside her away, and now she was taking Manoj away, too, she thought, just for a moment, before the thought passed like a cloud on a sunny day.

"Then I want to stay there," Manoj said. "They have these big classrooms and . . . they have chemistry labs where they mix things and make new things. And . . . Amma, they had a biology lab where they cut frogs and mice to look inside them. I want to be a doctor, Amma. I want to operate on people's brains and make things right when they're wrong. They call such people neuro-surgeons. Mona's husband, Vikas, he is a colonel in the army, and his brother is a neurosurgeon in New York."

He said the word *neurosurgeon* in English, and Asha couldn't even repeat it properly.

She hadn't seen him this excited in a very long time, if ever.

He had such a great need to absorb new things. She couldn't stand in his way, she realized. She would have to send him away.

Even when Manoj was just two years old, they had known that he was different. When he made drawings, he would make them neatly and then color them neatly, like he was ten instead of two. He had great command of the pencil, and by the time he was three, he could write his name on the pictures. They had been proud, Asha remembered, but also scared. He was so mature for his age, understood so much about his surroundings that Asha sometimes forgot that he was just five years old.

He was just a little boy. And he wanted to go away and learn.

Priya came again, and this time with the father's sister. Mayuri was very pretty, with long, straight hair. She wore tight pants and a bright-blue kurta. She wore beautiful, bright-blue slippers with golden designs on them. Her Telugu wasn't as good as the father's, but it was better than Priya's.

"You're so beautiful," she told Asha. "You have that pregnancy glow."

"It is what it is," Asha said.

"So your son is very smart," Mayuri said. "I mean, a one sixty IQ is stunning. Are you excited about sending him to a new school?"

"Excited and scared," Asha had answered.

"Don't be scared," Priya said then. "Don't worry about anything. The school is very good, and I think Manoj will be accepted after the interview. His test scores are so high that Mona thinks it won't be a problem. And she's setting up a scholarship for him."

"They must be very wealthy," Asha said.

"They are, but schools like this also subsidize . . . give a discount, when the child is as smart as Manoj," Priya said. "And they all loved Manoj. He's so bright, so clever. It was wonderful having him with us."

Manoj had talked more about the room he shared with Priya. He said that it had a big bed, but that everything in the house was big and smelled like sandalwood. He promised Asha that when he became a doctor, he would have a big house, too, and she could stay with him there, she and Pratap and Mohini.

"When will you take him for the interview?" Asha asked Priya.

"Today," Priya said. "It's at nine tomorrow morning. He'll stay with me at my in-laws' house. It isn't fancy like Mona's house, but he'll like it, I think."

"And we'll take good care of him," Mayuri said.

Asha felt strange handing over her child to another perfect stranger, but there was also a rightness to it. Priya and the father had handed over their child to her, and now she was handing over her child to them. Even though they didn't know each other well, there was a bond of trust between them, wasn't there?

"It's all happening so fast," she said.

"It's going to be fine," Mayuri said. "You'll see; it'll all work out. You'll buy a nice flat; your son will go to a lovely school."

Asha smiled unevenly at Mayuri. All these people had become a part of her life, the most unlikely people, but because of this baby, these people were here, helping her.

"Thank you, Priya," Asha said. This was the first time she had spoken the mother's name, and it made her feel good to say it.

"It's nothing." Priya looked a little embarrassed. "You're helping us and we're helping you. That's how the world goes round."

Doctor Swati talked about the school during the next exam that afternoon. Priya and Mayuri had left with an excited Manoj. He was already asking for the pad thing with the games from Priya as he got into the big black car with the driver.

Asha had been nervous about this conversation. She had expected Doctor Swati to be upset with her for choosing another school over the one she had recommended, and, sure enough, she had been right. Doctor Swati was annoyed that all the effort she had put in was for nothing.

"I was only trying to help you," Doctor Swati said. "I know you believe that Priya is helping, and I'm sure she is, but . . . your son will be fine in the school here."

"But Manoj is very smart," Asha said.

"Of course he is," Doctor Swati said. "But—"

"He has an IQ of one sixty," Asha said, even though she had no idea what that really meant. Mona had said something about it being a measure of intelligence, but Asha couldn't understand how something like intelligence could be measured in the first place. She had asked Manoj about the test, but he had been vague, saying something about boxes and colors and shapes.

Doctor Swati raised both her eyebrows. "One sixty? Really?"

"Yes," Asha said. "Priya took Manoj with her to be tested at some men . . . menses . . . I don't know. She's taking him today for an interview at the school. And they even found a scholarship for him. If it all works out, he'll start school this September."

Doctor Swati didn't say anything, digesting the information.

"That's a very high IQ," Doctor Swati said. "I didn't realize that he was such a smart boy. You must be very proud."

"Pratap and I are so happy," Asha said. "I can hardly believe it all myself."

"So the school thing is settled?"

"Almost, but . . . it's a boarding school. The school is in Hyderabad. And that will be very hard for us, but it's for Manoj's own good," Asha said.

"Well, I'm happy for you. Carrying their baby has really worked out for you, in more ways than one. I just hope the other mothers don't think things like this will magically happen for them," Doctor Swati said with a tight smile.

Keertana didn't like Priya one bit. She was one of those do-gooders, Keertana told Asha, and she didn't trust her. The other women in the surrogate house agreed that Priya was going above and beyond to help Manoj, and they couldn't help but be a little envious of Asha's good fortune. Even Kaveri chimed in on one of her visits.

"I'm so jealous," she said honestly to Priya. "First the gods smile at you and give you Manoj, and then they give you Priya."

"In a way, it's become harder because she is so

nice," Asha told her. "Before it was easier to hate her."

Asha had told no one that she sometimes fantasized that the baby was hers. She would stroke her belly and think about putting the baby to her breast when she was born, feeling that ache in her breasts when the milk burst out of them. She would soothe this child—and would take her home to Manoj, Mohini, and Pratap.

Asha didn't have to voice it; Kaveri knew. Kaveri had felt the same way.

"Next time when I do it, I'm telling Doctor Swati that I don't want contact with the parents," Kaveri said.

"So you are doing it again?"

Kaveri nodded. "We have to. Raman wants to start his own business. By then you will be back and you can take care of my boys."

"Have you talked to Doctor Swati?"

"Yes," Kaveri said. "And she said something should happen soon."

"Kaveri, if you don't want to do this, don't," Asha said. "If you feel so bad about it, if it weighs so heavily on you—"

"I don't have a choice, Asha," Kaveri said. "We need the money. If Raman has a business and regular income, then the boys can have an income, too, when they grow up. It's the right thing to do."

"Are you sure?"

"After the baby was born, I promised myself never again, but then time passes, you forget what it was like, and you think it's OK, it'll be OK," Kaveri said.

"I don't know what it will be like for me," Asha confessed. "But I will have to be OK. I'll have to go home and be Asha again."

"Just because you're carrying this baby, you didn't stop being Asha," Kaveri said.

"Yes, I did," Asha said. "I became someone I don't like. I have bitterness inside me. I feel there's a rot inside me, spreading. I argue with Pratap, which I never did before. I think mean thoughts about the mother . . . about Priya. And she's turned out to be so nice. You wouldn't believe the thoughts I've had about her taking my baby."

"Not *your* baby, *her* baby," Kaveri said. "You know that, don't you?"

Asha nodded. "I know."

Chapter Twenty-one

Priya went to the airport alone. She didn't want to share Madhu with anyone. They had never been away from each other for such a long time, nearly seven weeks.

The sight of Madhu with his backpack slung on his shoulder and a suitcase rolling next to him made Priya promise to herself that she'd never stay away this long ever again.

He dropped his bag, let go of his suitcase, and hugged her.

"God, I missed you," he said into her hair. "This was way, way too much."

Priya's heart stumbled. She had him, she thought. Why had she ever clamored so for a baby? He was enough.

On the drive back, Priya filled Madhu in on all the latest with Manoj's schooling.

"The boy is a miracle. Both Mayuri and I are in love with him."

His first day with them, Manoj had confessed to them that he had a girlfriend.

"Her name is Shilpa," he said. "And she's very nice."

"Is she now?" Mayuri said.

"She likes it when I kiss her feet," Manoj

said somberly. "And I told her that I don't mind kissing her feet, but I wasn't going to marry her."

Mayuri and Priya had burst out laughing. "This kid has already figured out the whole male-female relationship," Mayuri said.

Priya had given Madhu detailed reports about all the work they were doing for Manoj, and he had worried that Asha might misunderstand and think they were taking Manoj away from her.

"You think so?" Priya had asked; the thought hadn't even crossed her mind.

"She *might* feel that way," Madhu said. "After all, you're helping him go to a boarding school. Would you be able to send your child away like that?"

"No, but then we have the means to be with our child in such a situation," Priya said. "They don't."

"It doesn't seem fair," Madhu said.

Before Sush left for home, Priya had had the same conversation with her mother, who agreed it wasn't fair, but this was India—an unfair and difficult place for the millions who were poor.

Priya had confessed to her that after being here in person, she could see how her mother could see surrogacy as an exploitation of sorts. But she also admitted that, even knowing all she did, she would still do it again. "Plus," she added, "I'm helping Manoj; we got him a scholarship and admission to a great school. He would never have had a chance if he didn't meet us."

Sush had looked at her pointedly. "You have a good heart, Priya. I have never doubted it. But you're helping the boy to assuage your guilt as well. It isn't exactly a selfless act."

"Come on, Mummy, I'm doing all I can," Priya had said.

"But maybe you feel bad about using a surrogate, and seeing her, you worry about her feelings now," Sush said. She wasn't accusing; she was being supportive and understanding. She understood how Priya felt—a mixture of guilt and responsibility and striving to show that she was a good person. She was a good human being. Yes, she was using Asha, but she was also giving back. Were the scales even now?

"She walked into this with her eyes open," Priya had said.

"But did *you?*" Sush had asked, and Priya didn't have an answer.

She had to let go of Madhu when they got to his parents' house. Prasanna hugged him and made him sit down in front of her as she always did when she saw him.

"It's too long since we saw you," she said with tears in her eyes, holding both her son's hands in her own. "And you look tired."

"Amma, I have been on a plane for twenty

hours. I *am* tired," Madhu said kindly. "But one of your good meals and I'm going to be good as new."

"You know I didn't get this treatment when I came back," Mayuri said then. "I got grilled. 'Did you lose your job? Do you have a boyfriend? Is he white? We're going to arrange your marriage this time. No discussion.' She didn't hold my hands and say I look tired. And I was knackered."

"Oh shush," Prasanna said. "You did lose your job. You have no prospects right now. It's the best time to get married."

"I don't want to get married," Mayuri said.

"You're nearly thirty years old; if you were going to fall in love, you'd have fallen in love by now," Prasanna said. "We'll find you a nice Brahmin boy. A doctor, living in London. Will that work?"

"I can find a nice doctor in London if I want," Mayuri said, and looked at her brother. "Help me out here."

"I know some single Indian doctors in California," Madhu said, grinning. "Nice boys. Little *pappu* types with coconut oil in their hair, but excellent doctors, making tons of money."

"So, I should just sell my soul?"

"Nothing wrong with that," Prasanna said. "And you wouldn't be selling your soul, just marrying someone with a future. Which you don't have. Your fashion this and fashion that didn't work out."

"I was a designer for a major global retailer," Mayuri said, horrified.

"And now you're jobless," Prasanna said.

Priya looked on at the family and couldn't wait to have her own family with her child. Would they banter like this? How would their daughter be as a grown-up? Would she be a designer? A doctor? This was everything she had always wanted. Everything.

Chapter Twenty-two

We'll go to the village, Asha thought. *That's what we'll do. We'll take the baby, Mohini, and Manoj and go to the village. No one will be able to find us there. And then the baby will really be mine.*

As the days got closer to her due date, Asha woke every morning to the same thought. She wasn't as irritable as she'd been, but still her sadness was growing inside her, as big as the baby, as palpable. And then there was the guilt, just as big. This was Priya's baby. The good Priya who was helping her family, and she was thinking of stealing her baby, her happiness, and her future from her.

She didn't want to think these thoughts. She was a good woman. She wasn't a mean person. But her mind had a mind of its own, and Asha realized that she couldn't control her feelings. First, it had just been random thoughts—*What if the baby could be mine?* thoughts . . . by accident, that is, just by a miracle. Now she wished she could do something to make that miracle happen.

It made her irritable. This push and pull inside her. This large unhappiness. This melancholy she couldn't shake. It was almost time. She should be celebrating. Now she could go home and be with *her* family, finish this duty. She should be like Keertana, waiting to get that baby out and be on her way back to her life. Instead she was moping. She was making herself sick of herself.

"I can't wait for this baby to be out," Keertana said as she watched Asha pace the TV room.

"Neither can I," Asha lied. As long as the baby was inside her, she was hers.

"Are the parents visiting again today?"

"No, not for a few days. The father is here, and they had some things to do, they said, legal things to take the baby with them to America," Asha said.

"Are you going to get medication during labor?" Keertana asked.

"I don't know," Asha said.

"Get it," Keertana recommended. "It takes all the pain away. It's wonderful. Just the thought of the pain and I'm ready to wet myself. But last time I had the drugs and it was good."

"But isn't it bad for the baby?"

"It's not my baby," Keertana said. "Anyway, if it wasn't safe, Doctor Swati wouldn't give it to us."

"I wonder when it will happen," Asha said. "It's such an odd thing, isn't it? They can put some-one else's baby in my belly, but they can't predict the date that I'll have it."

PART V:
Labor and Delivery

Chapter Twenty-three

Asha went into labor at one in the morning. The pain started in her back, slow, ringing around her stomach. She knew what it was as soon as it began.

From her previous two births, Asha knew that the best thing for her in the beginning was to walk. So she got up, tentative because she knew that her water might break at any time. She left Gangamma sleeping in the room and went to find Revati. As usual, she was in the TV room, snoozing on the charpoy while the television was set at a low volume.

"Revati," Asha called out, standing next to her lightly snoring body.

She came awake almost immediately. Revati, everyone knew, was a light sleeper, used to being woken up at all hours.

"It's your time," she said as she sat up, and Asha nodded.

Asha groaned softly as a band of pain went from up her thighs to her tight stomach.

"OK," Revati said, and got up. "I will call Doctor Swati. What do you need?"

"I'm fine. I just need to keep walking," Asha said. She was tired, she realized, so very tired, and almost fell asleep standing up between contractions.

Revati called Doctor Swati at her house and was asked to take Asha to the clinic immediately. She put an arm around Asha and they walked next door.

"Almost there," Revati said.

"How far apart are they?" Asha asked, because she knew Revati was keeping time.

"About ten minutes," Revati said. "So you still have time, maybe a few hours."

A big groan burst out from Asha then, and she almost doubled over in pain. Her water broke right before they entered the clinic, wetting her feet and her *chappals*. Revati held her up and got them to the clinic.

Nursamma was waiting for them, and she asked Asha to sit in the wheelchair. "No," Asha protested. "It's better if I walk. If I sit down, the pain is unbearable. And I'm completely wet. My water broke."

Nursamma listened to her and then called out for the *dai*, the midwife. The clinic had five midwives, and there was always one with Doctor Swati in the birthing room. They wore white saris like Nursamma but not a white cap. Pratibha, one of the *dais*, rushed to Asha's side and walked her to the birthing room.

Revati didn't come with them, and Asha wished she had. She felt alone. The previous two times she had given birth, she had done it at home with Kaveri and a midwife. They didn't have money to go to a hospital or get a doctor. The village had a *dai* who had so much experience that everyone trusted her more than they would a doctor anyway.

In any case, the government hospital near the village was an hour's bus ride away, and it wasn't like the doctor always came to the hospital when you needed him. Asha had gone there a few times when Manoj was sick and had found out quickly that it was better to go to the village healing woman.

Asha had learned to give her children turmeric with milk when they had a cold instead of the pills that the doctors gave, and when they had a fever, she would keep it down with a decoction of ginger and raisins, as the village healing woman had instructed her.

Giving birth had never really scared Asha. Kaveri had had both her boys before Asha had ever gotten pregnant, so she'd had someone to advise her.

Puttamma, her mother-in-law, had always been on hand as well, which had been a comfort, because she was always so calm about childbirth. But this time there was no one. No family, no relatives, no one she knew. She was alone in this white sterile room with Pratibha and Nursamma.

"If you want to walk, just walk," Nursamma said, indicating the area around the bed. "If you want to lie down, you should do that. If you want help with the pain, you should let us know."

Asha nodded.

"For now, we would like you to take your clothes off and put this gown on, and then I want you to lie down for a short while so I can check you," Nursamma said. "Doctor Swati will be here soon."

Asha half listened, half waited for the pain to come back. Pratibha had to help her get out of her sari, which she was thankful to discard, as it was wet with birthing water, and into the pale-blue gown that had ties on the back. They didn't tie properly, and she felt embarrassed that her behind was bare. The embarrassment was short-lived; the contractions were starting to come faster and faster.

The baby would be here soon. Priya's baby.

"Has anyone called Priya?" she asked between contractions, her face relaxed as a wave of pain passed out of her.

"We have," Nursamma said. "You shouldn't worry about that. Just relax and breathe."

When Asha couldn't stand it anymore, she half sat and half lay down on the bed. Nursamma checked her often, saying that she was quite close now.

They asked her again if she wanted medicine, but Asha refused. Pain was part of the process. She couldn't cheat Mother Nature of this right.

Doctor Swati arrived an hour after Asha got to the clinic. She looked at the notes Nursamma had made on a pad that hung on Asha's bed, and she smiled. "Looks like you're going to have a baby soon. You're nearly ready."

Pratibha wiped Asha's brow and told her to breathe, keeping her calm through her contractions. Asha missed her village *dai*, the woman who had delivered Manoj and Mohini in their hut. Maybe that hadn't been as clean as this, and maybe she didn't have wires on her body measuring the baby's heartbeat, but it had felt much safer. Funny how here with all the solutions for problems that might arise at the ready, all Asha could think of were the problems.

What if something went wrong? It was a standard fear every woman had while giving birth. She screamed loudly as the contractions seemed to become harder, stronger, coming quicker.

Madhu's mobile phone rang at two in the morning. Asha had gone into labor.

They had been waiting for this call.

They were prepared.

They had the baby's bag packed. Small clothes, a blanket, diapers, wipes, a woolen cap. The bag was next to a car seat. Madhu had bought it in the States so it met US specifications. In California they wouldn't let you take your baby home if you didn't have a car seat for the baby.

Madhu woke his parents to tell them they were going to bring their daughter home. Prasanna promised to immediately set the house right. She was going to make sure the bassinet was ready with fresh sheets, convert Madhu's old study table into a changing table laid out with everything the baby would need—diapers, alcohol swabs, baby soap, and moisturizer. And yes, they would havea big meal with lots of sweets. A celebration.

Madhu drove like a maniac, and Priya took turns laughing and crying.

"Finally, Madhu, finally," Priya said.

The lights at Happy Mothers were on when they got there. Priya had run from the car, Madhu not far behind her. He caught up with her at the entrance and pulled her to him.

"Priya," he said. "You know I love you."

"Yes," Priya said, wanting to rush inside, but there was something about how he looked at her, so intently, that she stilled and said, "I love you. Very much. Baby or no baby, Madhu, I love you."

"Remember how you said that you were worried I'd leave if something happened to the baby?" Madhu asked, and when Priya nodded, he looked pointedly at her. "I won't. I never will. But . . . if something happened . . . you . . ."

"You're worried if I'll leave, go back to being baby-obsessed Priya," Priya said, and put her hands on his cheeks. She pulled him down to kiss him on the mouth. "I learned many things these past months. And one very important thing I learned is that you and I, we're family. Complete. Our child . . . makes our family bigger, changes the dynamic, but doesn't change the core of it."

You couldn't wash the past away. They couldn't just wipe away what had been said between them, what had happened, but they could move forward. They had moved forward, without even realizing it. The wounds had healed. Maybe when it had started out, Priya wanted the baby more than Madhu did, but as the child went from being an abstract fetus to becoming a swollen womb, Madhu was just as invested as she was. He loved this child as much as she did.

Madhu kissed her on the nose. "Should we go see if our daughter has arrived?"

As they walked inside the Happy Mothers clinic, Priya's heart was pounding.

She was scared. What if something went wrong? What if her baby died? What if Asha died? Would it be better if Asha died or the baby died?

Maybe this was why some parents chose not to know the surrogate. Priya was worried not only about the baby but also about Asha. She had gotten to know Asha and her family, had slept in the same bed with Manoj, held his hand and talked about his dreams with him. Asha was now family, and Priya wanted her to be as safe as her own child.

"We're ready to push," Doctor Swati said, her hands covered in long gloves, a green hospital gown over her sari.

"Push?" Asha said the word like it was alien to her; she rolled it on her tongue and felt a pinch It was time to let the baby go. It was time to push it out. She wanted to say she didn't want to. She wanted to keep the baby inside.

"Come on, Asha. With the next contraction, you must push," Doctor Swati said.

Pratibha took Asha's hand. "I will count, and when I say ten, you must push, OK? *Okati, rondu, mudu, nalgu* . . ." She went through the numbers in Telugu. When she said, *"Padhi,"* Asha pushed with all her might. It felt like her insides would tear.

"Come on, once more," Doctor Swati called out.

It began again, the counting and the pushing. Asha couldn't stop crying, couldn't stop wanting to hold this baby inside her, keep it for herself.

But after just four pushes, she felt the baby slide out of her and heard its first cry. It was the last time she felt the baby, the last time she heard it, the last time she was connected to it. Once they cut the umbilical cord, it was like a dam had broken, and Asha started to howl.

"Are you in pain?" Doctor Swati asked.

Asha closed her eyes and shook her head. *God, please don't make me see the baby,* she thought.

Please, let them take it away, far away from me. I can't bear this.

Even as her arms ached to hold the tiny life, making her cry in a pain more terrible than the contractions, she didn't ask to see the baby, couldn't ask for it. It wasn't hers. It wasn't hers.

"Asha, you need to tell me if you're in pain," Doctor Swati said.

"Is the baby here?" Asha asked, sobbing.

"No, we had to take her to another room to check her," Doctor Swati said. "Do you want to see her?"

Asha shook her head. "No." She tightly shut her eyes, shut out the world around her.

"OK," Doctor Swati said, and leaned down to hug Asha. "You did good, Asha. You did very good. You're going to be fine."

"Oh God," Asha said, opening her eyes for the first time since the baby had slid out of her. "Oh God, Doctor Swati."

"It's over," Doctor Swati said. "And the baby is—"

"Don't tell me," Asha said. "I don't want to know."

"OK," Doctor Swati said. "Priya and Madhu will be here soon. Do you want to see them?"

Asha wanted to say no, but she felt like she owed them one last meeting and said it would be OK.

It was three in the morning. It had taken just two

short hours to give birth, to give the baby up. Two hours. Nine months and two hours.

Asha lay crying softly, unable to stop the tears as Doctor Swati delivered the placenta. Pratibha massaged her belly to remove any excess blood, and Asha didn't speak, didn't say anything, just lay there, a weeping doll.

She put her hand on her stomach; it wasn't flat, but there was no baby inside. It was soft, like wet clay, and saggy. It looked bruised, black, like it had the previous two times she had given birth and held her babies to her bosom.

Nursamma opened the doors for Madhu and Priya.

"Is everyone OK?" Priya asked in English.

"The baby is born and Asha is well," Nursamma said in her thickly accented English. "You want to see the baby, I think."

"Already born? So quickly," Priya said.

"It was an easy labor," Nursamma said as she walked them to the nursery. "Asha didn't even take any pain medication. It went really fast."

Madhu grabbed Priya's hand.

The nursery was on the far end of the hallway where the examination and delivery rooms were. There was only one baby in one of the four cots. They had put her in a pink cap and a white onesie. She was asleep, a little pink burrito. On the side of the cot it read BABY RAO.

"Come, here she is," Nursamma said.

Priya picked her up, awkwardly, not sure how to hold her, but magically, she thought, she knew. She put her palm under Ayesha's head to support it; how did she know to do this? She looked at her in wonder and then at Madhu.

"She's ours," she whispered.

The baby opened her eyes briefly before closing them.

"She has blue eyes," Madhu said.

"And dark hair," Priya said.

"She's . . . my God, she's all here. Hello, sweetheart," Madhu said, tears rolling down his cheeks.

"Hello, Ayesha," Priya said, and hugged her close.

Madhu hugged both of them and dropped a kiss on Priya's head. "I love you both," he said. "I love you both so very much."

"It was a very good labor," Doctor Swati told Asha as she brought some Fanta for her to drink after they had cleaned her up and moved her from the birthing room. "Have some; you'll feel better."

Asha drank obediently through a straw, lying against soft pillows. She was in another room now, like a regular hospital ward. Sometimes the room had two or three women if they had all given birth at the same time. Doctor Swati had predicted that Asha would go into labor in a week or so. But nature had been in a hurry to part her from the baby.

"Why are you crying?" Doctor Swati asked.

"I don't know," Asha lied.

"It's normal to feel sad after giving birth," Doctor Swati said. "But you'll get over it, I promise. Sooner than you think, you'll not even think about it."

"Priya and Madhu are here?" Asha asked.

"Yes," Doctor Swati said. "They just came. They're very happy to see the baby. Will you see them?"

"Yes . . . but without the baby," Asha said. "I don't want to see the baby."

"OK," Doctor Swati said. "You did very well, Asha."

"Thanks," Asha said primly, in English.

"She'll see you, but she doesn't want to see the baby," Doctor Swati told Madhu and Priya when they met with her in her office.

Priya was still holding Ayesha, couldn't imagine letting that warm weight go. Nursamma had already made a bottle of formula, and Priya found that she knew, just knew, how to hold Ayesha and how to give her the bottle as she talked to Doctor Swati.

Why had she panicked so much? Why had she worried that she wouldn't know how to care for a baby? Yes, yes, the sleepless nights, the difficult days, they would come, too, but Priya wasn't worried. Madhu was with her.

"Is it normal for the surrogate to not see the baby?" Madhu asked.

"Yes, some see them once and some say they don't want to," Doctor Swati said. "She just gave birth. There are hormones involved. Of course she's emotional. But Asha is a strong woman and she did beautifully."

"Is she OK?" Priya asked.

"She will be," Doctor Swati said.

Priya put the empty bottle down on the table. Ayesha was asleep again.

"She's like family. I mean, I know her family, her son, and . . . I had hoped . . . ," Priya said, looking at Ayesha's beautiful face. Asha had given this to her. Had given birth to this child just a few hours ago. She had pushed her out of her body, nourished her for nine months, soothed her when she fluttered in her womb.

"Look, she's going to want to move on; this is normal. You shouldn't pressure her for more than she can give," Doctor Swati said. "Just because you sent presents and did all those things for her son, she isn't going to be your friend or your family."

Doctor Swati sounded snappish, irritated with them. It wasn't overt; she was still as patient as she had always been, but there was an undertone.

"I can leave the baby with Nursamma," Priya said reluctantly. "And then we can go see Asha."

Nursamma took Ayesha to the nursery, and Doctor Swati took them to the room where Asha was. There were three beds there; two were empty.

She looked small in the white bed. This mop of black hair and black flesh, huddled, lying on her side, looking away from the door.

Asha couldn't look at Priya or the father. She looked at the ceiling. Here, the paint wasn't peeling. It was all white with no ceiling fan—one wasn't needed, as the clinic was fully air-conditioned.

"She looks lovely," Priya said, holding Asha's hand, sitting next to her. "She has blue eyes. It's amazing."

Asha didn't want to hear about the baby, but she didn't say anything. She had managed to contain her tears, fill her insides with them, for this last meeting. She started to hum inside her head to block out the sounds of Priya's excitement.

"She's healthy and perfect," Priya said. "How are you feeling?"

"Good," Asha said softly. She didn't want to speak, as speaking made her tears come back.

"Madhu and I hope to see Manoj and Mohini . . . and your husband one last time before we leave for the States," Priya said. "We were thinking of coming by in a couple of days with the baby. What do you think?"

Asha looked at Priya then, her resolve to hold back the tears failing. "No," she said firmly.

Priya looked surprised. But then it seemed like she understood, and she nodded. She leaned down and kissed Asha on her forehead.

"You have given us the greatest joy imaginable," she said. "I can't thank you enough for your courage and your generosity."

Asha wanted to say something rude—but she couldn't. This woman had suffered, too, for years and years. Priya had told her all about losing her babies and not being able to get pregnant—Asha could imagine that pain. She knew women who couldn't keep their pregnancies and some who could never even get pregnant. They were treated poorly by their husbands, their own families, everyone around them. A woman had to get pregnant, had to give birth—it was part of being a woman, as natural as having breasts and a womb. A woman who never became a mother was incomplete.

"Thank you," the father said. He put an envelope next to Asha's pillow. "Here is our phone number and address. If you ever need anything, you can call. I have written down how you can call for free from here. You dial a number and ask for our number, and you won't even have to pay for the call."

Why would she call them? Asha couldn't imagine any scenario where she would call them for anything. They were no one in her life. There was nothing left for them to say to each other.

"If you need any help ever, Asha, please call us," Priya said. "Madhu's parents' phone number is there, too, so you can call them and they will let us know." Priya paused for a moment. "Doctor Swati said you don't want to see the baby. I just . . . are you sure?"

Asha could only nod, her eyes becoming glassy with tears.

"We'll write to you; will that be OK?" Priya asked.

Asha wanted to say no but nodded again. She would just throw the letters away without opening them.

"I'm tired," Asha said. "I need to sleep."

"Of course," Priya said, and she stood up. "We're sorry for bothering you, but we just had to thank you in person. Take care of yourself, Asha. And say hello to your family for us. I hope Manoj will enjoy his new school. Mona will be in touch with you."

She had done that for them, and Asha knew that she would never be able to repay that debt. Priya had saved Manoj's life and, in turn, Asha's as well. Maybe Asha had given them a gift that they couldn't get themselves, a gift they pined for, but they had given Asha an even bigger gift— a future for her son.

They were at the door when Asha finally

gave in. "Thank you for Manoj," Asha called out.

Priya almost stopped breathing, and then relief seeped through her. She turned around to look at Asha, into her eyes. Asha held her gaze for a moment and then turned her head and closed her eyes.

Through their social circumstances, their different worlds—they had touched each other in an irrevocable way. Their bond, not something that would be renewed, could nevertheless not be broken.

Their names meant "hope," and they had given hope to each other, and this was what brought them together, closed that gap between them, eliminated the social and class differences, made them sisters, mothers—made them equals.

Acknowledgments

This book would not have been published without my agent, Rayhané Sanders, who saved my life and gave me back what I had lost.

You wouldn't be reading this book without Danielle Marshall from Amazon, who brought me into the light and gave my book a home.

My friends and colleagues who have become my friends helped me keep my chin up while this book was written, edited, and published. My thanks to: Fatima Aller for the many, many great meals and abundant love; Alice Verghese for her support and a sympathetic ear; Monika Gram Ritter for making me believe people are good; Valerie Soulier for scolding, encouraging, and coaching me; and Oliver Brunchmann for listening to me whine and telling me to shut up when it was most needed.

And, as always, gratitude, love, and amazement for my babies, Tobias and Isaiah, and my husband, Søren Rasmussen, who bring out the best in me, in good times and in bad.

About the Author

Amulya Malladi is the author of six novels, including *The Mango Season* and *The Sound of Language*. Her books have been translated into several languages, including Dutch, German, Spanish, Danish, Romanian, Serbian, and Tamil. She has a bachelor's degree in engineering and a master's degree in journalism and works as a marketing executive for a global medical device company. She lives in Copenhagen with her husband and two children. She loves to connect with readers on her Facebook page at www.face book.com/amulyamalladi and on her website at www.amulyamalladi.com.

Center Point Large Print
600 Brooks Road / PO Box 1
Thorndike, ME 04986-0001 USA

(207) 568-3717

US & Canada:
1 800 929-9108
www.centerpointlargeprint.com